DECLINE

DECLAN REEDE: THE UNTOLD STORY
(BOOK 1)

MICHELLE IRWIN

COPYRIGHT

DEDICATION:

To those who've been with me since the beginning and have supported my books whether paranormal, contemporary, or anything in between.
Jenny, Jacky, Christy, Clare, Siobhan, Belinda, Jennifer, Amanda, Mandy, Donna, and everyone else in my (Para)normals.

To my husband for letting me live the dream and to my daughter for teaching me to follow my heart.

To the CS Crew, you know who you are and that you take support to the next level.

To everyone who came out swinging in support for Declan. Who wanted to see the results of his decision.

And finally, to those who like their hero with a potty mouth and dirty mind, I deliver to you Declan Reede.

CONTENTS:

GLOSSARY:

Note: This book is set in Australia, as such it uses Australian/UK spelling and some Australian slang. Although you should be able to understand the novella without a glossary, there is always fun to be had in learning new words. Temperatures are in Celsius, weight is in kilograms, and distance is (generally) in kilometres (although we still have some slang which uses miles).

Arse: Ass.
Bench: Counter.
Bitumen: Asphalt.
Bonnet: Hood.
Bottle-o: Bottle shop/liquor store.
Buggery: Multiple meanings. Technically bugger/buggery is sodomy/anal sex, but in Australia, the use is more varied. Bugger is a common expression of disbelief/disapproval.
Cock-ups: Fuck-ups/mistakes.
Diamante: Rhinestone.
Dipper: See S Bends below.
Formal: Prom.
Fours: Cars with a four-cylinder engine.
Mirena: An IUD that contains and releases a small amount of a progesterone hormone directly into the uterus.
Necked: Drank from.
Newsagency: A shop which sells newspapers/magazines/lotto tickets. Similar to a convenience store, but without the food.
Pap: Paparazzi.
Paracetamol: Active ingredient in pain-relievers like Tylenol and Panadol.
Phone/Mobile Phone/Mobile Number: Cell/cell phone/cell

number.

Ricer: Someone who drives a hotted up four-cylinder (usually imported) car, and makes modifications to make it (and make it look) faster.

Rugby League: One of the codes of football played in Australia.

S bends (and into the dipper): Part of the racetrack shaped into an S shape. On Bathurst track, the dipper is the biggest of the S bends, so called because there used to be a dip in the road there before track resurfacing made it safer.

Sandwich with the lot: Sandwich with the works.

Schoolies: Week-long (or more) celebration for year twelves graduating school. Similar to spring break. The Gold Coast is a popular destination for school leavers from all around the country, and they usually have a number of organised events, including alcohol-free events as a percentage of school leavers are usually under eighteen (the legal drinking age in Australia).

Scrag: Whore/slut.

Slicks: A special type of racing tyre with no tread. They're designed to get the maximum amount of surface on the road at all times. Wet weather tyres have chunky tread to displace the water from the track.

Skulled: (can also be spelled sculled and skolled) Chugged/Drank everything in the bottle/glass.

Sunnies: Sunglasses.

Taxi: Cab.

Thrummed: Hummed/vibrated.

Titbit: Tidbit.

Tossers: Pricks/assholes/jerks.

Tyres: Tires.

Year Twelve: Senior year/last year of high school.

Wag: Ditch school.

Whinge: Whine/complain.

Uni: University/college.

CHAPTER ONE

BATTLE AT THE MOUNTAIN

MY CAR THRUMMED to the tune of the V8 under the bonnet. Each time my foot grazed the accelerator, an angry growl reverberated around me. The sound coursed through my body like fuel burning through my veins and sent exhilaration rushing through me. Black bitumen stretched out as far as I could see, filling my narrow field of vision with the only sight I needed to truly feel alive. The track, and my place on it, was all I cared about.

In the distance, crowds pressed against the fences, pushing each other and vying for the best position to see the start of the race. They would watch me leap from pole position and gain further advantage over all of those lined up behind me. There was no one in front of me. No one to come between me and my victory.

No one but me—my fucked-up mind.

Realistically, I should have been buzzing with confidence, like I had been the last time I'd lined up for this race, but I wasn't. Instead, a constant loop of all the reasons I was going to fail ran through my mind, diminishing my purpose and causing my hands to shake. I tightened my grip on the wheel and took a deep breath to steady my nerves. Another press of the accelerator—another roar from my beast—reminded me of the power I wielded. The whole scenario was almost achingly familiar. My last eight starts had been from pole position, but my last five races had ended in a DNF. Did. Not. Finish.

I couldn't even get one damn car around a simple fucking racetrack in a series of clean laps. Not anymore. Not since Queensland Raceway. I couldn't explain it exactly, but every time I'd felt close to victory, something clicked out of place in my mind and for a tiny moment everything fell down around me. It shouldn't have been an issue; it was barely a lapse in concentration. It was a problem though, because it always happened when I was barrelling down a straight at speeds just shy of three hundred kilometres an hour. At that speed, even a fraction of a second was too long, especially if the straight ended with a sharp right corner.

This time, I was lined up for the fucking Bathurst 1000. A partnered endurance race. It wasn't only my arse on the line this time. My co-driver Morgan McGuire's championship hopes were resting on our joint performance. He'd already taken a moment before I'd climbed into the car to warn me of precisely what he would do to me if I managed to total the car this time. It involved a pair of rusty pliers and a part of my anatomy that I was particularly fond of.

I brushed my foot over the accelerator again, taking comfort in the snarl that issued. The car was the best it had ever been. No doubt that was partly in thanks to the complete rebuild it had needed after my last outing, but I chose to ignore that fact. I tried to focus on the roar of the engine and not on the fact that my team had informed me that I actually was close to getting one record this year.

According to Sinclair Racing's bean counters, I was one wreck away from passing the all-time repair cost in a single season. Suffice it to say this wasn't the record they, or I, wanted. In fact, Danny Sinclair and his board were so unhappy with me at the moment that it was highly possible one more wreck would see me lose not only the championship—which was all but out the window anyway— but also my career. And I fucking loved my job. I was living my dream.

It wasn't just the fast cars and loose women that excited me, although they were a benefit. A distinct benefit. My mind wandered to replay the previous night's activities with a pair of girls. There was nothing they hadn't let me do to them. By the end of the night, I'd screwed both of them in every way possible before sending them on their way.

Swallowing heavily, I discovered that thinking about my night-time activities at that moment was not the best idea. I needed the blood to stay where it belonged—in my head—and not be rushing south to fill my cock. I shifted in my seat and focused on the track in front of me and the chatter of my team in my ear.

In mere minutes, I would have to wrestle a six-hundred-horsepower, thirteen-hundred-kilogram roaring beast around a racetrack. That couldn't be done with a distracted mind. Especially not at Bathurst, a track that required the utmost concentration from even the best of drivers. Like I used to be. Before Queensland.

I closed my eyes, blocking out the track in front of me as the thought struck. Just twelve short months ago, I'd been at the top of my game. King Shit. No one was able to touch me when I was on the track. I had started the previous season as the dark horse, one that couldn't possibly be a threat, but I'd finished as the youngest driver ever to win the championship. At my age it was a fucking miracle I was in the car at all, let alone being discussed as a possibility for lead driver within the next few years. Or at least I *was* being discussed. Now, after a string of incidents, I was practically a wash-up who couldn't even finish a race. I was barely twenty-two, and my career was already hitting the skids. Unless I pulled a miracle—and a finish—out of my arse, I was finished. The chequered flag would drop on my career and I'd never see the track again. At least, not for Sinclair.

The drivers behind me revved their engines in anticipation of the start, reminding me of where my attention should have been. My mind raced with too many thoughts, and I tried to push them out, to focus only on the most important of them all. Number one: I needed to get away clean. Number two: I needed to keep my head on the track. At least that way I might have a fighting chance of finishing, which would be fan-fucking-tastic.

I can do it.

The thoughts I'd been trying to keep at bay, to keep off the track, started to flash in my mind. I beat back the vision, refusing to let her screw with my head before I'd even started.

Can't I?

My head spun as the doubt crept in. I pushed it down and decided that maybe that's all I needed to do: think positive or some shit. Be the change I wanted to see in the world and all that other bullshit.

Or maybe I should just try to stop over-fucking-analysing everything.

The simple truth was that I needed to spend more time focusing on the race and less time chasing the doubt that raced through the memories in my own fucking head. If I worked out how to do that, I might stand some chance of salvaging something of the shit that was left of my life. I just couldn't see a way past my particular issue. At least none that I wanted to do.

A voice in my ear confirmed the flags were due to go up in less than a minute. I allowed myself one second of solitude and closed my eyes. Pressing my foot deep onto the floor, I listened to the throaty roar that issued from my beast. It blocked out all other sounds and left me with a moment of peace.

My eyes snapped open as I heard the familiar sounds signalling me that it was time to go. The instant the green flag was raised, I jumped. Wrestling the heavy car into line was never an easy task—stalling was always a concern—but I got away clean.

Ride on instinct.

Don't think.

Don't overthink.

You know what you need to do.

Just. Fucking. Do. It.

I *would* do it. It was only one thousand kilometres, and I didn't have to drive them all. Morgan would have his shot—he would do it clean. The championship was his for the taking if he did his part. I just had to do mine.

Easy.

Starting in pole position had given me an advantage. I'd capitalised on that, and jumped from the starting line fast, which made it easy to stay at the front of the pack. My skills and awareness of the other drivers only helped to strengthen that lead.

My radio blared to life less than a minute after the start. The crew informed me of an incident in the first corner. It was already behind me, so I was ready to ignore it. There was only one thing I needed to know about it.

"No safety car," Eden, the woman I put my faith in on race days, confirmed a second later, alleviating the lingering concern.

Her statement meant there mustn't have been any major damage to the cars. That was all I needed to know. I didn't listen to the rest of Eden's information as she listed the cars involved. I didn't really care. My only concern was the track ahead of me.

My fingers danced across the instruments. Up. Down. Clutch. Accelerator. Brake. It was a rhythm I'd memorised years ago. The cadence of the movements matched the private symphony in my mind. Hard to the left. Up Mountain Straight. Hard to the right. Through the cutting. Reid Park. Past McPhillamy. The track, the car, everything came together to form a routine I'd done so often before that I probably could have done it with my eyes closed. Of course, taking the mountain for granted was asking for trouble.

Especially considering my recent performance issues.

In the last four years, I'd raced at the track a number of times. First, it had been in a production car, and then finally one year ago, I'd taken on the mountain in a Sinclair Racing V8. I'd fucking finished strong. My debut in a V8 and I'd finished second. It was almost unheard of for someone my age, but I was just that good. I'd driven with McGuire then as well. Buoyed by that win, as well as my other ones earlier in the season, I'd won the championship. I'd had such great fucking prospects. It was the stuff of legends—hall of fame worthy.

And then I fucked it up. Or more specifically, *she* did.

Refusing to linger on the thought, I focused on the track. I was coming into Skyline and I needed my head in the game. I'd learned from previous races and my many practise laps that with the time to enjoy it, the view from the top of the mountain was breathtaking. Under any other circumstances, I would have taken a moment to appreciate the scenery, but midrace it was more important to focus. To stay in the moment. To feel the car and let it guide me safely down the mountain. Especially with so much on the line. My balls being first on the list.

For a breathless moment, I hung suspended in the sunlight before the road dropped away beneath me and I paced through the S bends into the dipper.

A soft right. A hard left. Accelerate hard down Conrod Straight.

The start/finish line flashed away beneath me in a blur of white and black.

You've got this, I reminded myself as I exhaled a shaky breath.

One lap down. One hundred and sixty to go. Thankfully, I would only have to drive around half of those. Morgan would drive the rest so I just needed to get through the laps the only way I could at the moment—one at a time.

The track map was as strong in my mind as ever. Despite the fact that I'd driven Mount Panorama enough for it to be almost ingrained in my psyche, I'd spent hours studying it again over the last few days. It was never enough though; it was always a track that managed to surprise even the most experienced drivers.

I refused to let the doubt-filled thoughts creep in. I needed to keep my head focused on each lap, one at a time, and not think beyond my current stint. Thirty more laps, give or take, and then Morgan would take over and I would have nothing to think about while he drove his bit. I'd have nothing to do but watch on and be ready to take control again when the time came. Thankfully, the track in front of me was still empty and I'd already built a small buffer between me and second place.

THE LAPS continued to drop away in a haze of sun, heat, and speed as the cars behind me jostled for positions. My radio squawked to life at regular intervals, directing me to watch my fuel, my tyres, or just issuing directions for the small adjustments I needed to make inside the car. I fell into the comfortable pattern of the track and felt my mind start to drift. Brown eyes filled my mind, even as I resisted the urge to think about her.

"Safety car, Declan. Bring her in." Eden's lilting voice shrilled in my mind, focusing me back on the track for lap thirty-one. "Morgan's ready to go."

Thank Christ.

All I needed to do was bring the car safely into the pits and then I was in the clear for roughly thirtyish laps as Morgan took control of the car. If he crashed, well, that was all on him. I briefly wondered if he'd let me anywhere near him with the rusty pliers if that happened.

Once the car was in the pits, I breathed freely again. The love I felt for the job was fast becoming a noose around my neck, dragging me down to the depths of doubt—and it was all *her* fault.

The changeover between drivers was hectic as usual, but I was free and had done a decent job increasing the lead by fractions of a second at a time.

I pulled off my helmet and shook my head before brushing my fingers through my hair to return some shape to the dark auburn mess. I would hate if anyone saw my trademark spikes flattened against my head in a terrible case of helmet hair. Or worse, for some damn pap to catch a shot of it. Even though I earned my pay on the track, I had a reputation among the ladies that I had to maintain. Morgan and I both did really. Although he'd been all but taken off the market, we were still the poster boys of the series. Women wanted us and men wanted to be us. With his surfer-style blond looks and the blue-eyed charm I'd been gifted with by my Irish heritage, we provided the perfect package to the sponsors.

There was a time where I'd had issues with posing for the magazines and other duties. Then I saw the benefits. Especially on shoots with other models—it was rare that I didn't bring at least one of them home with me.

Knowing I had some free time, I headed into the garage to take a breather. As soon as I was clear of the immediate pit area, I unzipped my fire suit and pulled it loose. Freeing my arms, I tied the top half around my waist to give me some air. It was so fucking hot. Being October, the air temperature was easily over thirty degrees. On the track though—in the car—it had been closer to sixty. I grabbed my water bottle, downed it almost too fast, spilling some of it down my chest. Reaching for another, I was tempted to just pour the whole thing over my head before sitting to watch the race on the monitors.

By the time I was settled, Morgan had already pulled the car cleanly back onto the track and was working his way past the slower cars. He was a speed freak like me and, even though I would never admit it to his face, a fantastic driver. He had just the right balance of brains and balls to find success on the track. That was why he'd finished second behind me last year. He was older and more experienced—and the current lead driver for Sinclair Racing. If I had one or two more championships under my belt, our positions might have been different.

It was being fucking discussed.

But that was before Queensland Raceway.

Once, that track had been my main stomping ground. It was close to where I had grown up, was near where I'd gotten my start in karts, and also where I had eventually cut my teeth in the early stages of racing cars. I'd moved rapidly up the ranks while I was still in high school, before being offered a place on Sinclair Racing's team. They were *the* elite Holden team in the ProV8 world.

Danny Sinclair, the team owner, had courted me onto his team by offering me a five-year contract for a lot of money. No, not just a lot—a shitload of money. More money than a suburban boy like me had ever expected to make in ten years or more. The only problem with the offer was that it had meant relocating to Sydney. Which meant leaving my friends and family behind and saying a final goodbye to *her*.

We'd already broken up by the time I'd got the contract, but it was still devastating to say that final goodbye. Seeing her that last night—the night it ended for good—it was clear the hurt we'd inflicted on one another the day we broke up was still so raw for the both of us.

After I'd moved to Sydney to join his team, Danny had told me that as soon as he'd watched me race, he'd wanted me to be part of his "family" and everything else had just been a formality. I started as a junior driver in production cars almost straight away. Within two years, I'd moved up the ranks and had been given the chance to drive as part of their V8 team. I had more than exceeded everyone's expectations—I was just that damn good. Or at least, I had been. Until Queensland Raceway.

That was where I saw her again.

I had no idea what she was even doing at a race. She hated the sport. She'd always told me that she couldn't understand the fascination boys had with their "toys." Regardless, she'd been at that racetrack—my home track—mere metres away and separated from me only by a group of about twenty people. I'd wanted to speak to her so badly, but I didn't want to force open old wounds for either of us. That was if she even still bore any scars.

We hadn't spoken since I'd left for Sydney around four years earlier, and that meeting had been difficult. She'd tried to call, often in fact, especially in the beginning. I'd known that if I wanted to have a chance of making my career work I needed to avoid her. She was too small town for me, and her dreams would only drag me into a suburban life I would never be happy with. A clean break was the easiest option for her. For both of us.

Over time, her calls had slowed until, almost a year after I'd moved, they'd stopped altogether. Once the calls stopped, I'd almost been able to put her out of my mind for good. She still resided in my dreams and nightmares and in memories of both good and bad times—smiles and tears. Our past played out on instant replay every night, but other than that, she'd never crossed my waking mind.

Until Queensland Raceway.

Until I'd seen her in person once more.

She, Alyssa Dawson, the knobbly-kneed girl I'd loved, had blossomed into one hell of a woman. Her hair, mahogany brown and hanging to her waist, was silkier than I remembered it. My fingers twitched at my side as I thought about the feel of it tickling against my skin as we'd kissed. At some point, her hips and boobs had taken a womanly shape that her previously boyish frame had never hinted was even possible.

When I'd spotted her, it was clear that she was waiting for someone. Her gaze scanned the crowd at regular intervals. For half a second, I'd arrogantly assumed it was me. That maybe she'd come to beg for another chance. That she was willing to admit she'd been wrong and that my racing was a career after all.

With a satisfied smirk on my face, I'd begun to move in her direction. That's when I saw him. When her lips split into a wide smile the instant the hulking figure headed in her direction, I knew she'd well and truly moved on and had no further interest in me. The guy cut an imposing figure, towering at least a head over most of the crowd as he walked toward her from the concession stand. He held a hot dog in each hand and had two cans of Coke balanced in the crook of one arm, which proved it wasn't an accidental meeting.

His perfectly tanned face returned her grin before he planted a kiss on her lips and handed off her half of the food. Watching as their lips touched, my hands formed into fists at my side. It didn't matter how brief their kiss had been, it hurt like a son of a bitch to witness. In that instant, I wanted nothing more than to pound him into the pavement. Not just because he'd kissed my girl.

She's not yours anymore.

It was painfully obvious that she'd willingly come to watch a race with someone who wasn't me *and* seemed to be enjoying herself even though she'd protested against the series the entire time we'd been together.

It was clear that it was love—she'd never once come to watch me race when we were together. A new emptiness clawed its way into my chest as I watched them sit happily together and chat as they ate. When they'd finished, she ruffled her fingers through his jet-black hair. With a laugh, he'd picked her up and thrown her over his shoulder, caveman style, while she giggled and pretended to protest. Even though it was the last thing I wanted to see, I couldn't tear my eyes away from the pair.

I'd been the one to gouge a chasm in our relationship and walk out on everything we'd shared. I should have been happy for her. Instead, I felt like charging over to the fucker who'd claimed her heart and ripping him limb from limb before carrying her off myself. Maybe I could even show her some of the moves I'd learned in the time we'd been apart.

That was Queensland Raceway.

That was immediately before I climbed in the car.

That was the first race, ever, that had ended in a DNF for me.

That was why the former love of my life had become the bane of my existence. It was the memory of her that appeared and haunted me around the race track, leaching my concentration away for vital seconds at a time.

CHAPTER TWO

ON REPORT

WITH MY HEAD cradled in my hands, I tried to clear it of all thoughts of Alyssa. I tried not to think of her dark mahogany hair that curled at the ends and was almost unmanageable in the summer humidity of Browns Plains. It was vital I didn't focus on the memory of her light honey-gold eyes, or the long black lashes that framed them. Any thought of her boobs—so well developed since I'd last seen her—were strictly forbidden.

"Declan," a voice called.

I glanced up to see Gary, one of the pit crew, leading one of the roving pit reporters over to me. It wasn't the normal TV guy, who was an ex-V8 driver himself and now provided expert commentary on the race. Instead, it was a pretty young brunette who wouldn't have been out of place as a grid girl. I flashed her one of my winning smiles, even though she was officially off-limits—and not just because she was at my "workplace." With a growing blush, she held up a mic and made it clear she wanted an interview before I went back onto the track. I nodded. It was part of the job after all— the part that sponsors paid for, in fact.

Standing, I slipped the arms of my fireproof suit back on and zipped it up. The reasons were twofold. First, I wanted to be ready to take control of the car as soon as the mini interview was over and Morgan had arrived back in the pits. Second, all of my sponsors' badges were displayed prominently on my outfit. The more screen time I got them, the more they loved me. It was win-win.

The plump-lipped reporter—I probably should have known her name, it wasn't the first time she'd covered a ProV8 race that season—was already talking to the camera by the time I made my way to her side.

"I'm here with Declan Reede," she said before moving to cover the last inch of distance between us. Her boobs brushed my forearm as she talked. "Declan, how are you feeling about your chances today in light of your recent form?"

I bristled. Of course she had to bring that up. I chose to ignore most of the question and give the standard-issue response. "The car is feeling really good today. With a bit of luck and perseverance, I'm sure McGuire and I will both be on the podium at the end of the race."

"How about you?" She twisted her body in a way that forced her boobs to brush across my hand. "Do you have anyone special cheering you on today?"

I resisted the urge to roll my eyes at her. It was well known that Declan Reede did not have a personal cheer squad at any race meeting. I didn't have a significant other—didn't want one because it would only spoil my fun.

Instead of answering her, I checked the monitors. Morgan was just finishing lap sixty-two, and was being called back into the pit.

I was up. For a double stint at that—sixty-odd laps straight before handing it back over to Morgan to bring the car home. We'd agreed that would be the safest option; it was always sometime in the last ten laps that I choked . . . and crashed. I shuddered. *Not today.*

"So no special little lady here?" The reporter prompted when I didn't answer.

It almost sounded like she was fishing for a no. Maybe she was hoping for a ride with a champion. If so, she would be sorely disappointed. I didn't do brunettes, not anymore. It was my one rule when it came to selecting my "dates." The fact that she was asking such ridiculous questions only made me less inclined to dance the horizontal tango with her.

I cast her a withering glare.

"I thought you were here to cover a race, not gather juicy titbits for *Gossip Weekly*," I admonished before walking away, leaving her flustered and covering for the camera.

I'd probably get my arse kicked for being rude while we were live to air, but these rookie fucking reporters needed to learn that some questions were off limits. Especially by reporters with brown hair and big-arse doe eyes like the ones that haunted me on the track.

By the time I reached the pit area, it was clear that I'd been sitting in the corner of the garage for so long, not paying attention to anything but my meandering thoughts, that I hadn't even noticed the rain setting in. I should have known, really. Rain at Mount Panorama during the Bathurst enduro was almost as regular as the race itself. That didn't make it any easier to drive in though.

Unless the rain was a consistent downpour over the whole area, the track always ended up with dry patches. It happened because of way the bitumen stretched up over the mountain. That left all of the teams with a difficult choice: stay out on slicks and risk sliding all over the track if it's too wet, or put on wet-weather tyres and risk chewing through the tread and slowing the car down if it's too dry.

The decision came down to forecasting and the wrong decision could cost time later on. If we stayed on slicks and the rain continued we would need to pit that much earlier to change to wet weathers and vice versa. Luckily, we had Eden on our team. She had a knack for it, an innate ability to read a track. She very rarely got it wrong. I knew she'd already had a plan in place because she had the guys warming a fresh set of slicks. It seemed unlikely I'd be driving on a wet track for long.

I was flicking through the stats of Morgan's last laps, checking for any information, when Eden darted to my side. Her willowy frame was flattered by the team shirt, and even though her curves were fairly boyish, the presentation did the sponsors proud. Black pants wrapped her long legs which only served to make her appear taller and thinner than she really was. She pulled her mic away from her mouth so that whatever she had to tell me didn't accidentally get repeated to everyone.

"It's going to be a bit wetter at first, but I think it's clearing. You'll hopefully be all right on slicks. You just gotta keep your head these first few laps and you'll do fine. Watch yourself on Forrest Elbow."

I nodded absently, running over the information I needed on the car's handling and performance over the last few laps that Morgan had run.

"Dec," Eden said.

I glanced up at her in confusion when she didn't say anything further.

She grinned at me, her hazel-green eyes sparkling. With her sandy-brown hair pulled up away from her face and the giant headset on, the expression made her seem like an overgrown child.

"Relax out there," she ordered. "You'll do fine."

I gave her a genuine smile in return. Sometimes, especially lately, it felt like she was the only one on the team who was on my side. "Thanks, Edie."

I finished getting ready for my next drive and headed into position, ready to jump back in the car.

Minutes later, Morgan slid the car to a perfect stop and the frantic driver change occurred once more. The instant he was out, I climbed in, and set about reattaching everything and fastening my harness as fast as I could. The instant I'd finished, I clipped the window netting back into place and gave the thumbs up to let my crew know I was in and ready to go. I was acutely aware of the fact that most races were won and lost as much by fast pit stops and good strategy as by any actual driving. And of course, by not crashing.

The instant the car dropped back to the ground, I pressed my foot to the accelerator. Despite my rush, I was careful to keep the speed limiter on—the last thing I needed was a stop/go penalty for pit lane speeding. When I reached the end of the pits, I exploded out of the exit and onto the track.

In that moment, at that speed, I felt invincible. Thanks to my original lead and Morgan's perfect driving, we were currently in fifth position on track, but first overall after adjusting for compulsory pit stops. All I had to do was keep us there.

And so the dance began again.

CHAPTER THREE

HAUNTED

I'D BARELY REACHED Forrest Elbow on the first lap of my latest stint when I felt the tail start to slide. I hit the marbles on the edge of the track and struggled to retain control.

But I did. I got the car back where it needed to be, and it felt fucking fantastic.

Maybe I can do this after all.

I allowed myself to hope for a few seconds, but then my mind offered up a vision of her eyes. Red rims around honey-gold irises—the way they'd looked when I said goodbye a little less than four years ago. I shut down the images as quickly as I could when I felt my tail slide loose again. My rear kissed the side of a car attempting to come up my inside before I managed to right it.

My radio crackled to life and Eden's voice came through my headset. "Watch it, Declan. Morgan's asked me to remind you about the pliers."

Focus.

Just think about the track ahead.

Concentrate.

Three more laps and I'd found my groove again. Despite the incidents at the top of the track, the lighter fuel load and drier track helped me keep the car straight. The distance between me and the other cars behind me grew.

When I came down Conrod Straight, I overtook a Ford, which put me in third position overall and still outright first. My breathing steadied as I felt the car fall into a comfortable rhythm. It seemed impossible that we could lose, but I didn't allow myself to get too cocky. Not with my form, and certainly not at the notorious Bathurst.

Up. Down. Clutch. Accelerator. Brake. One, two, three, four. Hard to the left. Up Mountain Straight. Hard to the right. Through the cutting and Reid Park. Past McPhillamy and into the skyline. Breeze through the Esses into the Dipper. Soft right. Hard left around Forrest Elbow. Race down Conrod Straight.

Eden had been right about the track. By the ninth lap of my second stint, the bitumen was bone dry and the teams that had gambled on the rain staying were scrambling to the pits to change back onto slicks. I used the time to push even further ahead. Eden's voice squawked over the radio, telling me that I had just achieved the fastest lap time of the day. If I didn't have to keep both hands on the wheel, I would have given a fist pump in celebration. Things were finally going my way.

I was celebrating the small victories when I came across the top of the mountain again, across Skyline. The glare from the sun reflected in the top corner of my windscreen and I was blinded. Not by the light, but by the vision which the sun called to mind.

Alyssa.

My heart stopped and my eyes slammed closed.

Smiles and laughs; the sun glinting off her watch as we kept an eye on the time.

I could almost hear her voice bouncing around the car, laughing over some ridiculous shit we'd done during the day. We'd been so happy. So innocent. So fucking naive and stupid.

The memory was from one of the days we'd ditched school to hide out in our park. With a gasp, I swallowed oxygen down into protesting lungs. My hands shook and tremors raced through my fingers and into the wheel.

My stomach clenched as I remembered just how beautiful she'd been. She didn't have supermodel looks, she had something better. An honest to goodness girl-next-door quality that shone through from within and made her ten times sexier than any over glossed supermodel could ever be. The truth was, as bad as the visions of Alyssa's red-rimmed eyes were, the happy ones were worse. They became tangible reminders of how much she'd once meant to me, and I almost didn't *want* to suppress them.

With two more gulping breaths, I forced my eyes open and pushed the thought away. My grip tightened on the steering wheel, but it was already too late.

Though it'd been mere seconds, I'd been in my own world—my past—for too long and hadn't prepared to take the turn before falling into the Esses. I had no time to do anything but adjust the angle of my car as it smashed into the concrete barrier with a teeth-rattling bang. I prepared myself in the only way I could for a second crash as the car ricocheted off the wall, spun across the track, and then smashed into the side of a passing car. The sound of crunching metal and squealing rubber filled the space around me, but I could do nothing but hold on and hope for the best. My car lurched sickeningly toward the wall again, shunting hard into the concrete and rocking me into the hard surface of the door.

By the time I came to a rest, I was angled nose into the wall in a stationary car.

Unable to move, I panted as I struggled to comprehend just what had happened, aside from the fact that I'd crashed—that part I got loud and fucking clear. Closing my eyes, I mentally ran through my body to ensure I wasn't too badly injured. I wiggled my fingers and my toes and was relieved when everything did what it was supposed to. Except for my heart racing at a million miles a minute, and the fact that I couldn't breathe down nearly enough air to stay in control, I was okay.

My eyes snapped to the rear-view mirror when I heard the sound of protesting tyres.

Shit!

Another car, flying down from Skyline, hadn't seen me until it was too late. Although the driver was braking hard, he wasn't going to be able to stop or avoid crashing into me. I was too far out on the road. Waiting for the impact was maddening. It was as if time had stopped as I sucked down a breath and prepared for another jolt.

When time seemed to have restarted, it jumped to fast forward. The car slammed into the back of mine hard enough to lurch my whole body forward. My teeth smashed together, the impact rattling my skull until stars exploded behind my eyes. I said a silent thanks for the HANS device and harness holding me in place.

The nose of my car ploughed farther into the wall with a loud crunch before the tail lifted and spun my car again. The motion tossed me around like a rag doll as my car was hit once more. I finally came to a rest with the passenger side of the car hard against the barrier.

I risked a glance around to see two other damaged cars parked close to mine. The officials had the yellow flags out at last, and I had no doubt the safety car was already on its way around the track. At least it meant it was unlikely any other cars were going to join the pile-up.

"What the hell, Declan?" Eden's voice admonished me. "Danny's going to have your arse for this."

Yeah, yeah, tell me something I don't know.

I smacked the steering wheel hard before scrambling out of the wreck. The car was totalled. The once sleek red and black exterior now a mangled mess of broken glass, ripped stickers, exposed metal, and broken plastic.

I guess I win the record after all. Go me!

In frustration, I kicked the door. A sharp ache echoed up my leg.

"Fucking shitter of a fucking bastard of a fucking car!" I screamed as I ignored the pain and kicked the car again.

I knew I was supposed to leave the track immediately to avoid further injury, but I couldn't resist kicking the car a few more times to vent my frustration.

Finally, after a few more, "Fucks," "Fucking hells," and kicks for good measure, I climbed over the barrier.

Even though it was clear I was okay, I headed for the medics for clearance, ripping off the sleeve on my race suit as I went. Three of them came over to me and ran me through a series of concussion tests and other bullshit. Even though my ankle still ached from kicking the car, and a pain niggled along the right side of my body, I refused to tell them. I'd ice whatever I needed to when I got home, and deal with the rest later. I didn't have time for any of it. I just wanted to be gone. Not just from the car, but from the track. The team. The whole place. My life in general. The farther away, the better.

Eden was right, as usual. Danny was going to own my arse over the crash.

Fucking Alyssa "small town" Dawson. If it wasn't for her, none of this shit would have happened.

"Reede!"

I rolled my eyes at the sound of another driver's voice behind me—Hunter Blake, with Ford's Wood Racing. Ignoring the ache in my ankle, I walked faster to escape him. I couldn't deal with his bullshit.

Obviously uninjured, he covered the distance between us faster than I could walk. Grabbing on to my shoulder, he spun me around. "What the fuck was that?"

I shoved him off. "Go fuck yourself, Blake."

"You had to pull that crap didn't you? What's that, six in a row now?" His eyes narrowed.

"What the fuck do you care?"

"I don't give a fuck about your performance issues, until they affect me. They're affecting me, so you better fucking watch—"

"Hunter." His name was barked in a sharp tone by a unique voice on the circuit. Paige Wood, the owner of Wood Racing. She was a relatively new team owner, having taken over from her father when he retired, but she ran a tight ship and her team was second only to Sinclair. "Back to the pits."

Like the little lapdog he was, Hunter sneered at me once more and then spun around and retreated.

Instead of turning to follow him, Paige came up to me. Her

short blonde hair was pristinely coiffed, and despite her garish make-up she was kind of pretty. The team polo she wore showed the benefits of her fantastic surgeon—she was full in all the right places. All in all, she wasn't bad looking, for an older woman. A wild cougar displaying her true colours, and definitely someone I wouldn't say no to bedding if the offer arose. "Mr. Reede."

I nodded. "Mrs. Wood."

She chuckled, a throaty laugh which was clearly designed to be seductive. "It's Ms and please, call me Paige."

I nodded, and waited impatiently for her to get to her point.

"That was an unfortunate incident on the track."

Raising one eyebrow, I scoffed at her. "Unfortunate?"

She stepped closer to me, brushing her hands through the front of my hair.

With an eyebrow raised at the overfamiliar touch, I reached out and captured her wrist before lowering her hand back to her side.

A sly, challenging smile lit her lips. "Well, it wasn't exactly deliberate, was it? What else can it be called besides unfortunate?"

There were a hundred other things I could have called it, but I wasn't going to say them all. In fact, I was surprised how calm she was considering she'd lost a car in the tangle.

"You're not injured I hope?" she purred as she trailed her gaze over my body.

Glancing down at my ankle, I shook my head. "Nothing I can't handle."

"I assume Danny isn't going to be very happy with you?"

I barked a laugh. "That's an understatement."

She chuckled again, another throaty sound which echoed into my cock. "Well, maybe it's time you and I had a little chat about things?" She brushed her hand over my shoulder. "I like to give my boys extra-special attention."

I smirked at her. The attention she was lavishing on me certainly gave me something positive to concentrate on rather than the shit I was going to have to deal with back at Sinclair's pits. Some of the dealings I'd had with her in the past were a little less than desirable, and I had no interest in joining her team, but there was something about having the undivided attention of a woman who clearly looked after herself. Something told me she'd be a firecracker in the sack too.

"How about we have dinner sometime?" she said as she brushed her fingers through my hair again. "Talk about your future."

"I'm locked in with Sinclair for another year," I said. *Assuming he doesn't fire my arse.* "So I'm not sure what there is to talk about."

Another one of her throaty chuckles slipped past her lips. "Even if you're locked in for twelve months, there's plenty to discuss. I'd do almost anything to get you under me."

There was no missing or confusing the double entendre in her words. "Maybe it's worth having that chat one day then."

She brushed her fingers over my cheek. "Later then."

I turned around to go back to the pits, but stopped when I saw Hazel Sinclair—sweet Hazel, Danny's wife—staring wide-eyed at me in disbelief. When I gave her a wave to let her know I was okay, she frowned and turned away. It was a sign of the things I would be facing when I went back into the pits.

Fuck that shit.

CHAPTER FOUR

GETTING AWAY

INSTEAD OF REPORTING back to the pits to deal with the punishment I knew was coming, I fucked off. I climbed into my Monaro and drove straight back to Sydney.

The press would probably have a fucking field day at my expense, especially the snooty brunette reporter I'd spurned during the midrace interview. I didn't want to face them, or any of the drivers I'd taken out in my wreck. There were five of them who wanted my arse for the crash—Morgan more than any other. I just didn't see the point in hanging around the track long enough to get grilled, beaten, and investigated.

Or worse: fired.

My weekend was over by that point anyway. There was no way the boys would get the twisted mess that used to be my car back on the track. Which meant I wouldn't be getting back into the car for any reason, and unfortunately, neither would Morgan. I had little doubt he was already hunting down the pliers to follow through on his threat.

Only bad things waited for me back at the pits. If Danny was going to give me the sack, it was going to be easier to deal with later—after everyone cooled off. Hopefully in a private meeting where my dirty laundry wouldn't be aired all over the TV. I really didn't need my shame to be any more public than it already had been. It was almost a certainty that I would cop a fine for my outburst at the top of the track after I'd crashed. Short of a summary dismissal by Sinclair, it really couldn't get much worse for me.

Besides, by the time I'd finished with the paramedics, I barely gave a flying fuck what else happened to me. I was so far beyond caring about anything. All I wanted to do was get wasted and get laid. It didn't even have to be in that order.

I drove straight home. Throughout my drive, my phone kept ringing, but I steadily ignored it, hitting the end button on the steering wheel. There was no way I wanted to talk to anyone. It didn't matter who it was, they'd only destroy the little that remained of my sanity. When the caller still didn't take the hint, I turned the phone off completely.

After I'd parked the Monaro beside my Prado, I called a taxi so that I could have a good night without worrying about any of my cars being left unattended in the city. The trek from the garage to my upstairs bedroom had never felt longer. Weariness weighted my limbs and made each step difficult. The only thing that kept me moving was the promise of a drink at the end of the effort.

I jumped straight into the shower. Once the water was cascading around me, I thought about the accident and shuddered. I'd been in so many lately: six crashes from six starts. It wasn't possible to grow accustomed to it though—at least, I hadn't. Despite all of the safety precautions, there was always one instant where I wondered whether I would survive the impact. Somewhere between the brakes squealing and the metal crunching, my heart stopped beating. It only started again when I could feel my teeth aching and my brain swimming from the impact. As if reminded of the ache by the memory of the crash, my ankle niggled and my chest protested. I'd have to ice it before long, but that was something I could do later.

My body trembled as the adrenaline that had carried me through the three-hour drive home wore off.

I needed a drink.

Badly.

I couldn't think of anything else that would get rid of the shakes or the memories. I didn't bother washing my hair, it could go another day. I did wash my balls though, twice in fact, revelling in the fact that Morgan couldn't get his rusty pliers near them as long as I avoided him. It was more a precaution though. I wanted to make sure they got some special attention tonight from some lucky chick. Between the need to let off steam and Paige Wood's casual teasing, I needed to get off.

As I washed off the soap, I debated a quick wank to alleviate the pressure before going out; something to tide me over until I could find some little cutie willing to fulfil my wishes. The issue was, there was only ever one image which could get me off that way, and I definitely didn't want to be thinking about her just then. Not so soon after she'd caused me to crash. Again.

Turning off the water, I shoved open the door and grabbed a towel from the rack nearby. While I was towelling off, I caught sight of my own reflection and scowled at myself in disgust.

What have you become? You're fucking pathetic.

I threw the towel at the mirror, and turned to leave the room to find an outfit that was guaranteed to help me score. Black satin boxers were my staple item for a night out, and over the top I threw on a pair of slacks that did nothing to hide any boner I would have. I topped it off with a collared shirt that had sleeves easy enough to roll up to show off my arms—that always seemed to drive women crazy. I usually would have thrown on a team shirt, but I didn't want to be reminded of the fact that I might no longer be part of Sinclair Racing.

My solution to the whole situation was simple. I was going to do what I always did: hit the town, get absolutely shitfaced, and find some pussy to bury myself in. The problems would still be there in a day or two, but at least I could get some semblance of relief before I had to face them.

The taxi arrived while I was still getting dressed, but I just waved at the driver through the window to let him know I was aware that he'd arrived and then finished what I was doing. He could wait five minutes; it wasn't like he wasn't getting paid after all. Before I left, I downed a shot of whiskey to get a jump on things, and then grabbed a Corona from the fridge for the road.

Within half an hour, I was being ushered into the VIP room of my favourite club, Firebird. I loved it more than most clubs because I felt at home there. The whole place was themed with a garage motif. The sign out front was a bonnet from a Firebird, complete with phoenix, secured to a chrome bumper in front of an old roller door. Inside was more of a typical nightclub, with an ambiance aimed at privacy and secret deeds. The music was always loud, the drinks were always flowing, and the women were always loose. It was the perfect place to disappear and satisfy my cravings for booze and a wet pussy to sink myself into.

The VIP area was set up better than most I'd seen. Lining the edges of the space were six private booths, each with a set of black satin curtains that could be drawn for a little extra privacy. It meant I could take what I needed without having the hassle of bringing any girls back to my house. It certainly saved a taxi fare and awkward conversation in the morning.

I secured my booth, ensuring I had one regardless of how many people were allowed past the velvet rope, and then ordered a drink. Once I was comfortable, I sat back to scope out the talent.

There were three blondes, four brunettes, and a redhead. That meant my choices were instantly narrowed from eight to four. I couldn't do brunettes. I'd tried, a few times actually, but I just . . . couldn't. They'd all been absolutely fine pieces of arse too. It was just that every time I saw one of them sucking my cock, or bent over in front of me, I'd pictured Alyssa. And I couldn't picture her as one of these skanks—as some random piece of tail to use, abuse, and recycle. She was special.

The redhead and her blonde friend were dancing rather closely together on the dance floor. When she spotted me watching her, a smirk broke across her lips and their dancing grew even more risqué. I necked my beer and drank, all without taking my eyes off of the pair of them.

The redhead grinned at me, winked and then starting kissing

her friend, making certain that I saw every stroke of her tongue and every shift of her fingers over her friend's cheeks, neck, boobs.

Fuck me.

I was definitely up for another threesome. The way they were behaving, I was sure I could fuck them both multiple times before the club closed. I called over the private bartender. He knew what they were drinking—one of the perks of the VIP room—so I ordered them each another drink, and a Corona and a double shot of whiskey for me. I downed the whiskey while he made their fruity-arse cocktails. Once I had our drinks in hand, I ambled over to the pair.

"Hey, ladies," I said, oozing every ounce of charm I could muster after my shitty-arse day. "I thought you might be thirsty after all that dancing."

I flipped them my wicked smile, the one that practically guaranteed I got lucky, as I openly gazed over their entwined bodies. They both giggled in response.

This'll be easier than I thought.

The redhead moved closer to me. "You're Declan Reede, aren't you?"

"The one and only. And tonight I'll be your personal escort."

She giggled again, and it was clear she was already fucking wasted. I had the night in the bag; nothing could stop this score.

"I'm Tillie, and this is Talia." She indicated her blonde friend, who was kissing her way up Tillie's throat. They continued to bump and grind against each other as we talked. What little doubt I'd had about how easy a score it was going to be was swept away by their movements. The sight of them practically dry humping one another had me hard and ready to go.

"Well, Tillie, Talia, mind if I *come* between you?" I ensured I put extra emphasis in the right places to give them no doubt what my intentions were.

They both giggled and downed the drinks I had brought them like the glasses contained nothing but water. I skulled my Corona just as quickly and then they each grabbed one of my hands and pulled me between them. Within minutes, we were a meld of hands, mouths, and gratuitous grinding. I didn't think it was possible for me to get any harder.

Breaking free momentarily, I signalled my bartender for another round of drinks.

The two girls pressed themselves into me, and I was sandwiched between a wall of pussy and tits, fingers and tongues. It was my happy place, and I forgot about all the shit that had gone down on the track. I was even able to forget about Alyssa—almost.

I brushed my hand along Tillie's chest, gently at first, but when I got no negative reaction, I moved more deliberately. My fingers traced her nipples through the skimpy metallic shirt that barely covered her breasts. She moaned, so I captured her mouth with mine and her fiery red hair with my free hand. The position gave me enough control to push our way over to my booth, recessed in the dark wall. As soon as we reached our destination, I slid my hands up inside her dress, pushing it over her hips, and hooking my fingers into her panties. She reached for my zipper, pulling it down and pressing her hand over the front of my boxers.

I was tangled with her when another pair of hands traced the muscles along my back before joining Tillie's hand palming me over my underwear. I released Tillie's mouth to look behind me and met Talia's gaze as she leaned against my back.

"I was feeling lonely," she purred against my ear, as she moved her hand below Tillie's to stroke my cock.

"Don't worry, baby, there's plenty to go around," I said as I reached behind me, grabbing Talia's hair and guiding her head closer so that I could claim her lips to thank her for her help. The angle sent a sharp pain jolting through my side, but with the girls' magic hands touching me, I was able to ignore it. Tillie's fingers closed around my cloth-covered balls, drawing a moan of pleasure from me, which Talia kissed away with an open mouth and plenty of tongue.

My cock strained to escape and hide away deep within one of these girls, but Tillie's hand began working miracles even through the silky material as Talia held my face, running her tongue along mine. As Tillie stroked my cock, I felt her shift, drawing my attention to her. I watched as she sat up further, bringing her face to my stomach. She teased me through the cotton of my shirt, and ran her tongue between the buttons.

With one hand, I teased her nipples thought her shirt as I closed my eyes and relished the sweet ache of their combined touches. A flash of light erupted. For a fraction of a second, the world behind my eyelids shifted from black to red.

Shit.

My eyes snapped open just in time to be assaulted by another flash. And another. I pushed backward away from Tillie, knocking Talia to her arse as I did. I swung around just in time to see the filthy pap jump over the barrier and leave the club.

After helping Talia up, I made my excuses to leave the two women. Zipping up my pants as I moved, I gave chase to the pap even though it was too late. My ankle protested every step, and by the time I reached the door, I could barely stand on it. My night was ruined. The mood was officially killed and I needed to get ice on my injury more than anything else. One thing I liked about the club was its discretion, and yet they'd allowed a photographer in to capture the moment.

See if they'll get my fucking business again.

There was no doubt I'd soon be featured in *Gossip Weekly* again.

It was just what I fucking needed after the shit of the race meeting. One more incident for Danny Sinclair to nail me over. I didn't even want to imagine what he might have to say about it all. In pain, and ready for sleep, I gave up on the idea of an easy screw and headed home.

CHAPTER FIVE

SURPRISE ENDINGS

AFTER I GOT home, I camped out on the couch to assess my shitty-arsed weekend. With a cold beer in my hand, I tried to ignore the ghost of Alyssa dancing just behind my eyes. It was proving hard though, especially when I was inside my own head trying to concentrate on anything except the ache in my ankle and the pain that was blossoming steadily over my side.

I couldn't help but wonder how things had slid so out of control so fast. One thing was clear, Danny would demand some answers when I saw him next, and I knew I'd better have some damn good ones if I wanted to stay on the team.

I sighed. Maybe the first step to moving on was working out where my life had started to go wrong. The problem was that *nothing* had changed. Not really. I knew that—was acutely aware of it. The reality was before I'd seen Alyssa again, I was fine. After seeing her with the new man in her life, I was fucked. But the sighting hadn't *changed* a single goddamned thing.

When I'd first left Brisbane, I'd realised Alyssa was going to date again—so that hadn't changed. I hadn't *said* anything to her when I saw her—so that hadn't changed. I hadn't made any embarrassing cock-ups or done something which would sear myself into her memory or her into mine. *Nothing*. There was no fundamental shift or cosmic U-turn which had occurred. I still felt the same as I always had, only now she was *there* whenever I closed my eyes. Fresher in my mind maybe, and sexier than ever.

It wasn't like I wanted Alyssa back in my life though. Not really. She might have been the subject of my fantasies on the rare occasions I jerked off, but that wasn't a sign of anything serious. Neither was it new. It had been that way ever since I'd left her. There was logic in that though. She'd been the one woman who'd had something of a semipermanent role in my sex life when we were younger, during my formative years at that. With my revolving bedroom door and buffet of choices, I never had time to study any of the women long enough to actually remember faces or specific details. That was all it was, I was certain of it.

Besides, I doubted there were many red-blooded men who wouldn't fantasise about Alyssa if they'd seen her naked. Especially the way she'd bloomed in the last four years. I swallowed hard just thinking about it. Some things hadn't changed though: she still had the ideal girl-next-door look, clearly still didn't slather her face with inches of make-up, and I was certain still had just enough snark in her personality to guarantee a wild night in bed.

Is she wild in bed? My palm slid down to caress my cock before I'd given it a thought. *I bet she is.*

Those new curves . . . My mouth went dry as I cupped myself.

Stop!

Fuck!

The fact that Alyssa starred in my dreams or kept me awake every night wasn't entirely unusual either. That had been happening for as long as I'd been in Sydney. It certainly wasn't a sign that I wanted her back. If I'd wanted that, I never would have left Brisbane in the first place. I would have at least returned one of her phone calls. Or something.

Even after I'd seen her at Queensland Raceway, the reasons we'd broken up were still as true as the day we'd parted. She was too focused on her small-town views—she had wanted the regular life. The husband, white picket fence, and two point four kids. She didn't understand racing—the excitement of being behind the wheel and overtaking someone or standing atop the fucking podium holding high a trophy that was earned through blood, sweat, and tears. She didn't understand the perks that came with it—the fame, money, and hot women.

No, I definitely didn't want her anymore.

I didn't want that life.

Closing my eyes, I relaxed against the couch. At some point, I must have drifted off because the next thing I knew, a pounding filled the house. A second later, the pounding stopped but then the doorbell chimed. With a glance at the clock on the wall, I confirmed it was almost four thirty in the morning.

Who the fuck makes unannounced house calls at this time?

The doorbell rang again, and again. Whoever it was, they were persistent.

"I'm coming!" I shouted over the noise as I limped to the front door. "Hold your fucking horses." *This better be fucking important.*

I pulled the door open, but before I even had a chance to get a look at who it was, I was greeted by a fist connecting with my left eye. A second fist smashed hard into my gut and my breath flew from my body, expelled in one painful burst. Doubled over, and with blurry vision, I could only make out vague shapes and not specific details.

"What the fuck!" I wheezed out while trying to suck in some air around the piercing agony in my chest. Even though the attacker was unarmed, images of a knife embedded in my skin swum in front of my eyes. It couldn't have been more painful even if I had been stabbed. Stars danced in front of my eyes. Gasping for air, I couldn't get enough.

"Just repaying what I owe you." I recognised Morgan's beachside drawl the instant he spoke. The purpose of the visit was clear—my accident, and our subsequent DNF, had all but put him completely out of championship contention. "And delivering a warning. If, against my better judgement, we're ever partnered again and you fuck up my chances for the championship again . . ."

The sound of my desperate attempts for breath filled my head and darkness overtook me. Pressing one hand against the doorframe to support myself, I tried to pull myself upright and met his gaze. His lips twisted in a grimace and fire flickered in his hazel gaze. The expression, coupled with the lack of any words in his threat, was more potent than any words that could have come out of his mouth.

A few weeks ago, I would have called him a cock, punched him back, and then we would have fought until one of us was on the ground. We would've laughed, had a few beers to get over it, and then he would have left my house after we were back on okay terms. As it was though, with me unable to force air into my lungs, it was taking everything I had not to fall in a heap at his feet. I staggered forward, leaning against him. My hands groped at his shirt as I tried desperately to suck down oxygen—any air.

"Fucking hell, man!" Morgan snapped at me, shocked by my lack of retaliation and by the wetness that was threatening my eyes. "Seriously, Reede! You need to get your shit together."

I coughed around the ache, but the action caused the vice around my chest to tighten and squeezed the last of my breath out of me. I fell to my knees in front of Morgan. Despite trying to force the oxygen in with gasp after gasp, I couldn't get the oxygen I needed. My mind spun and I sank to the ground.

"Shit," Morgan muttered as he looked at me.

The last thing I saw was Morgan's frowning face swimming in front of me before the darkness claimed me.

"DECLAN." ALYSSA'S voice filled my mind and I knew I was dreaming.

I was too comfortable, felt too light. It was as if all the weight in the world had been lifted from my shoulders.

"What are you doing to yourself?" The worry echoing through her voice didn't touch my euphoric mood as the familiar scent of coconuts and everything that was *her* surrounded me. I inhaled deeply, and as I did, a sharp ache echoed through me and stole my breath. I cried out in agony.

Something wet dropped onto my hand, and I tried to force my eyes open but they refused to cooperate. All I got were blurry images that I couldn't piece together properly.

"Is this really your dream? Is *this* what you gave up everything we had for?"

What I could see through the haze was dark mahogany hair, frosted with streaks of blonde near the top—just like Alyssa's had been when I saw her at Queensland Raceway.

"Lys," I croaked, still certain I was dreaming and wanting to hold on to the image as long as I could. Her nickname slipped from me despite the years it had been since I'd used it last.

An answering sob filled my ears as a hand gripped mine more tightly. A cool sensation flowed up my arm and I sank back into the darkness.

I WOKE alone in a hospital bed.

It was a sad indicator of the hole my life had become that no one was there to fuss over me. I pushed the call button to get the attention of a nurse to at least find out why the fuck I was even there. A matronly woman walked in—nothing like the nurses I would have liked to be treated by—and started to check my vitals with a string of questions on her lips. While she spoke, I recalled Morgan's visit. Fucker. He'd put me into hospital—he'd never gone that hard on me before.

She was halfway through her examination when she brushed her fingers over my hand. The sensation reminded me of the vision I'd had of Alyssa crying at my side. *Is her vision stalking me even here?*

"Was there someone here?" I asked.

The nurse shook her head. "Not that I saw, hun," she said. "I do have instructions to ring a"—she paused to read something off the chart—"Danny Sinclair when you're awake and lucid."

I offered what I hoped was a winning smile. "Can I not be awake and lucid for a little while longer?"

She frowned and waited for me to elaborate.

"He's my boss. He's going to chew me out as soon as he gets here. I just . . . need a break first. Please?"

A moment passed without her saying anything. Then she nodded. "I'll wait until you've had some food at least. How are you feeling?"

I scoffed. "Do you want the truth?"

"Best not to sugar-coat it otherwise we won't know if you're healin', will we?"

"In that case, I feel like shit."

She chuckled before stifling it. "I'm not surprised. You've fractured two ribs and strained a few muscles to boot."

"Well, fuck me." It meant I would be out of the car for at least a month—maybe more. My season was all but over, and that was assuming Danny didn't just fire my arse.

"There'll be none of that for a little while," the nurse said with a chuckle.

"Shit, really?" I pushed myself upright, and regretted it instantly as the pain in my chest vice-gripped my lungs.

"You need to give your ribs a chance to repair without undue stress."

I didn't tell her that a severe case of blue balls would *be* undue stress. "So a couple of days?" I asked, wondering whether I could do it.

"A couple of weeks, just to be on the safe side. And no heavy lifting in the meantime."

Even though it was tempting to crack a joke about not being able to hold my junk then, I kept my mouth closed as I considered a couple of weeks without sex.

"What about . . ." I glanced around to make sure we were definitely alone—the last thing I needed was for some pap to overhear me asking if I was still okay to jerk off. "Wanking," I added in a whisper.

"The doctor will talk you through the dos and don'ts, I'm sure, but you'll have to listen to your body. It's the muscle spasms that will do you in."

I winced as I thought about the ab-tightening, chest-compressing euphoria of an Alyssa-induced self-loving orgasm. "Damn."

True to her word, the nurse didn't call Danny until after I'd had something to eat, and was practically ready to be discharged. Instead of him coming in person, I was just left with a message to be at his office in two days. I doubted the meeting would bring anything good.

TWO DAYS later, after the team got back from Bathurst, I limped into Danny's office and sat staring at the trophies that lined the wall behind him. It was easier than meeting the slate-grey gaze of the man I'd disappointed—and forced into spending a fortune in the process.

"You're still hurt." Somehow Danny's observation came out as an accusation.

I hid my foot under the chair. Both my ribs and my ankle still hurt like a son of a bitch, but I'd done a decent enough job of managing by myself at home in the time since I was discharged from hospital.

I swallowed down my nerves. "It's nothing."

After narrowing his eyes at my assertion that I was still fit, he launched into a ten minute tirade about being a team and how my actions affected other people.

Even though it was almost impossible to hold my tongue, I did. Anything I said, any words I let loose in a sarcastic comeback, would only add fuel to the fire. Fuel that was definitely not needed in light of the crash, my injuries, and everything else.

After he'd finished his lecture, he laid three things in front of me—the latest issue of *Gossip Weekly* with my public threesome gracing the cover, a letter from the ProV8 officials, and a plain envelope.

"You've really messed things up for yourself this time, Declan," Danny said, his voice firm. His grey hair looked like it had been through a wind tunnel, probably because of his nervous habit of running his fingers through it when he was stressed. Given the pressure of managing a ProV8 team, it was a wonder he wasn't bald. He'd raked his hair no less than fifteen times since I'd entered his office.

I just nodded in response to his statement. What could I say, really? I couldn't exactly deny any of it, the evidence was irrefutable.

"You've been fined ten thousand for your outburst at Bathurst," he continued.

I nodded again. Ten grand. It was painful, but not unmanageable.

"And another ten for that display." His hands indicated the magazine cover. "For bringing the sport into disrepute."

Fuck.

Twenty thousand in fines in one week. I wondered whether maybe it was another record. As if my life wasn't screwed up enough already. I knew better than to argue though; it wasn't as though Danny had set the fines. Besides, he might have exuded calm at all times and seemed to be the very picture of patience, but I knew just how explosive he could be if you argued back.

Despite his short stature and thin frame, I'd seen him bring grown men to tears. I knew only one person who could put Danny in his place, and that was his wife, Hazel. Over the years, she'd made her thoughts on my womanising very clear, so I couldn't count on her leaping to my defence anytime soon. Especially not after she'd seen me talking to Paige Wood. I wouldn't be surprised if Danny brought that up next.

I waited for Danny to continue, but he just sat, hands clasped together, and assessed me. He knew how to psych out the competition, and at that moment, that was me. Leaning back in his chair, he crossed his arms with the accompanying sound of the creak of leather as his old jacket refused to move as swiftly as he did.

For a brief moment, I wondered whether I was excused. I hadn't been explicitly dismissed from his office though, so I didn't think I had been. I gulped down a breath and met his gaze again. There was still the matter of the third item. The plain envelope. The one I was almost certain held my marching orders. I almost hoped he'd say that it was just to put me out of my misery.

When Danny stared impassively at me for a moment longer—locked in a silent battle of wills I was sure to lose—the air in the room thickened into a palpable presence surrounding me, clawing down my throat as if trying to force words from me and the envelope loomed larger before me, magnified by my fear of it.

"Is—is there anything else?" I asked when I couldn't handle the waiting any longer.

Danny frowned. "What do you think?"

"I—I don't know."

He stood and circled his desk, perching on the edge of it and gazing down at me. "What's going on with you, Declan?"

My mouth went dry. I was tempted to say I didn't know again, but I knew that wouldn't satisfy him. Panic gripped my chest as I waited for him to say the words I knew were coming. He was going to ask what was wrong, I was going to tell him nothing, and then he was going to fire my arse.

I dropped my head. "It's a ghost from my past," I muttered down at my lap.

"And what, precisely, does this ghost have to do with me?"

"Nothing. It's just something I need to deal with."

"How?"

"What?" I looked up at him.

"How are you planning on dealing with it?" His gaze was steady, unwavering as his cold slate gaze assessed me.

"I just need some time?" It wasn't assertive, or cocky, or anything of the things he probably expected of me. It was a sign of just how far I'd fallen in a few short months.

Danny spun around and grabbed the plain envelope, sliding it closer to me.

"What's this?" I asked timidly as I took it into my hands.

He pushed himself off the desk and crossed to his window. "Open it." His tone gave nothing away.

Swallowing down my fear, I peeled open the envelope slowly. There was no point speeding to the end of my career—or my dreams. Inside was a key and a smaller envelope with airline details printed on it.

"What's this?" I asked again, my voice lifting as I examined the contents. It certainly wasn't what I'd expected. Instead of the dreaded notice of dismissal, I'd pulled an airline ticket from the envelope and then inspected the details. It was a ticket to London on a flight due to leave the following day.

Danny crossed the room again and sat in his chair, his slate-grey gaze steady on me again. "You are taking the rest of the season off."

It wasn't what the doctor had indicated. After assessing the damage to my ribs—just a hairline fracture—she'd said there was a chance I could be back in the car again before the end of the season. There was no question in Danny's voice though. The time off wasn't a choice I was being offered, but a directive from the boss. Something I couldn't argue with, not with the tenterhooks I was already hanging from.

That didn't stop me from trying.

"What about the sponsors?" The team's sponsors paid for a certain amount of track time each year, and the sponsorship money was refundable if that time wasn't met.

Danny laughed sardonically. "This isn't open for discussion, Declan."

He leaned forward in his chair, placing his elbows on the desk, and then stared at me.

"Do you honestly think any of them will miss a crash every single meet? It'll probably end up being cheaper for us to back out of every deal than to have to build a new car every couple of weeks. Besides, the way you've been driving, it's unlikely we'll meet the track time requirements anyway."

I hung my head in shame. My cheeks burned red and I longed for a drink to take the edge off the guilt eating at my stomach.

"This is a one-time offer, kid. A last chance, so to speak," Danny said. There wasn't a trace of anger in his voice, but somehow that made it seem all the more serious. "Take the time off like you wanted. Go to London; the doctors have given you clearance to fly. Get your shit together, and then come back fresh next season and get back to winning me some races."

I didn't need to ask what would happen if I refused or if I couldn't do what he wanted; the answer danced in his eyes. The ticket wasn't much more than a stay of execution if I didn't do as he ordered.

That didn't stop me from questioning him though. "Why London?"

"Because you sure as shit haven't sorted yourself out here. I think you need a change of scenery. Plus, it'll keep you away from Morgan until he's calmed a little."

I nodded. "But what's the key for?"

"An apartment I own in London. You'll have free access to it while you're there, but that's the only thing I can offer you until you return for the preseason testing."

"Thank you," I whispered, even though I wasn't sure that it shouldn't have been, "Fuck you."

I didn't want someone telling me what to do, or where to holiday, but maybe he was on the right track. Maybe it was exactly what I needed—to get out of the country and away from any possible reminders of Alyssa.

It was a chance to try to get my head together. To break whatever hold it was that Alyssa had over me after one chance sighting of her happy smile in the arms of another. Happy without me.

"You do realise this means your pay will be suspended?"

I nodded, mentally calculating what I had in liquid assets. With luck and good management, I should've had enough to make it through to preseason without compromising too much of my lifestyle. I would miss the twenty grand I had to pay in fines that much more though.

"And I shouldn't have to remind you that your contract is up for renewal next year. I'm a reasonable man. I'm willing to overlook this last six months, providing you can prove to me that you are back on top next season."

After standing and gathering up the documents with all the fines, I offered him a small smile. At least it wasn't an outright dismissal. There had certainly been enough grounds for one. "Thank you, Danny."

"I meant it when I said you have the potential to be a great driver, Declan. Nothing's changed since then. You just need to get your head back in the game."

"Thank you."

"That is all."

I knew not to hang around after getting dismissed from his office, lest he change his mind.

As I walked down the corridor away from his office, I kept staring at the plane ticket in my hand. The flight left the following day, and I had three months before I needed to be back for preseason testing for the following year's races. That gave me three months to sort myself out.

Three months to get Alyssa "small town" Dawson out of my head for good.

CHAPTER SIX

CHANCE ENCOUNTERS

AFTER I ARRIVED home, I sat on the edge of my bed, staring at the plane ticket. It felt heavy in my hands, much heavier than a piece of card rightfully should. It was weighted with expectation and fear. If it didn't work . . . nothing would. I would be done. My career, the one thing I'd worked so damn hard for, would be gone. I'd given up everything for it. If it were gone, I'd be left with nothing. I'd have to crawl back home a failure and watch Alyssa flaunt her new love at every turn.

Realistically, the ticket should have felt light in my hands. It should have felt like the life preserver it was designed to be. One last lifeline thrown in to stop me from sinking further into the deep shit filling my life. For that reason, I was willing to cling to it with both hands. However, it also raised the question of how exactly I was supposed to get my head back in the game. How did I even start to try? It wasn't as though I hadn't tried to sort myself out.

I sighed as I threw the ticket onto the bed beside me and fell backward to stare at the ceiling. Almost two hours passed that way, with me lost in the same cycle of thoughts as always, before I decided that if I was catching a plane in the morning, I really needed to get some shit organised. Like clothes . . . and a suitcase.

In my head, I ran through a list of tasks. I thought it would probably be polite to contact my parents at some point before I left, to let them know I was leaving the country for a while. It was the sort of thing they liked to be kept in the loop about. For a second, I debated calling them. Mum would no doubt have already heard about the whole *Gossip Weekly* thing though, so I decided a text would probably be easier and involve a little less lecturing.

I turned my phone on and instantly regretted it. The thing went crazy, beeping and vibrating with all the missed calls and texts I'd received while it was off. I ignored them all, sent Mum a quick text and then turned the phone off again. I wouldn't have time to call Telstra in the morning to turn on international roaming so no one would be able to contact me. I would be unreachable—which sounded fucking fantastic.

My list of things I needed to do before I left grew with every passing second. I realised I would definitely need my passport, so I'd have to hunt it down. The last time I'd used it was the team trip to Bahrain, but the trip back home had been a bit of a blur and I struggled to remember where I'd put my passport after that. I ran downstairs to check in the study, and saw my passport on the desk next to my old answering machine. The sight made me pause. It was a relic of the days when I'd first moved to Sydney and was no longer used. It wasn't even plugged in to the phone line anymore. All it was good for anymore was storage. With everything running circles through my head, it would be dangerous to listen to a single message, but I couldn't help myself.

With a deep breath that hurt like a motherfucker, I steeled myself and pushed play.

"Hey, Dec. I hope you don't mind your mum giving me this number, but I need to talk to you. Call me. Please?" Alyssa's voice filled the room. Even though she started strong, her words were teary at the end, especially as she added her quiet plea. The recording wasn't the first time she'd tried to call—I didn't have those early ones.

Instead, it was from after I'd first moved into something slightly more permanent than Morgan's spare bedroom, a little over a month after I'd arrived in Sydney. I didn't know why I kept it, but I just couldn't bring myself to delete it.

I frowned as my finger hovered over the delete button. She'd moved on anyway, why should I keep her old messages? Before I had a chance to act, the next message started.

"Dec, please. I need you to call me." Her tone was harsher, but still filled with sorrow and the weight of expectation. *"What happened to you always being my friend? To you always having my back? I need—"* The message cut off as I yanked the machine off the desk, pulling the plug on the power with the movement. With Alyssa's tear-filled voice echoing in my ears, I hurled the answering machine across the room, turning away before it smashed against the wall. She'd moved on from that—moved on to smiles and races with another man.

"Fuck you, Alyssa," I said to the empty house.

Maybe I didn't have her to keep me company, but I had something better: I had my wet bar. Screw the doctors and their no alcohol with the pain medication rules.

WHEN I woke the next morning, it was with a throbbing headache. A strong urge to just crawl back under the covers overtook me. At least until I remembered why I'd set the alarm in the first place.

The flight.

I jumped out of bed and called a taxi. While I waited, I dashed madly around the house getting the last items together.

For the first time in ages, I missed my family. I regretted not having someone to help me get to the airport. Mum and Dad were still up in Brisbane and other than Eden and Morgan, I hadn't really made any friends in Sydney. All of my time, spare or otherwise, was spent with the team. With Morgan's foul mood over my crash, and the team's attitude toward me in general since the crashes started, I didn't think any of them would help me out. Truthfully, I didn't want any of them there to see me off. Especially when Morgan had no doubt shared the gory details about what a pussy I'd been when he'd confronted me.

Despite the early morning, I grabbed my sunglasses to cover the deep purple shade that still covered my left eye, and also to protect my bloodshot eyes. Throwing on a baseball cap, I pulled it low over my face in an attempt to remain as incognito as possible. My stomach protested every movement I made, and I seriously thought about cancelling my flight entirely. Even though I'd managed to swallow a couple of painkillers, they hadn't taken the edge off the throbbing ache in my skull or in my chest down at all. The thought of having to face a trip through the airport, and then onto a plane full of strangers, was just too much.

Still it was go, or leave Sinclair Racing. Danny wouldn't offer me another chance for redemption.

The taxi beeped when it arrived out front and, with a head filled with all the reasons I needed the trip, I rushed out to greet it.

BEFORE LONG, it was my turn to check in. I tossed my bag onto the scales and dropped my ticket and passport onto the desk, waiting while the chick behind the computer did her thing. She tried a few times to engage me in conversation, but it was too early and my aching skull left me too pissed off to do much more than grunt responses back at her.

What the fuck am I doing here? I wondered.

What was it exactly that I expected the trip to give me? Did I really expect three months would change everything? What did I want to change anyway? I mean, obviously it would be nice to get around the racetrack without crashing out. Did that mean I had to exorcise Alyssa out of my mind completely though? I wasn't sure I wanted to do that. I didn't have feelings for her, I was sure of that much at least, but my chest still clamped shut at the idea of never thinking about her again, of never seeing her face while I dreamed.

I briefly considered calling Danny and just cancelling my

contract to save everyone the hassle of the charade. Maybe I would be able to find a job on the sidelines of racing that would give me the thrill without the repair bill. It was the coward's way out though, and I was no fucking coward. Besides, I didn't want to throw away my dreams just because of some stupid visions that stopped me from completing a race. That would change . . . somehow. I just needed to figure out how.

The simple fact was that I needed to do what Danny had commanded. I needed to go to London and get my head back in the game. Or at least give it a red-hot go. It was my only chance and if it didn't work, what would it have cost me?

Even after I'd checked my baggage and gotten my boarding pass, it was still a little too early to deal with security. There were a couple of hours before my flight and I needed to recover from the overly cheerful girl at the check-in desk before I wrangled with any other airline employees.

Instead, caffeine was the next item on my agenda.

After finding my way to one of the airport coffee shops, I ordered a double-shot latte. Once I had my coffee in hand, I walked straight into a booth at the back, which was unfortunately close to the counter but put me away from the general public at least. I slumped down into the booth, hiding my face as much as I could. The last thing I needed was for a roving photographer, or worse, a desperate fan, to find me and ruin my day.

The warm coffee was slowly bringing me to life when I saw a ghost from my past. Alyssa Dawson's meathead older brother, Josh, walked past my booth and headed for the counter. I shook my head to clear it because it wasn't possible that he could be there. The only explanation I could come up with for his presence was that I'd gone completely and certifiably insane. I wondered whether Morgan's fist had been one knock to my head too many. Josh had to be a vision, just like all the ones I'd had of Alyssa. There was no other reason I could think of for him to be in Sydney. Especially not at the international departure lounge just metres from where I was.

Regardless of how small the possibility was that it was him, I did everything I could to avoid any eye contact and limit the chance of him spotting me. I sank further into my seat and dropped my gaze. The last time we'd met, he'd almost put me in hospital just for breaking Alyssa's heart. I really didn't feel like adding another black eye to my current collection of complaints, or risk him turning hairline fractures into something much worse.

The man I hoped wasn't Josh headed for the counter. I turned my head to the right to stare at the wall to avoid catching his eye. The instant his booming voice greeted the cashier, I was left with no doubt that it was him. The sound sent my heart racing. Even though I hadn't seen Alyssa for years, and he had no reason to have any continuing beef with me, I wasn't willing to take the chance that he wouldn't smack me in the mouth just for the fun of it. After our last meeting, I wouldn't put anything past him.

He was built like a brick shithouse and had fists to match. For a while, Ruth and Curtis, Alyssa's parents, had thought Josh might end up playing Rugby League professionally. I wasn't sure whether he'd followed through on that dream, but I hadn't seen him in any games so I doubted it. He'd probably followed Alyssa's career advice and given up on those dreams because they were too impossible.

He ordered a short black and a caramel macchiato. I froze and my mouth went dry. I may not have seen Alyssa in years, but I could easily recall her favourite drink. She'd tried a few different things before settling on the caramel macchiato. Her voice echoed through me, filling my mind with the words she'd said when she'd raved to me about it after she'd gone into the city with her other best friend, Jade. Alyssa's smile had been bright as she'd told me about this drink she'd found that was heaven in a cup.

I closed my eyes and focused on naming each of the corners of Bathurst in my mind in order to block the memory. Nothing positive could come from reliving the good times Alyssa and I had once shared. It was a long time ago, before I'd shattered her heart to follow my dreams.

When I thought of Forest Elbow, my mind spiralled back into the place I'd been straight after crashing at Bathurst. I put my head on the table and groaned. Surely my own personal demon could not be at the airport to haunt my escape as well as my races? My heart pounded in my chest and it became harder to breathe.

It doesn't mean she's here, I reasoned with myself as I brushed one hand through my hair. After all, how many people in the world must drink caramel macchiatos? It wasn't like Alyssa was the only one and had invented something completely unique. It was a standard menu item, for fuck's sake.

Get a fucking grip, Reede!

Without lifting my head from the cool surface of the table, I turned slightly to glance at Josh. He gave no hint why he was there, or what he was doing in Sydney in general, as he casually flirted with the barista before collecting his drinks. To go.

I kept my head down until he'd walked past me again without giving me a moment's consideration.

My mouth twisted and my stomach plummeted. With him gone, I would never know whether or not she had actually been there. I felt the loss of that information acutely before I pushed it away. It wasn't like I cared about her or wanted to see her anyway. Not really. No more than I would have wanted to see anyone from school who had suddenly materialised in my vicinity. I downed the last of my coffee despite my protesting stomach.

Pushing the sighting out of my head, I made a beeline for the newsagents, determined to pick up the latest copy of a few of the various Holden magazines so that I'd at least have something to read on the plane. I hadn't even entered the newsagency when I saw part of the reason for the trip staring out at me from the stands at the front of the store. Multiple copies of the latest *Gossip Weekly* lined the wall. I pulled my hat down even further and ducked my head as I pushed past the display.

Please God, don't let anyone recognise me in front of the Gossip Weekly *stand*.

I moved straight into the men's magazines section. The one housing the magazines filled with cars, bikes, girls, or some combination of the three. Once I was there, I breathed a little easier. It would at least be less embarrassing to be recognised away from that wall.

I had three different magazines in my hand, debating the merits of each one, when I heard Josh's booming voice again.

"God, that Declan Reede thinks he's all that and a bag of fucking chips, doesn't he?"

Holy fuck! Instinctively, I ducked down lower than the top of the shelves. A grunt of pain rushed from my lips as the movement strained my injury. I pressed myself against the magazines to ensure he didn't see me if he spun around.

Even though my first thoughts were of avoidance, and my second were wondering why he was there, I had enough sense to figure he was commenting on the *Gossip Weekly* cover. If he'd seen me, I doubted his voice would still hold the jovial edge it had. Just in case though, my gaze darted left and right to ensure he wasn't beside me. I practically rested against the shelves, trying to ensure I was well and truly out of sight. Why couldn't he just disappear already and leave me alone to get on the plane in peace?

"Yeah right, babe, you need to face facts."

It was clear someone had responded to him, but I hadn't heard what they'd said or even whether it was a male or female. My fists clenched and my teeth ground together. I wanted so badly to look, but stayed crouched on the ground instead. I may not have been a coward, but I wasn't a fucking idiot either. The dude was at least twice my size, had fists like tenderising mallets, and I couldn't be certain whether he was over his vendetta against me or not. Considering the way I'd left Alyssa, I wasn't willing to put my head on the chopping block on a maybe. The vivid memory of him pounding me into the ground over and over again, and then of the long recovery, was enough to force me to keep low and out of sight.

"That boy is so far up himself he'd need a compass and a flashlight to get out again."

I thought I heard a female laugh. With my heart smashing against my ribs, I straightened a little to get a look. My hands shook as I reached up to try to move closer to the top of the magazine stand. All I could see was Josh's back as he paid the cashier for whatever he'd purchased. When he left the store, he walked just behind the person he was with; almost stalking them like a bodyguard would. Because of his position, I didn't get a clear view of his companion.

I didn't want to risk following them to find out. My curiosity was not worth the pain, and not just the physical one. If by some unfortunate miracle, he was with Alyssa, I didn't necessarily want to see her when the whole purpose behind my trip was to get her out of my head. Just before he disappeared around the next corner, I heard him ask, "So how do you think Phoebe's going to go while you're off on this little adventure?"

I didn't hear the reply. Once I heard his voice retreat far enough away I moved out of my hiding spot and toward the counter. I purchased all three magazines I'd been looking at. The covers were warped and bent due to the sweat from my palms seeping in as I'd wrung them while hiding. Besides, I wasn't willing to risk hanging around the newsagency any longer than I needed. Josh and his friend might realise they'd forgotten something and return. If they did, I didn't want to risk running into them.

While I debated possible safe hiding places, I thought about Josh's words.

"You're off on this adventure."

I presumed that meant he was saying goodbye to someone and not flying himself. On that assumption, I headed straight to security. At least if he didn't have a ticket, he couldn't haunt me through there.

I shoved the magazines into my carry-on luggage and placed it down onto the conveyer belt. After checking to ensure that Josh was nowhere to be seen, I put my wallet, keys, sunglasses, and hat into one of the little boxes and slid that behind my bag. The security officer called me through the metal detector.

He looked a little bored as he waved me through, but then he did an almost comical double-take as I walked closer to him.

"Holy fuck! You're Declan Reede."

Oh really? I'm glad you told me because I'd been wondering who the fuck I was. I bit my tongue and smiled as politely as I could manage. "Yeah."

"Can I get you to sign something for my son, he's a huge fan."

Sure, your "son." I resisted the eye roll that was building. Most people asked me to sign for someone else, but I often wondered how many were just using it as a ruse rather than admit the autographs were actually for themselves.

"No problem," I said. "Have you got a pen and paper?"

He hunted for something, and I wanted more than anything to just tell him to forget it and walk away rather than let him waste any more of my time. It was the usual issue though, and the biggest problem with doing autographs. If I refused to sign things, the fans thought it was because I was too arrogant. If I did sign stuff, anyone who saw me assumed it was because I was full of myself. It was absolutely a lose-lose scenario.

My jaw tightened as the guard took another minute to find something. I didn't owe him anything—not my time or my squiggle. I was on holiday, not there in any official capacity.

Maybe Danny won't be too pissed if I tell this guy to fuck off.

The only thing that stopped me was that I'd learned long ago the two groups of people to never be rude to: those who prepared anything I ate or drank and those who had special potential to make my life more difficult. The guard definitely fell into the second group. I'd likely be held in some interrogation room, strip searched, and probed if I was too rude.

When he shoved a pen and paper in front of me, I quickly scribbled down a note. It was just the usual, "Race hard! Declan Reede" crap, but it made him happy. Handing it back to him, I breathed a sigh of relief that no one else had noticed. Or at least, no one else had approached. I understood that fans were important in the grand scheme of things, but when I was at a fucking airport trying *not* to draw attention to myself, the last thing I needed was a pack of autograph hounds chasing after me.

I quickly slipped my cap and sunglasses back on, ready to return to some semblance of anonymity, but it was too late. I'd barely taken two steps when the people who came through security behind me raced after me, calling my name loudly before asking for my autograph. Half an hour later, with a severe cramp in my hand, I'd finally signed autographs for almost everyone who wanted one.

The one I hadn't signed was a copy of *Gossip Weekly* thrust in front of my nose. Even I had my limits in vulgarity.

Once I'd broken free of the pack, I headed straight for the airport lounge, thankful that I had a membership considering Danny had only sprung for premium economy rather than the usual business class seat. I hid away in the corner with my back to all the other passengers and my cap tipped low over my face. I just wanted everyone to leave me the hell alone. There was enough shit going through my mind without needing to worry about other people.

I waited until the last normal call before I boarded. I really didn't want to be stuck on the plane any longer than necessary, but I also didn't want the airline to call my name over the loud speaker, effectively telling everyone in the airport that I was one of those arrogant people who think the whole plane should wait for them. Not to mention the risk that they'd announce my name on the plane as well, thereby informing everyone that they had a celebrity in their midst.

Walking up to the attendant at the gate, I handed over my boarding pass. When I did, I flipped her the best smile I could manage in the circumstances. Although I was positive it was more of a grimace, she let it slide and returned with a lifted lip of her own. She directed me through to the tunnel and then I entered the plane.

The next flight attendant looked at my ticket and pointed me in the direction of my seat. When I followed her directions, I smiled. There was a fine piece of tail bent over across the seats already. No doubt that gorgeous arse belonged to the person who would be sitting next to me for the duration of the flight. Or at least the first leg of it. More than enough time to find out if I'd have her joining the mile-high club, regardless of the doctor's no-nookie rule.

As I walked closer, I admired the view. Whoever it was, she was struggling to get something out of her carry-on bag. Then I saw it. The now sickeningly familiar cover of *Gossip Weekly*.

Fuck.

At least ten hours, and possibly another twelve if we shared similar seats on the next leg, stuck next to someone who not only read *Gossip Weekly*, which would have been bad enough at the best of times, but who also had the issue with me ungraciously gracing the front cover as their early inflight entertainment.

The woman stood, and, if possible, things got worse for me. She was a fucking brunette. Which meant there wasn't even a chance of me trying to add another notch to my mile-high club belt if by some miracle she was impressed by public displays of lewdness and wanted an example of my prowess.

Great.

It was crystal clear the flight was going to be an hours-long torture test.

She pulled her bag up from the seat and tried to stow it in the overhead compartment, but was just a little too short to balance it properly. I watched her struggle for half a second, her blouse pulling up away from her stomach and displaying a sliver of her silky-smooth, milk-coloured skin. When it was clear she couldn't do it alone, I closed the last of the distance between us and reached my hands up to help. Even though I wasn't really in the position to be lifting anything, the bag looked light enough.

"Would you like some assistance?" I offered.

At first, I assumed that I'd startled her, because she froze and everything she held in her hands came toppling down on top of both of us. I wasn't prepared for it, so the bag slipped straight through my hands, knocking off my hat and sunglasses as it fell.

I stumbled to catch my hat and then dropped to the floor to retrieve my sunglasses. "Fuck!" I cried out as the move caused a sharp stabbing in my injured side.

Not wanting to be an arse, despite my injury, I put my hand out to help my seat-neighbour with her carry-on. At some point, she'd bent down too. Her breathing was shallow and her hands quivered as she reached to grab her bag off me. I thought she must have been a fan or something, so I raised my eyes to offer my assistance again.

Holy fuck!

CHAPTER SEVEN

UNDISCOVERED TERRITORY

I COULDN'T MOVE.

I couldn't think.

All that kept running through my mind was *holy fuck*!

A flight attendant tapped me on the shoulder and I felt some semblance of feeling return to me. Too bad it was a hollow feeling that churned my stomach and stopped my breath. Finishing the coffee earlier despite my roiling stomach was an infinitely stupider decision than I'd thought. My stomach coiled back on itself and the taste of stale coffee rose in my throat like bile.

"Are you two okay here?" the attendant asked. "We need to get everyone seated for take-off."

I nodded vaguely as I saw the red blush run up *her* cheeks. Her gaze hadn't left mine since I'd met it, and she held me captive like a proverbial deer in the headlights. I wondered if she felt as breathless and empty as I did.

Hollow. Empty. Cold.

Finally her honey-gold eyes turned from me to the cabin crew member, releasing the hold she had over me and leaving me free to think again. As if a levee wall burst, my mind was filled with images, memories of the last time I'd seen those eyes. That blush.

Alyssa.

Her name was on my lips, but I couldn't speak it. My mouth was dry and my eyes burned. The memory of the vision I'd had while in hospital filled me and I was rendered completely mute.

"Sorry," she mumbled before picking up her bag.

The flight attendant helped her stow it away securely and then tossed mine in too. Although I'd stood up, I still couldn't move or think enough to offer any further assistance. I watched as *she* slid into the seat closest to the window. I couldn't do this. I couldn't be stuck next to my past for the better part of a day—or more. Not the way my heart raced and my palms sweated. Not now. Maybe not ever.

"Excuse me," I asked the attendant as quietly as possible. "Is there any chance of getting another seat?"

"I'm sorry, that's not policy."

"Even in economy? Or first?" I begged urgently. "*Any* seat *anywhere* else on the plane? I'll pay extra if I have to."

She frowned. "I'm sorry. I'm not able to help with that. Now, please take your seat and fasten your seatbelt."

Fasten my seatbelt is right.

Hours stuck on the plane next to Alyssa fucking Dawson was not a good start to the whole getting her out of my system plan. The worst part was that the way she stared steadfastly out the window, her face a shade of red so bright she would have put a tomato to shame, made it clear she'd heard me asking for another seat.

After I'd sat down, I threw my sunglasses and hat into the storage pocket and then pinched the bridge of my nose before realising that fucking hurt with my still-black eye so I tugged at my hair the way Danny did when he was pissed.

I had no fucking clue how to handle the Alyssa situation. Talk? Don't talk? Reminisce? Ignore? If someone wrote a book of helpful hints that dealt with running into your ex on an almost day-long flight to another fucking country, I wanted ten copies.

"Alyssa," I finally murmured in greeting, the feel of her name rough and awkward on my tongue. Even though it was tempting I couldn't just ignore her, or the giant fucking elephant between us.

Her head shifted almost imperceptibly in my direction and she seemed to be having a similar internal debate. Then she closed her eyes, sighed, and nodded. "Declan."

Why did my name have to sound so fucking good on those lips?

At that exact moment, the safety announcements started. It provided me with a few precious moments where I could ignore Alyssa without feeling guilty. I'd never been more fucking interested in having an emergency situation before. All too quickly the video was over, and then the uncomfortable silence began as the plane started its run-up for take-off.

Of all the fucking shitty luck I had; only I could end up stuck on a plane next to the very reason I was leaving the country.

The plane vibrated as it raced faster and faster down the runway. The sensation set me on edge. I wasn't a bad flyer necessarily, but I figured it would be just my luck to crash on take-off or something equally as crappy. When the vibration increased to a bounce, I instinctively reached for the armrest, ready to dig my fingernails in and hold on for grim life. Only Alyssa had beaten me to the one between our seats. My hand grazed hers before I pulled it back. She turned her head away and moved her hand to her lap. When her hand was gone, I moved mine back. There was no point neither of us using the damn thing.

Once we were settled in the air, she pulled out her magazine and I could have sworn a small smirk crossed her lips as she looked at the cover.

I rolled my eyes and pushed myself back against the seat. *Fucking great!*

She buried her face into the magazine, holding it up so every time I looked at her all I saw was myself sandwiched between two strangers whose names I didn't even fucking remember. Their faces were blurred and unrecognisable both in the photo and in my mind.

I don't know what compelled me, but I had to speak to Alyssa again, if only to dispel whatever thoughts she must have been having reading that trash.

"You can't believe everything you read," I whispered to her conspiratorially.

She dropped the magazine onto her lap. "Oh really? So you're not really a megalomaniac arse who finds it impossible to keep your pants on? And you're not more interested in screwing random women than you are in doing your job properly?" she replied in a curt tone.

Ouch. I deserved it, but it still hurt to have the confirmation that she thought so little of me. I'd somehow managed to convince myself that after I'd left, she would just hold onto the memory of what we'd had. That she wouldn't look for anything else about me—that she'd care enough to forget me and ignore whatever mistakes I made. It was clear I'd been wrong.

I glanced around, wondering how long it would be before the cabin crew started to serve the drinks, because I desperately fucking needed one—or ten. It would be the easiest solution to my current situation—just get so shitfaced that I couldn't speak even if I wanted to. It fixed almost everything else in my life, or at least made the crap more manageable. This wouldn't be any different.

"Josh is still a huge fan," she said, with a sarcastic edge to her voice. A definite smirk twisted her lips. Was she enjoying my obvious discomfort that much?

"Yeah, I heard." It slipped out before I thought about what I was saying.

She froze. "What do you mean you heard?"

Fuck. "I was in the newsagents when I heard his voice."

"I didn't see you there."

I scoffed. "You really think I'm going to show my face anywhere near Josh? I'm not a complete fucking idiot. What would I even say to him? 'Hey man, how've you been? Haven't seen you since the day you beat the shit out of me. Wanna give it another go?'"

For a moment, her face was aghast, but then she chuckled. To my ear, it sounded forced and nervous, but maybe that was just the way she laughed these days. How was I supposed to know? It wasn't like I knew anything about her anymore.

"There are some benefits to having a big brother like him. He keeps the fuckheads away at least."

My smile fell to form a scowl. We'd almost had a civil conversation—our first conversation at all in almost four years—and she'd used the opportunity to call me a fuckhead. It was no less than I deserved, but still . . .

I turned my body away from her and stared out into the aisle instead. Despite picking a random spot and devoting my entire focus to it, I heard her laughter behind me. I didn't want to know what she found so fucking funny, but inch by inch my body betrayed me and drifted back toward her to see what it was about.

"Did I offend you?" she asked when I caught her gaze. Her lip twitched and I frowned. The action made her laugh louder.

"Why the fuck would you think that?" My voice was ice and steel. I didn't want to talk to her. She obviously didn't want to talk to me either. I didn't know why we were wasting each other's time—aside from the fact that neither of us could escape.

"Yeah, because the way you just turned away from me wasn't a dead giveaway."

I rolled my eyes and turned away again.

"You're acting like a three-year-old, you know."

I resisted the urge to twist my head and poke my tongue out at her.

"Look, I don't need this," she snapped. "Frankly, I couldn't care less whether you're offended or not. I'm not sitting here to please Declan Reede. I just thought I should try to be pleasant, considering it looks like we're stuck together for the better part of a day."

She pulled out her purse and grabbed a small box of pills.

"What's that?" I asked.

"None of your business," she snapped back.

"Maybe not," I said. "But I'm still curious."

She sighed and closed her eyes. I could almost hear her counting in her head as if it would ease her frustration. "If you must know, they're sleeping pills. I had them prescribed for this trip. It just struck me that spending as much as possible of the next ten hours unconscious seems like a pretty good option considering the alternative."

"The alternative being me, the megalomaniac arse? Or as you implied, the fuckhead."

Her lip twitched. "I thought that much was pretty clear."

"Well, if that's the case, are you sure you can trust me to keep my pants on?"

"Who would know?" she asked. She took a deep breath and glanced at me again. Buried in her gaze was a pain I didn't understand. "You're still making friends I see," she said after a moment.

At first, I thought she was referring to the magazine again, but her gaze was locked on my face. *Oh right . . . my black eye.* A mirthless chuckle slipped from me as I touched my fingers to the swollen skin and winced. "Yeah. My co-driver wasn't too impressed by my performance at Bathurst."

"Right." She nodded and her fake half smile was back in place. It was as if she had a mask she'd slipped on to hide her feelings. I hated it, only I wasn't sure why. It was only her eyes that gave away any emotion at all, and that was pain. "What's up with that anyway? You've crashed out of the last, what, five meets?"

What the fuck? How does Alyssa "I Hate Cars" Dawson even know that?

After a moment, I remembered. The bloke she'd been with at Queensland Raceway. He'd obviously changed her in ways I never could. It must have been fucking love if he'd turned her around to the point where she actually knew how many rounds I'd crashed out of. At that thought, the coffee I'd forced down twisted in my stomach until I was certain I was going to retch. The image of her lips on his seared into my brain and raced down my spine in a shiver.

"Why?" she asked.

"Why what?" I snapped as I was forced back to the present by the sound of her voice.

"Why do you think you've been crashing?"

"If I fucking knew don't you think I would have stopped by now?" My tone was still harsher than I'd intended, mostly because the vision I'd had of her kissing that other fucker had twisted into something more in my mind. I swallowed hard to force down the bile that rose in my throat.

"Sorry for asking."

We sat in silence for a few minutes.

"You, uh, ended up in hospital after the last one, didn't you?"

I scoffed. "That wasn't the crash." I pointed to my black eye. "That was Morgan."

"Why would he do that?"

"Why does Morgan do anything?" I laughed as memories of Morgan's past exploits ran through my mind. Even though he'd delivered the blow that had landed me in hospital, I couldn't stay pissed at him for it—I'd have done the same if the roles were reversed.

"You were in hospital. How can you be so blasé about it?" Even though I didn't see what business it was of hers, Alyssa seemed aghast at the idea.

"It's just the way it is between us."

"What happened to you, Dec?"

I frowned at the way she said the words, as though my not being pissed at him was something terrible. "What do you mean what happened? I'm living my fucking dream."

She nodded and her lip quivered. "Of course. How could I forget?"

Turning away from me, she ended the conversation.

After a while, she sighed and reached for the box of pills. She slid out one of the blister packs.

"I'd really rather you didn't do that," I murmured before she could pop the tablet out onto her hand.

"Like I said before, it's hardly your business. I don't see why it matters to you. It doesn't affect your dream after all." She was clearly exasperated with me. I wasn't sure I could blame her.

"Because I have a problem with gratuitous drug use." I didn't feel ready to spill all the gory details. She didn't need to know them.

Considering I'd likely never see her again after we stepped off the plane, there was no need for her to ever know. "Those things are addictive."

"Well, it's my body."

"Your body is a temple." The instant the words were out, I realised the possible double meaning. *Holy fuck—I did not just say that to her*.

"Really? Well, I can see how well you treat your *temple*." She pointed to the magazine cover. "I guess you practise open worship?"

Now it was my turn to blush. "Fuck! You know what? Whatever. Do whatever the fuck you want," I muttered as I turned away from her again.

The silence enveloped us both. It called to me, tempting me to say something more and not just let the moment rest.

With a sigh, I turned back to her. "What I meant is that you've got to look after your body. Too many of those things and you won't be able to get sleep naturally." *I should know*, I added in my mind. "Why don't you at least wait? You can't need sleep, it's still only morning. I promise that even though you're stuck here next to me, I'll try and keep out of your way as much as I can. If you really can't sleep later, take them then." I was beginning to ramble. *Not good*. "Just don't use them only to avoid talking to me." *Please*? I couldn't voice the word; she didn't owe me favours.

She didn't answer, but she did lean over to her bag, I assumed to put the pills back away. I smiled slightly at my small victory.

"Thank you," I said.

She nodded, but rubbed her fingers against her temples. Her eyes seemed damp, her lashes sticky. The sight burned my insides. Something was wrong, and I wanted to question her about it. She didn't owe me an explanation though, and to ask for one would just open up a can of worms too big to be able to close again after the end of our journey.

"Are you just going to Hong Kong?" I asked after a brief pause.

She shook her head. "London."

My heart leapt at the word, even though it shouldn't have.

"You?" she asked a moment later.

"Same."

"Do—do you think we'll be sitting together on the next flight?"

I couldn't tell whether her tone was hopeful or fearful. My throat was sticky and dry as I grabbed my boarding pass for the next leg. "Only one way to know."

Instead of demanding that she show me hers in exchange, I just handed my pass over to her. She compared it to her own and frowned. I wondered whether the frown was because she wouldn't be seated next to me, or because she would. I was almost afraid to ask, but I needed to know. Maybe she wouldn't be beside me. My chest ached a little at the thought of losing her so soon.

"So?" I found the word eventually.

With shaking fingers, she handed the boarding pass back to me. "Looks like we're in this for the long haul."

Her words dredged up ancient memories of the reasons I'd left Brisbane. I hadn't wanted the long haul—I'd wanted the freedom to pursue my choice in career. As if her words had reminded her of similar things, she wrapped her arms around her legs and stared out the window.

We sat in silence for a while. I was doing my best to fulfil my promise of pretending I wasn't there, but it was impossible. The familiar bubble which always seemed to encapsulate us whenever we were alone was back in force, pressing on me and urging me to speak to her. While I sifted through topics, trying to find something that might be safe to discuss, I remembered something. A curiosity. Josh's words at the airport. I tried to push it out of my mind, but it nudged back. Finally, after who knows how many minutes of silence, I turned back to her.

"Who's Phoebe?"

She looked at me with wide, startled eyes. Her hands traced into her long, dark locks before finding the ends. Her breathing sped as she twisted her hair relentlessly around her fingers. "What?"

"At the airport, when you were leaving the newsagency, Josh said something about a Phoebe."

Alyssa's gaze darted away from me as if searching for an escape. "She's . . ." A sigh crossed her lips and she closed her eyes. "No one you know."

I could tell that Alyssa was going to say something else before her evasive answer, which piqued my curiosity even more. "Is she like a girlfriend or something?"

She rolled her eyes. "Yes, Declan. I was so ruined after you, I knew no men would ever compare, so I turned into a lesbian."

Even though I knew she was being sarcastic, a part of me was turned on by the thought of Alyssa with another girl. I'd had enough experience with multiple girls to know how hot it could be—especially if it was Alyssa.

Stop! There was no doubt if I lingered on that image for too long, I'd be in urgent need of a trip to the loo.

"No, I meant of Josh's," I said.

She laughed.

"What's so funny about that question?"

"I just couldn't imagine Josh dating."

My confusion must have been clear on my face.

"He's married. Has been for about three and a half years now."

"What?" I couldn't deny that her revelation surprised me. He'd been dating a stuck-up cow the last time I'd seen Alyssa. He must have moved on pretty quick, unless . . . "To Ruby?" I asked incredulously.

She smiled. "The one and only."

"That sucks for you." Alyssa and Ruby had never gotten along.

"Actually, not really. She and I get along great now."

"Really?"

"Yeah, apparently she used to question my taste in men. She doesn't have the same problem anymore."

"So she had a problem with me?" I snapped. *Fucking bitch*.

Alyssa chuckled. "Yeah, something like that. She has the same high opinion of you as Josh does."

"Is there anyone in your family who doesn't hate me?"

She shrugged. "None that immediately spring to mind."

I guessed that I shouldn't have been surprised, what with the way I'd left things, but it was pretty fucking nice to have it confirmed so bluntly.

"How are things back home anyway? What's everyone been doing?" Surprisingly, I found myself *wanting* to talk to Alyssa, more and more with every passing second, but I couldn't think of any decent topics of conversation that wouldn't end in an argument. Old friends and reminiscing about the way things used to be seemed a safe-ish topic—providing I avoided the topic of *us* at least.

She shrunk away from me and frowned. "Good."

"Just *good*?" I raised an eyebrow at her.

Her frown deepened, but she didn't say anything else.

I twisted to face her. "Seriously, that's it? I've been away for four years now, and all you've got for me is *good*?"

She sighed and closed her eyes. "You're the one who left, Dec. You're the one who doesn't check in with anyone. What do you want me to say?"

"But surely *something's* happened since high school? Someone's gotten married, had kids, something?"

"Don't you talk to your mum?" Her voice was quiet, reserved. Her body curled inward, as if she wanted to get as far from me as she possibly could in the small space.

I shrugged. "Sure, but not about home."

"I guess your life is much too interesting to care about those of us who were left behind in the backwater town you grew up in." Her voice rose higher with each word. No doubt the result of four years of repressed feelings.

I scowled at her. Just because I'd been slightly cordial, she had obviously decided to make a big deal out of the fact that I was successful in the ways she'd doubted I could ever be. "It's not like that, and you know it. All I wanted to know was whether there was some hometown scandal that might offer up a few minutes of conversation in this long-arse plane trip so that we didn't end up talking about the fucking obvious white elephant."

"Fuck you, Declan."

"What?"

"You can't sit here and ask me about the town fucking scandals when you have no fucking clue what's been going on in anyone's life but your own. You can't talk about white fucking elephants when it's obvious you don't even care let alone know anything real. Do you have a single clue what I've been doing for the last four years? Did you even care enough to ask *anyone* about me at all? I could have died for all you cared, you arse. You don't have to answer, because I know you never once even checked in to see if anything major had happened to me!" She was screaming by the end of her tirade and tears welled in her eyes before spilling onto her cheeks.

The flight attendant came over to her. "Excuse me, ma'am, I'm going to have to ask you to calm down. You're disrupting the other passengers."

"Fine. Sorry." Alyssa's face was burning red and her voice was clipped but apologetic.

I blinked at her, wondering where the fuck her anger had come from or how it had dissipated again so quickly.

"Can I have a glass of water, please?" Alyssa asked.

The flight attendant nodded. While she was gone, Alyssa reached into her bag. I heard the tell-tale sound of two blister packs popping. As soon as the attendant came back with a small plastic cup in her hand, Alyssa dropped the pills into her mouth and skulled the water. She turned her back to me and pressed her head against the window.

"I'm sorry, Alyssa," I murmured, even though I wasn't sure I really needed to apologise. Her reaction seemed far too over the top for what should have been a meaningless conversation. Then again, her reactions to simple things had always left me a little confused. "I shouldn't have asked."

Her body stiffened, and I thought I heard her sniff. She didn't turn back to me or acknowledge my apology. I guessed the conversation was over. I closed my eyes and wondered what the hell her reaction was all about.

"And you're right. I never cared enough to ask." I lifted my chin, pressing the back of my head against the headrest as a stifled sob sounded from beside me. *Fuck her.*

Half an hour later, Alyssa was fast asleep. As she slept, she drifted closer to me and soon her head was resting against my shoulder. I was inundated with the scent that was unique to Alyssa—cinnamon and sugar. With a sigh, I gently coaxed her head back off me onto her chair. The sensation was just too much for me to handle. I needed space to roam, to pace, but the small aisles of the plane were far too narrow. Instead, I tipped my head back and stared at the vents above me. What did I do to deserve the fresh hell being delivered by Alyssa's presence?

Before long, her body was curled against me again, only this time I couldn't find it in myself to move her. Her breathing was steady and she looked too peaceful. I couldn't help but wonder what might have happened if I hadn't left Brisbane. She murmured in her sleep, and the sound was enough to set me on edge. My body grew rigid beneath her and I held my breath. It was a hideous reminder of the last time I heard her talking in her sleep—the last time we were happy together.

The night after our school formal, we'd given ourselves to one another.

It had been a night of highs and lows, but in the end we'd overcome the difficulties of locked hotel rooms, embarrassing lamp breakages, and an up-do filled with booby traps to have one of the best nights of our lives. The moment we'd shared was better than I could have ever imagined—possibly better than any I'd had since if only because it was real. It was raw. With the memory in my head, and the weight of Alyssa's body against me, my chest tightened. The ingrained reaction was exactly why I had run from her. That night as she'd slept, she'd murmured an acceptance to a marriage proposal. One I'd never even planned to make. It was just the push I'd needed to leave. A perfect reminder that she wanted me to settle down with her—a life filled with kids, weddings, and the death of my dreams.

I glanced down at Alyssa's sleeping form and wondered what might have happened if she hadn't uttered those words. They'd been the catalyst for everything that happened after. I'd broken up with her shortly after she woke in the morning and then she'd run from the room in tears.

That afternoon when I arrived back at my house Josh was waiting to beat me into a bloody pulp. Despite the concussion I'd suffered, the whole day was seared into my memory. It haunted me as I stared, unseeing, at the screen on the back of the headrest in front of me. Being with her would have cost me everything. She'd wanted to follow the path from uni, to marriage, to kids and had never believed that I could earn a living from racing.

If things had gone differently, it was likely that I would have been trapped in a small-town life. I would have been forced to give up my dreams of racing in the ProV8 series.

CHAPTER EIGHT

REVELATIONS

ALYSSA ROLLED IN my arms, and muttered the names Phoebe and Flynn before a small frown furrowed her brow. With the weight of the memories in my mind, her closeness was too much. I lifted her off me and once more coaxed her back to her seat.

I closed my eyes and leaned back against my own headrest. Fuck I was tired. Not just from the long night, but tired deep down in my soul. I'd experienced the sensation before, but it was usually easy to push aside. Now, the darkness around my heart seemed as thick as molasses and threatened to swallow me down into its depths. With a sigh, I let it take me.

ALYSSA STALKED out of the hotel bedroom. In her hand, she held her bag and the remnants of her formal dress—torn apart in just one in a series of stupid moments the night before. Without another word, she pushed the hotel room door open and stormed out. With a frown, I watched as the door swung closed. Just before the click, I heard the elevator ding and everything caught up to me. We'd just broken up. Again. After what had been the best night in my life, I'd thrown it all away because of some words muttered in her sleep. Fuck!

I threw open the hotel door and ran down the hall, arriving just as the elevator doors closed in front of her tear-streaked face.

"Alyssa! Stop!" I flew forward out of my seat. My heart pounded in my chest and my mouth was dry. I was disorientated for a moment as I glanced up at the screen in front of me which showed an airplane closing in on a flashing circle.

It was just a fucking dream.

"Declan! What the fuck?"

I froze. Alyssa's voice was right beside me. When I turned to look at her, the events of the last week crept into my mind. I blinked a few times at Alyssa before realising that my scream had obviously startled her, and she'd spilt coffee down the front of her shirt.

"Shit, sorry," I whispered, pushing the call button for the cabin crew.

I clambered out of my seat to allow Alyssa the room to wipe off her shirt. Despite the bundle of napkins she had in her hand, she wasn't making any progress.

"Oh, fuck it," she said. "I'll have to change. Can you just grab my bag down for me?"

I nodded like an idiot and grabbed her bag before passing it to her. She dug around in it for half a second before producing another shirt. Before I realised what she was doing, she pulled her soiled shirt off and handed it to me. I should have turned away. I shouldn't have stared, but shit, how the fuck was I supposed to look away?

At least three seconds passed before she pulled her new one on. The delay had given me more than enough opportunity to scope out her bra and the silky white skin of her breasts spilling over the top. Beneath her left breast was a new tattoo, but I couldn't make out what it was. Her belly-button ring, once a turquoise to match my eyes, was just a plain silver barbell now. Her boobs were fuller than I remembered them, and I itched to see whether her skin was as smooth and tasty as I remembered. The shirt she'd given me was still warm from the proximity to her body and I found myself gripping it tighter, unwilling to let anyone steal it from me. With a strength I didn't even know I possessed, I resisted the strong urge I had to put it to my face and inhale. While she changed, I stood, no doubt looking like an idiot, gaping at her with her shirt bunched between my hands.

She snatched the dirty shirt from me and then turned to the toilets to rinse it off. I could have sworn I saw a hint of a smirk on her lips. That's when I realised she'd been awake while I was asleep. She'd been awake while I was dreaming.

Fuck.

She knew I was dreaming about her.

Can this plane trip get any worse?

I looked at the time. We were less than a half hour from Hong Kong. Not quite halfway to London, but nearing the end of the first leg. *Thank Christ for that.*

I stood in the aisle until Alyssa came back to reclaim her seat. When she passed me, her smirk was unmistakable.

"It looks like gratuitous drug use suits you," I commented as I climbed back into my seat.

She gave me a quizzical look.

"Well, you look much happier now."

"Did it occur to you that I was happier because up until a few moments ago you were unconscious?"

Despite the urge to react to her words, I didn't. Instead, I chuckled. "Ah, but I'm not unconscious now, and you're still much happier."

She shrugged, but her smirk grew into a genuine smile—if only for one nanosecond. "We'll see. I guess it depends on the quality of conversation that my neighbour on the next flight is willing to engage me in."

"Well, I'm steering clear of Browns Plains—that's for sure." I laughed and she joined in.

"You were dreaming about me," she accused, the smile dancing on her lips again—as if that thought gave her great pleasure.

It was my turn to shrug again.

"What was it about?"

I closed my eyes and debated what to do. We'd finally started a somewhat pleasant conversation, joking around with each other the way we used to. I'd even started to hope that maybe we could have made it through the next ten hours without another argument. That would likely change if I dredged up the memory of our formal and of me breaking up with her. It was especially dangerous considering we were about to land and even though she'd indicated we'd be side by side for the next leg, I hadn't confirmed it for myself. Maybe she'd just said that because she'd thought it would get a reaction from me.

"Aren't you going to tell me?" she asked.

I opened my eyes and turned my head to face her. "I'm worried it will upset you."

She laughed. "*You're* worried about how *I* might feel?" She sounded incredulous.

"Don't be so surprised. I'm not the prick the media thinks I am."

"Not always," she mused. Her smile disappeared as she turned pensive. "But I've seen you do some pretty fucked-up things."

"You have." She hadn't seen the worst of it, but she'd seen enough.

"Please tell me?" she pleaded quietly. Her bottom lip even stuck out in a cute little pout.

I frowned. "I don't—"

"I have a right to know," she argued when I didn't respond appropriately enough for her.

"How exactly do you figure?"

"Well, apparently, I was the star attraction. I think that allows me certain privileges."

I debated again, before going with a half-truth. "It was about our high school formal."

She narrowed her eyes at me. "The formal? Or what happened after?"

Shit. What did she hear? I stared at her in silence.

"You know, Josh thought you'd raped me." Her statement was

a quiet, almost-whispered confession.

I choked on the air as the statement left her lips. Pushing myself forward in my seat, I coughed as I struggled to comprehend what she'd said. The action caused a redoubling of the pain in my chest, and I coughed harder. "What?" I managed to utter between convulsions.

"What else would you expect him to think? I turned up at home, early, alone, in tears, my feet sore from walking from the bus stop, my dress in tatters, and calling you an arsehole. He put two and two together and came up with rape. You have to believe me that I didn't know about what he planned, or what he did to you, though. Not until after I found out why you weren't in school that last week." The sorrow in her eyes confirmed her words. She had no reason to make any of that up, not now after so long. It would gain her nothing.

"Well, at least that explains his reaction," I murmured when I got my breathing back under control. I'd always thought he was delivering a message from Alyssa—to tell me to back off because I didn't want to follow her rules. I'd simply assumed he'd gone a bit over the top with the delivery as punishment for breaking his sister's heart again. I'd never suspected that he thought I'd hurt her. The truth was, he'd probably gone easy on me. If I'd thought someone had raped Alyssa, there would be no *almost* about the hospital stay part. In fact, they'd be lucky if they didn't find themselves in a morgue.

"He copped a bit of a serve from me once I found out," she said with a sad smile on her lips.

"I really am sorry." I buried my head in my hands as I considered what I was about to say—and how dangerous the words might be. "I mean about the freak-out I had that morning. I just, I don't know. I felt trapped, I guess. It felt like we were barrelling along at a million miles an hour. I could already see myself as a grandfather sitting on a porch wondering what the hell happened to my life and when my chance to go racing would come."

She nodded, but her brow bent into a frown. "I know. I get it. I felt like that too sometimes. We were pretty . . . intense." She

85

chuckled darkly after the last word.

We lapsed into silence, both deep in thought about what could have been. It made me remember the fucker at Queensland Raceway. I wanted to ask her about it, but didn't want to admit that I had seen her there or the impact—literally—she'd had on my life since.

"So is there anyone in your life now?" I asked, almost silently. I wasn't sure whether or not I wanted to hear the answer. Before she had the chance, an announcement was made that we'd be landing soon and instructed the cabin crew to prepare.

After a moment, Alyssa said, "Not really."

It took me a moment to realise it was a response to my question. "What does 'not really' mean?"

"It means . . . I don't really want to talk about it."

"Okay." Even though I was desperate to know, I didn't want to press her and end our civility.

"I'd ask you the same question," she said, "but we both already know the answer to it."

I nodded; she had me there. The whole world knew that Declan Reede liked to screw random women in clubs thanks to *Gossip Weekly*. Not to mention the fact that I had declared, on numerous occasions, that there was no way I was going to settle down for anyone. That I didn't need a woman in my life telling me what to do. By Alyssa's side again, it was almost embarrassing to consider the various things I'd said over the years.

"Declan, there's something I do need to talk to you about—"

She was interrupted by a crew member and after we were alone again, seemed more interested in packing her belongings into her handbag than continuing the conversation.

After the plane had landed, I pulled both of our carry-on bags from the overhead cabinets while Alyssa collected her handbag. Grabbing her bag from me, she hastily shoved everything inside with no real rhyme or reason. Her hand hovered over the *Gossip Weekly* magazine in the pocket of the seat in front of us. For a moment, I was certain it would continue to haunt me for the rest of the trip, but eventually she moved her hand away and left it where it was.

I packed my cap and sunnies away in my bag because I wouldn't really need them in Hong Kong airport. ProV8 may have been big in Australia, but it hadn't taken over the rest of the world yet. At least, it wasn't popular enough to see me inundated with autograph hounds in a foreign city.

Alyssa slung her bag over her shoulder and slid into the aisle in front of me.

"I'll see you in a few hours, I guess," she said and the dismissal in her tone was clear.

It certainly left me with no doubt where I stood—only worthy of being spoken to when there was no other choice. "Yeah. Sure."

I let a few other people go before making my way into the aisle. If she didn't want me to be anywhere near her in the airport, that distance might as well start as early as possible.

Once I was free of the gate, I thought about the things I needed to do in the five hours I had free. Having a shower was certainly on the agenda; I'd spent too long cramped up in the airplane seat and needed to clean. A decent coffee was also on the must-do list.

Convincing myself not to look for Alyssa, I headed off to try to find a shower. Eventually, I found a lounge that offered food, showers, and a space to relax. Within fifteen minutes, I was under the steady stream, trying to wash away the tension that being near Alyssa had elicited within me. Unfortunately, there was only one way I knew would work for sure.

Clasping my cock in my hand, I closed my eyes and let Alyssa in. The sight of the few genuine smiles she'd granted me on the trip, the smell of the coconut body wash she clearly still used, and the feeling of her warm body against mine as she'd slept. With her right there in my fantasies, fresher than ever before, I stroked along my length. Visions of the glimpses I'd been given of her new body danced through my mind. The tattoo, her new belly ring, the swell of her breasts. I groaned with need as my hand worked faster.

Before long, I was tumbling over the edge into a painful bliss. My stomach clenched and released as my orgasm ripped through me, and I gritted my teeth as the agony in my side grew steadily with every spasm. Despite the pain, the relief that filled me was worth it. It'd been too long since I'd come, and it was a literal load off. Especially when I'd have to see Alyssa again before long.

After drying and dressing in the other outfit I'd packed in my carry-on, I went in search of a coffee and something to eat.

BY THE time I headed for the gate, it'd been almost four hours since I'd seen Alyssa. I'd considered going to the airline desk and asking if there was any chance I could get bumped to the next flight to London. When I was halfway there though, an ache, which had nothing to do with my ribs, invaded my chest. It was possible the next twelve-hour leg would be the catalyst for purging the memories of Alyssa—even if the first half of the journey hadn't been.

My gaze scanned the waiting passengers until they landed on the one person I wanted to see. Pretending not to notice that she was across from where I wanted to sit, I sauntered over to the row of chairs and took a seat. It was only after I was settled that I risked a glance up and acted as if I'd noticed her for the first time.

"Alyssa." I nodded and couldn't help the tiny smirk that twisted my lips as I considered that less than two hours earlier, I'd gotten myself off with thoughts of the first part of our trip. It was like a dirty little secret only I knew, and that was so fucking hot.

When she looked over to me, her eyes were red-rimmed and filled with sorrow. All thoughts of my happy ending were wiped away at the sight. It was clear she'd spent the better part of the time crying.

I frowned. Had she been crying over me? It just didn't seem likely. I mean, I was a fucking catch, but I doubted she had any tears left to cry for what we'd shared. It was too many years ago to still affect her.

I moved from my position across from her to sit at her side. "Are you okay?"

She shook her head.

"What is it?"

"I just miss—" She risked a quick glance at me and then swallowed heavily. "Home."

"Haven't you only just left?"

She shook her head. "I've been in Sydney for a week already."

Holy fuck! She'd been in Sydney for a week and I hadn't known. My chest burned at the thought. What would I have done if I had found out? I frowned. Really, the least she could have done was contact me to let me know she was close. We could have had dinner or some shit.

Why would she? It's not like you have a fantastic track record for answering her calls.

I frowned and leaned back in the chair.

"There's just so much going on," she murmured. "I can't deal with it."

"You can talk to me if you want," I offered.

"Don't do this, Dec."

"Don't do what?"

"Don't act like you care, when you've made it clear you don't." She stood and moved away from me.

I sat dumbfounded as I watched her walk away. Did I care? Scarily, the answer might almost have been yes. At very least, I cared much more than I should have.

Deciding that I didn't really need to buy into her crap, or invade her life, any more than I already had, I stayed where I was and considered what the fuck I'd said which could have tipped her over the edge like that. And what the fuck she'd been crying about.

MORE THAN a little pissed at the way Alyssa had stormed off after I'd offered her my shoulder to cry on, I decided to wait to board. I didn't want to be stuck sitting next to her for a minute longer than I had to be.

I gladly became the arsehole who waited until his name was called before boarding. Of course by the time I found my new seat, Alyssa was already seated. Her ears were already covered with headphones and she stared unblinkingly at the screen in front of her—even though the in-flight entertainment wasn't on. The closer I got, the clearer I could see that she was still upset. Tears wet her lashes.

Without a thought, I yanked my bag up to push it into the overhead lockers but the movement was too rapid and sent a jolt of blinding agony through me. I dropped my bag and clutched at my chest. In an instant, Alyssa was standing in front of me with my bag in her hands.

"Are you okay?" she asked.

As if you care. I clenched my jaw and snatched the bag back from her without a word. Ignoring the renewed pain, I carefully lifted my carry-on and forced it between other bags in the overhead locker. Then, without a further word, I plonked myself down on the seat.

"God you're such an arse," she muttered before returning to her seat.

"Well, I wouldn't want you to have to act like you care," I retorted with a sneer.

A frustrated growl left her lips, but at least her tears had stopped. She jammed her headphones on again and I thought about how similar the take-off would be to the last one. As the thought ran through my head, a chuckle escaped me.

She glanced in my direction when she heard the laugh, but didn't say anything. After a minute of silence, she turned to me with a frown. "What's so funny?"

I shook my head and laughed again.

"Dec." Her voice was filled with a deadly warning. "Tell me."

"Just *us*."

Her confusion grew. "I don't see anything funny about us."

"C'mon, Lys." I laughed. "We've barely spent a day together and we're already doing exactly what we've always done."

"Which is?"

"This. Fighting. Talking. Rinse and repeat. Throw in a kiss for good fucking measure, and it's a condensed version of our entire relationship."

She didn't say anything, but instead turned back to sit in her seat properly, clearly lost in thought.

"Dec, there . . . there's something I need to tell you," she said after another beat.

I spun to look at her, and saw that her face was pale. She looked like she was about to hurl. I wondered whether she was getting motion sick, but the last flight hadn't seemed to have caused her any issues.

Her eyes shifted to the window, she stared out of it for a few seconds as if steeling herself. "I . . ." She met my gaze and her expression fell. The tension in her body released and she slumped like a puppet cut from its strings. "I might be leaving Australia soon."

"I've got news for you. You already have," I whispered with a chuckle.

She shook her head. "No. I mean for good."

"Oh." For reasons unknown to me, that news made my heart plummet to my stomach. "Why?"

She looked away from me, staring out the window as she spoke. "Well, I've just finished my last round of exams at uni. Once I do, I'll have my Honours in Law."

"What's that got to do with leaving? You can practise law in Australia, can't you?"

"I've been offered a position with Pembletons. They are the preeminent barristers in London. Well, the world really. They have offices all over."

I had no air left in my lungs, and I couldn't draw any in. The ache along my side intensified as I struggled to breathe. I wondered if the cabin had depressurised in the seconds that she'd spoken. No oxygen masks dropped from the ceiling though, so I considered that maybe it was just me.

It couldn't just be me though. My lungs felt too tight—too sizes too small. And my heart . . . it was aching like it would burst at any second.

My fingers clawed the armrests as I glanced around searching for signs that anyone else was struggling for breath.

Alyssa kept her focus on the window. "They look for the best of the best of the best, and they've offered me a position in either their

91

Sydney or London offices. I just have to choose."

I couldn't breathe. *Seriously, shouldn't those oxygen masks fall soon?*

Alyssa kept talking, but I wanted to scream at her to shut up. The most important thing was the fact that the plane was losing air, not her happy fucking plans for the future.

"London seems like the smart choice for the opportunities it will provide. It means a little bit more study but the client base is fantastic."

My lungs tore painfully with each breath I tried to gasp down. The reason settled over me with a thud as I looked up into Alyssa's eyes. I didn't want her to leave.

A wave of nausea washed over me and my body started to shake. How the fuck could *that* be the issue? Why did it matter if Alyssa went to London permanently? I hadn't spoken to her in almost four years. What difference would distance make to that sort of relationship? Surely having Alyssa be on the other side of the world would make it easier to focus on the racetrack? So why did it feel like she'd just ripped my heart out with her bare hands and was now consuming it while it was still beating in her palm?

"Don't go," I whispered as I clutched at her arm. My voice was broken, pleading. "Please."

She gave no indication that she'd heard me, except to close her eyes for half a second. Then she turned toward me, but stared blankly past me and into the aisle. "Dec—"

My next move shocked even me, but I could only blame the lack of oxygen. My brain was screaming, "No!" even as I moved in toward her. Something compelled me forward though. My lips were on hers in an instant and I felt alive in a way I hadn't in so long. A tightening sensation washed over my stomach, twisting it in ways which made me almost instantly hard.

She pulled away from me, her eyes were wide, and her mouth opened into a little O.

I was still trying to come to grips with what I'd done when her hand whacked across my cheek. The area heated and burned, but was nothing compared to the pain that ripped through my heart after her action. I put my hand over the spot where she'd just slapped me. Shock filtered through my system and tears sprung to my eyes. It took every ounce of willpower I had to stop them from falling.

"I'm sorry," I whispered, trying to keep my voice low and even. I didn't even know what exactly I was apologising for—the kiss or . . . everything else.

Alyssa sighed and closed her eyes. "No, I'm sorry. I shouldn't have slapped you." She paused. "God knows you deserved it"—she sighed—"but I still shouldn't have done it."

The thing I couldn't explain to her was that my lips burned more than my cheek. They wanted to taste her once more, to claim her again. Her mouth became a beacon for me, drawing the attention of my gaze.

"When?" I asked after a minute of silence, forcing my eyes to meet hers rather than stare at her lips.

"When what?" she asked. Her voice was quiet and cold. Tired.

"When are you leaving?"

"If I decide to go, it'll be after graduation, next February."

"That's the reason for this trip, isn't it?"

She nodded. "I've got to decide whether the London branch is right for me. That's why I was in Sydney; I've spent the last week in that office."

"Then how long are you in London for?"

"About the same, I guess. I'm anxious to get home as soon as possible though, especially if I'm going to be moving away for good. There are things I need to get sorted out."

"Like?"

"Like, none of your goddamn business," she snapped.

"Sorry." She'd practically just cast me aside and proved that she had a life that I wasn't a part of, and it made me want to know more. Moving to London was a far bigger dream than she'd ever had before. Despite how desperate I was for more information, I didn't want to press her and piss her off.

"No, I'm sorry. It's hard to explain, but I just don't think I'm ready to let you into my private life again. Not when you'll waltz off into whatever party will have you, to throw down with whatever random chick you can find, as soon as this plane lands."

"I don't have to," I said.

She paused, even her breath stopped for a time. "You don't have to what?" she asked in a quiet voice.

"I don't have to waltz off to any party. Or throw down with any random chick. All I've got going on over there is a key to an apartment. That's it. I'm free to do anything I like."

"And?"

I didn't know how to answer her "And?" but I knew I didn't want this leg to end like the last one. I didn't want whatever it was we had developing between us to end so soon. I wanted to extend our time together for as long as I possibly could. "And, well, maybe we can go out to dinner while we're both in London?"

She closed her eyes and shook her head slightly. "You want me to go on a fucking date with you? After everything you've done?"

"No," I said but only to stop her from shutting me down. It was exactly what I was asking. "Not a date. Just two old friends catching up." Maybe from there, I could figure out some way to get her out of my head.

"I don't think so, Dec. I'm sorry, but I don't want to get involved with you again. I—I don't know if I can." Her voice was brittle, like the thin ice I was no doubt treading on by even asking for more time with her.

"I understand." Her words shattered me. I didn't understand any of my emotions anymore, but I knew pain when it sliced through my heart. I fixed my eyes on the seat in front of me— desperate not to let her see how deep her words had cut. My lip may have quivered as tears pricked my eyes.

"Fine . . . a drink," Alyssa said and I turned my head toward her. She had her eyes closed and looked pained.

"What?"

"I'll go out with you for a drink, *one drink*, once we get off the plane. But that's all. Then I need to be on my way so I can live the life that you left me to."

"That would be nice," I said. One drink was at least a start.

We fell back into silence again. After a few minutes Alyssa put her headphones on and concentrated hard on whatever was happening on the TV in front of her. I felt myself drifting off to sleep again. It had been so long since I'd had good, natural, uninterrupted sleep, but something about the airplane made it almost easy. Perhaps I needed to fly more often.

CHAPTER NINE

PANICKED

BY THE TIME I woke again, we were only about five hours out of London. I wasn't sure whether I was relieved or disappointed by that fact. The one thing that struck me was how amazingly comfortable I was. More than I'd ever been on an airplane. More than I had been in a very long time in general if I was being honest.

It took me another second to realise that my arm was wrapped around a sleeping Alyssa, and my fingers rested on her hip. Her head rested on my chest, and her shoulder was tucked into my underarm. In fact, her whole body was turned toward me and her arm draped across my stomach. The position left her fingers brushing across my thigh, and dangerously close to my now raging hard-on. My head turned toward her, leaning against her hair, and every breath filled me with the comfort of her presence.

It was clear just how dangerous the position was. *How the fuck did we end up like this*?

I carefully tried to extract myself without waking her but failed miserably. At the worst possible moment, when my hand hovered just near her boobs, her eyes fluttered open. She took a second to take in our position, and my hand at groping level, and sat bolt upright. Her hand connected with my face for the second time in less than six hours.

"What the fuck, Dec?" she snapped.

"Fucking hell, Lys," I hissed back at almost exactly the same time.

"How the hell do you expect me to react when I wake up with your paws all over me?"

"You were all over me!" I protested.

"Yeah right," she said. "As if I would come near you with a ten-foot pole." A small smirk crossed her lips.

"I wouldn't want you near me with a ten-foot pole," I joked. "That would fucking hurt."

She chuckled. "You know what I mean. There is nothing that I find attractive about you."

"Come on, just admit it . . . you want this." I ran my hands over my body.

She blushed, even as she shook her head.

Holy fuck! "You do, don't you?" I asked incredulously. Then I realised I was seriously close to another slapping, and I definitely didn't want that. If her hands touched me, I wanted it to be for altogether more pleasurable reasons.

She managed to rein her blush in a little and controlled her slap-happy hand for the moment. "Been there, done that. Not interested in an encore. Especially not with all the other *guests* you've had lately."

I raised my eyebrow at her words, which contradicted the look in her eye as her gaze roamed my body as if seeing me for the first time. "I seem to remember you saying to me once that you planned on doing *it* a lot."

Part of me wondered whether I secretly *wanted* to be slapped by Alyssa again. I was certainly going the right way about it.

"Who says I haven't?" she said with an almost innocent look on her face.

Fuck, she's a sex goddess.

My mouth went dry as I pictured her in various positions, but then I recalled that other fucker and had to stop the image when he invaded the visions. Seeing that would do nothing more than make me hurl. An ache built in my chest and my hands quaked. I wanted to demand names, addresses and phone numbers of every man she'd been with after me so I could hunt them down and kill them.

"It may surprise you to learn that you're not the only man on earth."

It was hypocritical considering how many women I had been with—I couldn't even *begin* to tally numbers—but the thought of anyone else being with Alyssa that way made my fucking blood boil.

"You mean that fucker who took you to Queensland Raceway?" The words tumbled out of my mouth before I thought about them.

"What?" she asked. Her eyes were wide and unblinking. "How do you even know about that?"

"I saw you."

Her brows pinched together and she wiggled on her seat. "You saw me? When?"

"After qualifying. Before the first race. I saw both of you, getting food." I couldn't work the accusing edge out of my voice; not that I tried too hard. "And you looked pretty fucking comfortable in his arms."

She chuckled. "Trust me, there's nothing going on between Flynn and I."

Flynn. That's the fucker's name, is it? I recalled her dreamy words on the earlier flight. *She was fucking dreaming about him with me sitting right next to her! Motherfucker!*

I thought of his lips touching hers and my fingers curled into a fist. "Sure, it looked like nothing."

She burst out laughing. Her whole face lit up with a smile brighter than any she'd worn since I had the fortune—*misfortune?*—of sitting next to her. "Declan . . . he's gay!"

"What?"

"He's just a really good friend that I met through uni."

I shook my head. Her statement didn't make sense, not with what I'd seen. "But he kissed you."

She raised one eyebrow. "If you think *that* was a kiss, I think you need to brush up on your bag of tricks. Here I was with the impression you were some sort of sex god or something."

Maybe you should show me what you regard as a kiss. I couldn't bring myself to say the words even though they danced the tarantella on my tongue. I'd already been slapped twice, and I didn't really want to try for a third . . . *Do I?* "If he's just a friend, how the fuck did he convince you to go to a race when I couldn't the whole time we were dating?"

She bit her lip and it was clear she didn't want to tell me something. She nestled back into her seat, facing the front of the plane once more. "Umm . . . he's into all that car crap too. He helped me out a lot; taking him to a race was the least I could do."

There was something more, I knew it. Even with the years that had gone since I'd last spent any time with her, I could read her expressions like a fucking book. I was about to ask her to clarify, but the cabin crew interrupted with a meal for each of us. I'd missed the last one because I was asleep, so I was famished. Even airline food was acceptable in my empty-stomached state.

By the time I'd finished talking to the flight attendant, Alyssa had slipped her headphones back on and the conversation was over again for a while. While I ate my meal, I thought about everything that had happened over the last day. How much information I had learned, but how much more she still seemed to be hiding. Then again, it wasn't like she owed me anything at all.

Except her company for a drink like she promised.

When I'd finished, I glanced over at Alyssa just in case I could get her attention, but she'd started an in-flight movie. Instead of talking to her, I watched as she smiled and laughed at what was on the screen. She really was as beautiful as ever, maybe even more so now she'd grown into her curves. I thought about all the shit that had happened between the night in the hotel and the last time I saw her. The night we'd sat side-by-side at our picnic table as I'd said goodbye. I hadn't allowed any room for negotiation and didn't let her say anything that might convince me to stay. After I'd shattered her heart, she slapped me and stalked off into the night.

I hadn't seen her again.

Until Queensland Raceway. Until the dude I thought must have been fucking her, but was apparently just a friend. Would the last five races have ended differently if I'd known that piece of information? I dismissed the thought as soon as it came into my mind. That would mean I felt more for her than I allowed myself to, and that couldn't be right.

"What are you thinking about?" Alyssa's voice was soft beside me. I didn't even realise her movie had finished, or maybe she'd just grown bored with it.

I didn't see any point in lying to her. She'd be able to see through me as clearly as I could her. "You."

"Why?"

"I was just thinking about all the fucking mistakes that drove us apart."

"What do you mean?"

"Well, I thought Josh attacked me because you asked him to. I never even realised he thought . . ." I couldn't even say the words. *How could he ever think I'd rape her*? "I just thought it was your way of telling me you didn't want me anymore."

"But I told you after that that I did want you," she said. The smiles and happiness she'd worn when she'd been watching the movie were completely wiped away. "Repeatedly. Even after you moved to Sydney, I tried to call you, but you never answered the phone yourself and no one seemed to pass on my messages." Her voice sounded close to tears.

"They passed them on," I whispered, leaning forward and putting my head in my hands. "I'd just shut down the part of myself that still cared about you. Maybe it was callous, but I couldn't be there in Sydney and still be in love with you. It would have torn me in two."

I closed my eyes as I felt her hand rubbing a small circle on my back. My tears were dangerously close again. I bit the inside of my cheek to try to hold them off.

Just as I was relaxing with her touch, the plane dropped and my stomach lurched.

Fuck. What was that?

The plane plummeted and jumped.

Fuck!

I reached for the armrests, clawing the material as I tried to grip harder. My teeth clenched together as the plane bounced again.

"Fuck!"

The beginnings of a panic attack crashed over me. My palms felt itchy and sweaty and I couldn't breathe. The plane felt suddenly too claustrophobic and tight as it fell through the air again before leaping back up. I leant back in the chair, squeezing my eyes shut as I started to hyperventilate. I tried to open up my lungs and force oxygen in, I tried all the techniques my quack had given me for this situation, but nothing did anything. It wasn't working. Nothing was working. Nothing *would* work.

Even though I recognised the start of a panic spiral, there was nothing I could do to stop it. My teeth clenched tighter, practically grinding the surface away, as I tried to no avail to breathe through wave after wave of blinding panic that threatened my hold on sanity.

"Declan?" Alyssa asked softly. "Are you all right? It's just turbulence, and it's stopped now."

"Talk to me," I whispered to Alyssa through my laboured breaths.

"About what?" Her voice was full of concern. The sound of her worry made my panic intensify. "What do you need?"

"Talk to me about anything, just say anything. I need . . . I need a distraction." The last words came out as a high-pitched squeak. I was getting dizzy and I couldn't breathe.

I'd done a good job of hiding the full force of my panic attacks from everyone else. Only my ex-psychiatrist knew about them. Never in my wildest nightmares would I have thought I'd have to suffer through one on a plane. In a public place no less; where gossip and lies easily started and could spread like wildfire. And with Alyssa at my side. When I could, I started to repeat my mantra to myself silently in my mind, *I can get through this, I've had one before and I made it through then. I can get through this, I've had one before and I made it through then.*

"I went to Queensland Raceway to see you," Alyssa's voice cut through my mantra and her words left me stunned.

"What?" I turned toward her, my internal monologue forgotten.

"I've been to every race of yours I could get to."

I wasn't sure if her admission was easing my attack or not. It was definitely distracting, but I couldn't decide if it helped me — and my decision to leave her all those years ago — knowing that.

"Why?" I asked. After a moment, I realised it was definitely helping. My breathing had started to come a little easier. My heart slowed almost back to a normal speed.

"Because you were right. When you said I never thought of it as a real career, I mean. I never thought you could make a living from it, and I never went to a single race when we were together. When you left, I kind of wanted to see what all the fuss was about."

I shook my head. "But that explains one meeting. Why did you keep going?"

She laughed a little and her cheeks grew a little pink. "I . . . well, I found I actually enjoyed the thrill of being there at the track. Especially with Flynn. He was full of information and was always patient with me while teaching me the rules. Now we go on friend-dates whenever you come to town." While she was talking, her eyes had taken a faraway look, as if she was reliving some memory. I wished I could see what it was. In that moment, I felt every single day of the years I'd shut her out of my life. After a moment, she chuckled and ducked her head. "Actually, he was surprised when he found out I used to date you, and a touch jealous."

"Jealous of you or me?"

"Of me." Her chuckle grew into genuine laughter. It fucking killed me that her smile was so genuine, real, and carefree when she was talking about that other fucker. "After the first meet, I got grilled for three hours on what it was like to kiss you and whether your body was really as smoking hot as it looks when you're walking around with your race suit on."

Before I could stop myself, I was laughing in response to her honesty. "I'm not sure whether to be offended or flattered."

"Oh, you should be flattered. He's quite the catch."

I laughed again.

"Better?" she asked.

For a moment, I wondered what she meant, and then I recalled the reason for her admission and the conversation that followed. My panic attack. She'd certainly helped to sweep it aside. "Much. Thanks."

She put her arm around me and guided me closer to her side. I rested my forehead on her shoulder and I breathed deeply. The proximity worked even better than her talking had. I raised my gaze to meet hers and was pulled toward her lips once more, but this time I resisted it.

Leaning back out of her embrace before the siren call of her pink pout grew too strong, I rested my head back against the seat and closed my eyes. A moment later, she pushed headphones onto my head and then my ears were full of the calming sounds of classical music. I closed my eyes as her fingertips traced gentle lines over my face. I allowed the music, and Alyssa's touch, to calm me completely.

I didn't even realise that another hour had passed until I opened my eyes again. I was more relaxed than I had been in, well, ever. I pulled off the headphones and then smiled at her.

"Thank you. I'm all better now."

"What was that?"

I shrugged, not really wanting to make a big deal out of my weakness. If Danny or his boys found out about the attacks, they might never put me in a car again. "Nothing really. Just a panic attack." I tried to make a mental note of how easy they were to dismiss when I wasn't in the grips of one.

"Are they the reason you've been crashing out?"

I shook my head. "No, I've never had one while driving. They usually only hit at night when I can't sleep." *Or when I wake from dreams of you.* I sighed.

"You suffer from insomnia?"

I nodded. "For . . . quite a while now." I'd stopped myself from saying four years before it was too late.

She seemed to consider this information for a while. "Is that why you have a problem with gratuitous drug use?"

"Maybe. Like I said, it's easy to grow reliant on those pills." I shrugged, still unwilling to get into the full nitty-gritty of that story with her. We fell into silence, but it was at least a slightly more comfortable silence than the last time.

A few minutes later, Alyssa spoke again.

"It was actually really nice running into you, Dec," Alyssa said. Her words reminded me that we only had about half an hour left before the plane was due to land. She chuckled. "And those are words I never thought I'd say."

"I still owe you that drink." I wasn't ready to give up my time with her just yet.

"It'll be like six in the morning when we land. Why don't we catch up tomorrow after we're both rested?"

I nodded, but then I had a thought. "Where are you staying?"

"I was just going to find a place somewhere in the airport to shower and maybe crash for a few hours. My hotel room isn't ready until later this afternoon. There wasn't much point booking anything when the plane landed so early."

"I have free unlimited use of the apartment I mentioned earlier. Why don't you have a shower and catch some sleep there?"

"I'm not really sure that's such a good idea," she said with a hesitant edge to her voice.

"Come stay. Please?" I begged, pouting a little to get my point across. "I promise I'll keep as far away as you want me to. I just want to know that you'll be safe. I wouldn't feel right letting you wander off into the night in a foreign country with nowhere to stay."

She pursed her lips together in thought for a moment before nodding. "Okay, but only if we can change the drink to breakfast."

"Why don't we start with breakfast and see where it takes us?" I offered her my panty-dropping smile and turned on the charm.

When she nodded, a worried grimace crossed her features instead of a smile. I wasn't sure what it meant, but I was happy to celebrate the small win I'd had.

Finally the plane began its descent, and I couldn't help thinking that Danny had been right to send me on this trip. It may just change my life after all.

CHAPTER TEN

NO COMPLICATIONS

ONCE WE'D BOTH arranged our things, I carefully pulled both my and Alyssa's bags down from the overhead and slung them onto my shoulders. Even though I knew she was more than capable of carrying her own, there was no way I was going to risk her darting off on me and disappearing into the crowd like she had after the first flight. Not when I felt so close to a breakthrough on my crashing issue. It wasn't sorted yet, I was sure of that much. Deep down though, a certainty grew that more time with Alyssa was going to be the easiest way to find a solution. She was the cause after all. I just needed to pinpoint why.

When we headed into the terminal, I managed to convince her to stop at the duty-free shops for a few supplies. When she said she didn't want to buy any alcohol, I used both of our quotas to grab some premium grog for my stay. We walked side-by-side as we went through the motions of customs and baggage collections. Our conversation wasn't exactly awkward, but it was weighted down in ways it had never been when we were kids.

A little less than an hour later, we were free of the bustling Heathrow Airport. We found our way to the taxi ranks and waited in line for our turn. I gave the driver the address of Danny's apartment in Kensington. Alyssa was silent through it all, but she never stopped chewing her lip. It felt like she had something she wanted to tell me, but wasn't sure how to start. I decided if it was really important, she would let me know when she was ready. All I hoped was that she wasn't regretting her choice to agree to spend a few hours in the apartment with me.

On the drive to the address Danny had given me, I grew anxious. I hadn't asked anything about it really, assuming it was going to be just me for the length of my stay. Well, me and any titbits I brought home to satisfy my urges. Either way, I hadn't considered needing more than one bed. Panic coursed through me that it would be a tiny studio with only a bed and not much else.

Maybe it was a bachelor pad style apartment filled with all the latest tricks for snaring the ladies. The nearer we got, the keener my anxiety became over inviting Alyssa to stay without having seen the space first. What if it was some sort of semi-brothel sex den? Would she believe it wasn't mine? Or maybe it would be a shithole with rats and cockroaches breeding on every surface. Truthfully, I couldn't see Danny owning anything that even remotely matched either of those descriptions and I definitely couldn't see him giving *me* the keys if he did. Still, the panic was impossible to shake.

Here goes nothing, I thought as the taxi pulled up in front of the building. The facade of the building gave me some hope that it wouldn't be a hovel inside. It was so old school it was almost art. I didn't know one era from another, but it reminded me of my childhood, of hours spent watching *Paddington Bear* with Alyssa at my side. It was so different to what I was used to—the hustle and bustle of modern Sydney—that I could almost have believed that I'd stepped back in time. I gave the driver my credit card for payment, letting him run it while I unloaded our bags.

My heart pounded in my chest with each step as I led Alyssa to the front door. I tentatively turned the key and took one last deep breath before I pushed open the door. It turned out all my fears were unwarranted. She followed me with her suitcase as I carried our carry-on bags and my own suitcase up a short flight of stairs into the large open-plan living, dining and kitchen area. Although the apartment was long and narrow, the colour choices and furnishings gave it a dramatic feeling of light and space, even in the dark grey of the early morning.

Despite the historic facade, the interior was very modern. It looked decked out with every luxury you'd want on holiday.

The kitchen was an expanse of stainless steel, including a giant island in the middle. Monstrous ovens and equipment filled every cavity. Looking at the array of knobs and dials, I decided I was best leaving them alone. At least the ice maker on the fridge looked easy enough to use. That fact alone meant that I would at least have ice and water for the duration of my stay. Takeout would have to suffice for the rest of my needs. At least nothing would be too different from home there.

Opposite the kitchen, in the only enclosed section of the area, was a staircase which I assumed must lead up to the bedrooms and bathroom.

The dining area led off from the kitchen, to the left of the main living space. A large oak dining table, with pews running down each side for seats, rested in the middle. The colour scheme of the whole apartment seemed to be based on a natural palette, a mix of dark hardwood floors, sea grass carpets, and eggshell walls. In the living area, a chocolate-brown leather sofa and two plush beige linen armchairs clustered around the fireplace. Three large windows behind the sofa gave panoramic views of the cobblestone street below. To the right of the windows was a wood and glass door which appeared to lead out onto a terrace.

Dropping the luggage I held, I walked slowly through the open space, absorbing all the little details. On top of the fireplace, flush-mounted and blending almost seamlessly into the wall, was a huge flat-screen TV. An antique roll-top desk sat in one corner of the room; the top was open so I could see there was a desktop computer and phone tucked inside.

The wall behind the armchairs was lined with open

bookshelves, filled to bursting with old leather-bound books, lending the space just a touch of the old-world charm that covered the exterior. I ran my fingers along the spines, wondering whether they held some old treasures or were just there for decoration.

"Wow!" Alyssa murmured from the kitchen.

"Yeah," I replied, turning to look at the area from just in front of the fireplace. Between the money I was on, and the team I belonged to, I was used to a touch of opulence. My own house was a multi-million-dollar McMansion that I'd probably be repaying until the day I retired, but it had nothing on the apartment. With a perfect blend of old-world charm and modern technology, the place took my breath away. Looking at Alyssa as she spun a small circle, no doubt to take in all the details like I had, I figured she thought the same thing. In that moment, it felt like I'd come home at last. Who knew I had to travel halfway around the world to find a place I'd feel so instantly comfortable?

"Whose place is this?" Alyssa asked, running her fingers along the stainless steel of the kitchen island.

"Danny Sinclair's," I replied. "He's the one who made me take this trip."

"Why?"

"Can't you guess?" I raised one eyebrow and made the sound of squealing brakes and a car crash.

A small chuckle escaped her; it had an edge to it that I didn't understand. "Oh, I see. Well, at least he didn't just fire your arse, I guess."

"Yeah, well, that's next if I don't get my shit sorted."

"What's to sort?" she asked, seeming genuinely confused. Her gaze met mine and offered the perfect answer to her question. It was the memory of those eyes that haunted me around the track. I wasn't about to admit that to her though. How could I tell her that she was the reason my career was in the fucking toilet even though we hadn't spoken two words to each other in years? Before I'd wound up seated next to her on the flight at least.

There was a softness to her stare that I didn't want to acknowledge. A compassion almost, which I certainly didn't need. I couldn't cope with her looking at me like that. It set me on edge, making me clench my fists even as my cock swelled.

"I don't fucking know, all right?" My jaw pressed together tightly as I twisted free of her gaze. I leaned against the fireplace mantle. "That's the hard part. How do you fix something when you don't know what's fucking broken?"

She issued an exasperated sigh from behind me. I wasn't sure what I would see if I turned to look at her, but I was certain it wouldn't help me.

A minute passed, then two, and neither of us said anything more. I stared steadfastly at my own reflection in the darkened TV and regretted asking her to come back to the apartment. It had seemed like such a good idea on the plane, but I didn't expect her to launch straight into questions that cut to the crux of my visit. I wasn't sure I ever wanted to discuss those questions with her.

"Um, okay, well." Alyssa was no doubt trying to break the tension that made the room stifling when she spoke, but her voice sent the image of her eyes and the sound of crunching metal coursing through me again. "I'm going to take a shower and then try to get some sleep. I want to be awake when it's time to get settled into my hotel."

I nodded before allowing my gaze to leave my own reflection and focus on hers. With a few deep breaths I was able to purge the emotions that had taken me in their grips. The reminder that she would be leaving in just a few hours made me more inclined to hurry up and work out what the fuck I needed to do to get her out of my mind when I was driving. I could have said something to invite her for a drink and get the process started, but I didn't feel up to it yet.

"Sure. I'll try to find you a towel," I said instead.

I carried Alyssa's suitcase up the stairs. There were two bedrooms; one had a king-size bed, the other two singles. I put her suitcase on one of the single beds before thinking better of it. She'd always loved her space when sleeping. Even in primary school, she'd slept on a double bed. Whereas I could sleep anywhere, and had when the occasion had called for it. With her in the next bedroom, I doubted I'd get much sleep anyway. My insomnia was bad enough when she was almost one thousand kilometres away, I couldn't begin to imagine how terrible it would be with her just metres away.

"Would you prefer the king-size?" I asked.

"No, it's fine. You're the one staying here for your holiday. You may as well get settled as soon as possible."

Nodding again, mostly because I couldn't find adequate words to say anything else at that point, I left to hunt through the cupboards for a towel. I hoped the fact that it was a guest accommodation would mean everything was fairly strategically placed. While I searched, I heard Alyssa start on the water in the bathroom. The door was shut when I passed again, so I didn't enter. Even though the thought was somewhat tempting—after the glimpses I'd got on the plane, I longed to see all of the changes in her body up close and personal.

When I spotted the open door for what would be her bedroom for the night, I decided I would just leave the towel on the bed for her. It hadn't taken her long to get somewhat settled in and the contents of her carry-on bag were scattered all over one of the beds. Her suitcase sat next to the mess; open and practically calling out an invitation to snoop. Even though I tried to resist the call, my gaze slid across the contents as I laid the towel on the bed. Everything was mussed up in the suitcase, as if she had been looking for something.

Holy fuck!

At first, I couldn't believe my eyes, but the longer I looked, the less I could deny what I was seeing. Resting pride of place on top of the messy mountain of clothes was a pink vibrator. It wasn't the first time I'd seen one of course, but the thought of it being Alyssa's made my cock hard and my cheeks burn red. I spun to leave the room before she caught me intruding so absolutely on her privacy. In my haste, I hadn't noticed that the water had stopped in the bathroom or heard the footsteps in the hall, but I collided with Alyssa in the doorway. In her hands, she clutched a shirt I recognised as the one she'd spilt coffee over when we'd been on the plane.

"Hey, I was just rinsing this again . . ." Her voice trailed off as she took in my blush. Her eyes flicked over to her suitcase, and then it was her turn to blush. She walked over to the bed and flicked the lid of her suitcase shut. When I looked over to her, she had her eyes closed and her hand rested on top of the black material of her luggage as if it was trying to burst open again. I could almost hear her silently willing the ground to open up and swallow her whole. Something needed to happen to relieve the tension in the room or it just might kill us both.

"So how long are you over here for?" I asked. My brain chose that exact moment to see the hilarity in the situation, so my voice was infused with laughter.

She covered her face with her hands and groaned into them. When she pulled them away though, it looked like she had a small smirk on her face. "A week."

"Wow, only a week?"

She turned to me. She was definitely smirking now. "I'm a woman, Declan. I do have needs."

It was clear that I'd been right when I'd assumed she must have grown into an absolute sex goddess. "Needs that must be met regularly, I see."

"Well, it's not like I get loads of external offers like you."

I cast an appraising eye over her body and moved closer to her. "I find it hard to believe you wouldn't get all the opportunities you wanted."

Her smile fell a little in response. "You'd be surprised. Besides, I've found it easier to make my own opportunities. That way I don't have the messy complications after the fact."

"What complications?" I asked, lifting one shoulder up in a half shrug. I was so close to her now, I could reach out and touch her — so I did. My fingers brushed the hair off the back of her neck so that it fell over one shoulder. A slight shudder raced across her skin at our contact. "If you really want it, there's always someone willing to give you a bit of wham, bam, thank you ma'am without the strings." I whispered the last words against her neck, my lips practically ghosting her skin. If I was any closer, she would have felt my erection poking into her back.

I ran my words over in my head again after they were out. Had I really told her she should go and screw a random stranger?

She moved away from me, climbing onto the bed to escape. When she looked back at me, there was sorrow in her gaze. "There's always strings."

I shrugged. "Not in my experience."

Which was plenty enough.

She narrowed her eyes at me, and then she swallowed hard. "Maybe." She moved to the side to get around me, a change of clothes and the towel I'd brought in held tightly in her arms—almost as a shield. She danced just outside of my arm's length and as she moved, kept her front to me the whole way. "I guess I've never investigated it that thoroughly. I've always been too busy with uni and Ph— stuff."

She only turned when she reached the door. I took that as an indication that she was ready for the conversation to be over. I wasn't sure that I was, but I wasn't exactly sure about anything since I'd realised I'd be sitting next to her on the plane. Following her out, I wondered what the hell was going on with my head. If he wasn't such a quack, I would have almost considered calling Dr. Henrikson, my former psychiatrist, to figure it out.

"I'll, um, I'll be downstairs if you need me," I said as she retreated to the bathroom. I leaned against the wall and watched her fight with the bathroom door with her arms full.

"I'll be fine. I'll just shower and then head to bed."

I nodded. "I'll go next."

"Oh shit, actually, is there a phone here?"

I frowned at her question. "I don't know if it is connected, but I saw one on the desk when we came in. You can give it a try."

"I have to make a phone call first, if you don't mind? Mum will probably send Scotland Yard if I don't call her soon."

It was something I could see Ruth doing—at least the Ruth that I remembered. "Easy fixed then, you make your call and I'll shower first. I'll be done before you've finished saying hello."

Grabbing one of the towels, I headed out of her room. At the very last second, I stopped and my eyes trailed back into the bedroom—to her suitcase—and then back to her. She blushed again, and I couldn't help but smirk at her before I left.

When she went down to make the call, I followed her to the stairs to see if she'd get through. After a moment, I heard her say, "Hi, Mum," so I assumed the phone must have worked. I tried not to listen as I turned for the bathroom, but the occasional sentence, like, "How is she? Is she eating?" and, "Put her on," floated up the stairs to me.

While I showered, my brain was running loops around our conversation. Not only had I learned that Alyssa couldn't go a week or two without an orgasm, but she didn't get them from other people very often. At least, she hadn't until then. I just *had* to go and convince her to fuck random guys because it wasn't that difficult to fuck without attachments.

Fucking idiot!

How on earth had that conversation gone so far off track?

CHAPTER ELEVEN

WHISKEY AND ICE

AFTER I'D HAD the briefest of showers, focused on hygiene and not much more, I headed downstairs. Alyssa was just hanging up and offered me a small smile.

"See you in a few hours," she said.

I nodded and headed toward my goal. My suitcase was still by the kitchen and held a rather bountiful supply of duty-free alcohol. I opened it only far enough to pull out a bottle of top-shelf whiskey and set about hunting down a glass in the massive kitchen. Once I'd found one, I pushed the glass under the ice-maker on the fridge, half filling it with cubes. I poured a triple shot of the whiskey over the top.

My intention was to relax and enjoy the flavour, but once the glass was at my lips I tipped it all down my throat. I hadn't realised how much I needed it after the flight and subsequent revelations. It was still difficult for me to process the fact that at that precise moment, Alyssa was in the bathroom upstairs—naked.

I poured another, larger, drink and carried it with me over to one of the oversize armchairs. I flicked on the TV but didn't pay attention to it. My mind was occupied thinking about what it might be like to be upstairs in the shower with Alyssa. Instead of wild imaginings of what she would look like, I recalled the time we had a shower together, in the hotel room after our year twelve formal.

Even as I sat on the sofa, removed by years and proximity, I could easily recall the feel of my hands running along her water-heated skin. The lather from the soap removing all the friction between our bodies. The taste of the water as I sucked it off her breasts. I downed the second glass of whiskey in a rush. I was so fucking hard it was uncomfortable.

After getting a third drink, I returned to the couch and turned the TV off. It was pointless noise that I didn't really need. I tried to savour the taste of the whiskey instead of gulping it down like a lifeline. For the price, it was a drink designed to be enjoyed, not skulled as fast as possible.

I put the glass to my lips again and sucked a small sip into my mouth and let it rest on my tongue. While I did, my mind supplied me with the incredibly hot, but unhelpful, images of drinking it off Alyssa's skin. I decided that maybe I needed to make *opportunities* of my own.

Alyssa was safely tucked away upstairs in the shower, and apparently had no intention of coming back downstairs. She'd said she was going straight to bed after her shower after all.

I raised the glass again taking another, slightly larger, sip. While I did, I sucked one of the ice cubes into my mouth and rolled it around on my tongue, imagining I was swirling it around Alyssa's nipple. I moaned at the thought.

The cold focused my attention on my mouth, making it a little less noticeable that it was my own hand sliding up my thigh. It was almost easy to pretend it was Alyssa's.

I popped the button on my jeans and slowly slid down my zipper. Closing my eyes, I concentrated on the taste of the ice and alcohol in my mouth as I pushed my hand into my boxers. I thought of Alyssa under the shower, wet and glistening, and so fucking tasty.

The water in my mouth from the ice seemed to become infused with her flavour. I grabbed hold of my cock and slid my hand along the length. *This* was my perfection. It was the sort of relief I'd sought with hundreds of nameless, faceless women and never found. The sort of relief which only fantasies of Alyssa could provide. I closed my eyes and leaned back into the chair, sinking further into my fantasy and allowing my hand to glide up and down the length of my exposed shaft to the image of Alyssa imprinted in my brain. It wasn't me holding myself—it was her. Her hands. Her mouth. Her body.

Her on her knees in front of me, her head in my lap and her lips wrapped around my cock.

Oh fuck, baby.

The ice in my mouth grew smaller and smaller as my body heated with the lust and excitement that raced through me. It had been so long since I'd let myself truly enjoy a fantasy about her. I rolled the ice cube around my mouth one last time before swallowing the mouthful. I left my hand on my erection as I leaned forward with the other to grab the glass and claim another piece of ice. I opened my eyes to locate the side table and met an amused, honey-gold gaze staring at me. Her delight only increased as a warm blush crept up my cheeks.

"Don't stop on my account," she said with a chuckle.

Holy fuck!

I pulled my hand out of my boxers and zipped myself up. My erection was almost painful, pulling my pants tight as it sought desperately for the release promised only moments earlier. It would have to wait though. It wasn't polite to masturbate in front of guests.

"Fuck. Sorry, Alyssa." I said, running my hand—the one that hadn't been down my pants—through my hair quickly before downing the rest of the whiskey.

She laughed. "I guess *everyone* has needs."

She had *no* fucking idea.

My *needs* grew exponentially when I saw the tank top and pants set she was wearing. It was thin white cotton with small pink flowers all over it. She had no bra on and the white cotton was almost completely see-through. Through the material, I could see the thickest black lines of her tattoo, and could clearly make out her erect nipples. The sight was too much. I wanted to put my mouth on her tank top and make out *with* her nipples. She wasn't wearing panties either; I could see the dark triangle of hair between her thighs. As if I hadn't already been hard enough before she came downstairs.

"I just came to get a drink." She smiled, seeming completely oblivious to her lack of adequate coverage.

"You want some whiskey?" I croaked, holding up my empty glass. Fuck knows I need some more.

She gave a half-hearted shrug. "Sure. Why not?"

When I stood, my erection rubbed uncomfortably against my boxers and jeans. With some difficulty, I walked with an air of nonchalance toward the kitchen. I tipped the mostly melted ice from my glass into the sink and topped it up with some fresh cubes. Then I grabbed another glass for Alyssa, put some ice in it and poured us both a double shot.

The whole way through the actions, which should have been routine and easy, my heart pounded. My head swum, but I wasn't sure whether that was from the alcohol or from the lack of blood in my brain. I turned to take Alyssa's drink to her but found she'd followed me into the kitchen.

"So . . ." Alyssa said awkwardly as I handed her one of the glasses.

"So?" I responded, finding it difficult to understand what she wanted to say. In fact, I was finding it difficult to even stay upright or think. Processing anything other than the need for another sip, and my aching desire for her touch, was so far beyond my capabilities it wasn't funny.

"So, do you really think two people can just fuck with no complications?" She rolled the glass between her hands, sloshing the liquid around and clinking the ice cubes together.

Confused why we were back on the topic, I struggled to keep up. She'd ended the conversation about it pretty abruptly when we'd been upstairs. "Sure. What I mean is, I've done it before. If everyone's upfront about what they want, what's the issue?"

"And you'll do it again." I wasn't sure if it was a statement or a question.

"I guess." I wondered what her point was. Was she going to have a go at me about sleeping around? If she was, she was going to have—

"Good," she said, stopping my thoughts in their tracks. She smiled and held up her glass. "To fucking—with no complications."

After she clinked my glass, she threw her drink back like a pro.

I placed my untouched glass back on the island in front of me as I frowned in confusion. Alyssa rested hers beside it. I tried to get my head around the conversation, but nothing added up like it was supposed to. I'd had far too much to drink for it to make sense.

Before I could register what was happening Alyssa's lips were on mine. She tasted like the alcohol and her tongue was cold from the ice in her drink.

I was asleep. It came to me in one blinding realisation. It was the only thing that made a lick of sense and the best explanation I could come up with for why Alyssa's tongue was in my mouth and her hands were tangled in my hair.

It was only logical that I'd fallen asleep during my little fantasy while I wanked, and my subconscious was torturing me for letting her in. It was exquisite torture, but torture nonetheless. Later on, I would wake up and have to face Alyssa and try to drive the thoughts of the dream out of my mind.

Despite knowing I was going to pay for the dream in the morning, I was sick enough to run with the fantasy. My hands found her hips and she moaned at my touch.

Her hands clutched at my hair and she pulled me against her. Her lips wrapped around my bottom lip and she sucked on it in a way that drew a sound from me that was new and utterly unique to her. With her body wrapped around mine, her breasts pressed against my chest and I could feel her erect nipples brushing against me.

"Lys, oh, fuck, Lys," I muttered around kisses. I'd thought I was hard and desperate before, but it'd been nothing by comparison. After the way her kiss blazed through me, my dick was probably harder than the stainless steel bench she'd backed me against.

I pushed my hand against the waistband of her pants and slipped inside with no resistance. My fingers brushed across the smooth, naked span of her arse.

Fuck.

My erection strained and ached, the exquisite pain being the physical evidence that maybe, just maybe, it wasn't a dream after all.

I broke the kiss off, but my lips didn't move from her skin. I traced a path over her chin, onto her neck, and then down along her breastbone until I reached the material of her tank top. My mouth sought her nipples through the material. A fresh sound of needful pleasure ripped from me as I caressed her perfect peaks with my mouth. Teeth and tongue worked in unison, dragging the cotton around her tight buds. Even though bending over strained my already sore ribs, I honestly didn't give a shit. I could have had two broken legs and I still would have found a way to stand there and worship her body.

"Oh, fucking hell, Dec!" Alyssa cried. Her voice dripped with pleasure and need.

I spun us around, picked her up—swallowing down the whimper of pain that threatened to escape—and placed her onto the kitchen island. She yelped a little as her arse hit the cold steel, but I stood between her legs and she quietened. Dream or reality didn't matter any longer. I was going to take everything offered and I wasn't going to let either of us leave the kitchen without being thoroughly fucked first.

Grabbing my glass, I took a small mouthful of the amber liquid and then I met her mouth again. Our tongues twisted around each other, swapping the liquid back and forth until it was finally warm. Little by little, it trickled down the back of my throat, but it wasn't enough. With my eyes open and my gaze firmly meeting hers, I swallowed what was left in my mouth. Fuck, it tasted like Alyssa. A moan of delight left me before I claimed her lips again and my fingers rubbed the wet circles on the front of her shirt.

She shifted against me, leaning into my touch.

After a beat, where I thought I might just burst from the perfection of the moment, I pulled back.

"Do you really want this?" I asked.

"Please, Dec." She reached for my cheek and traced her fingers over the corner of my mouth. I sucked her finger between my lips and stroked the tip with my tongue. Her eyes rolled back as the pleasure of the sensation rolled through her body.

I pulled her hand away from my mouth and grinned.

"In that case, I have plans for you," I murmured before grabbing an ice cube from the glass with my fingers.

Holding it between my teeth, I rubbed the ice across the front of her tank top, tracing the cube across her already tight nipples. A hiss of pleasure escaped her and she squirmed in my hold. I used the fingers I'd grabbed the ice with, cold and dripping with whiskey, to trace patterns along her inner thigh. She mewed with pleasure as her body bucked away from the cold even as she leaned into my touch.

Her hands tugged at my shirt, unbuttoning it as quickly as she could. Once it was loose, I shook it off to give her free access. Her fingertips moved to gently caress the swollen bruise around my ribs. Ever so gently, she pressed her lips against each rib. The alcohol haze I'd been suffering from was clearing more and more by the minute, only to be replaced by an Alyssa-induced one. All I could see, hear, smell, and taste was her. I was completely and utterly lost in her.

In *us*.

How in the hell had I ever let her out of my life?

I'd forgotten just how fucking good she was at getting my body to react. How fucking tasty she was. How the sound of a moan or my name on her lips was almost enough to do me in without any kind of touching.

Her hands ran up and down the length of my back excruciatingly slowly, until finally she circled them around to my front. Fingertips traced my muscles, and I wanted to let her take control and fuck me the way I knew only she could, but I had things I wanted to do to her first.

I alternated between using my tongue and the ice cube on her nipples, drinking down the water as the ice melted. The cold cotton was the only barrier between me and perfection. When I went to lift my head to free her from the material, her fingers found my hair and she directed me back to her breasts. Using my fingertips at the hem of her tank top as an indicator of what I was going to do, I went to pull away again. I leaned back and pulled her tank top off in one swift movement. She relinquished her grip on my head only at the last second but then reclaimed her purchase to guide me straight back to her breasts the instant her shirt was off. I used my mouth on one breast while I worked the other with my hand, pinching and rubbing and caressing. God it felt good to have her in my hands again. It was something I had barely known I was missing, but despite the countless times I'd tried to replicate the feeling, there was no one else in the world who made me feel the way she did.

Looping her legs around my waist, she bucked her hips against mine. Her arse slipped off the bench when she did, but I had her. She was pinned between my hips and the bench. Even though she wasn't particularly heavy, her weight was enough to cause the constant niggle in my side to blossom into an ache. Her body, and her touch, were enough to soothe it down again.

More than anything, I wanted to rip her pyjama bottoms off, bend her over the bench and fuck her silly, but it was Alyssa. I owed her far more than that. I reached down and slid her pants off before pressing my palm against her mound.

Her hands were at my waistband, tugging on the button and zipper on my jeans. I pushed her back up and onto the counter, pressing her backward until she was lying on it. She squirmed a little at the cold but it warmed quickly on contact. My jeans dropped away as soon as her weight was off my hips.

Taking a moment, I gazed up her body, absorbing every inch — like a man granted just a glimpse of heaven. Who knew how long

I'd have with her, whether she'd call a stop to everything and I'd have nothing but the memory to satisfy me. The first thing that drew my eyes was the tattoo under her left breast. I could see now that it was a constellation or something, but fucked if I could tell which one. I longed to trace it with my fingers—or my tongue.

I noticed a new mark running across her stomach, near her pelvic bone. I'd memorised all of the scars on her body one time, and knew where each one had come from. I wondered what sort of accident she'd had to get the new one.

"Declan," she moaned desperately, drawing my focus back to the moment and letting the question give way to far more important matters.

Lifting the glass of whiskey to my lips, I drew a small mouthful of the amber liquid and another ice cube into my mouth. Hooking my arms around her legs, I lifted her hips up to meet my mouth. I kissed her inner thigh, rolling my tongue through the alcohol to taste her. I twisted my head to the other side and repeated the process. Catching the ice between my teeth, I swallowed down the whiskey.

I rubbed the ice against her clit, fighting the urge to smile as her hips writhed in my hold. In an agonisingly slow circuit, I traced the ice cube from the top of her pussy, down over her lips before brushing it against her entrance. I repeated this a few times until she was screaming and panting for more. Then I swallowed everything that was in my mouth, moaning at the combined flavour, before burying my tongue inside her.

"Holy fuck!" she cried out. Her hands twisted into my hair and she guided me to the position she wanted. I pressed my tongue up against her and she bucked. I ran my nose along her clit and she yanked on my hair again. I traced a small circle around the area and then rubbed at her clit with the tip of my tongue over and over until she was quivering against me. Placing her arse back on the counter, I added two fingers and continued my assault with my tongue until she came hard, screaming out my name and clutching tightly to my shoulders, my hair, anywhere she could get purchase to hold me firmly against her.

Once I felt her orgasm slowing, I pulled back to look at her. With her head tilted upward in pleasure and her body shaking from the way I'd made her come, she was a fucking goddess. More than ever before.

In high school, she'd still been a little clumsy and awkward, still growing into her body. Now, she'd flourished into a woman, and knew exactly what to do with her curves.

After a moment, she'd gathered her breath and sat up. Her arms wrapped lazily around my neck and she pressed her face into my shoulder, licking and sucking at the crook of my neck. I downed the rest of my glass of whiskey. There was no point in letting it go to waste after all.

When I set the glass down, I picked Alyssa up to head to the stairs. She was coming to bed with me and I wouldn't accept any arguments. I'd barely taken two steps before the pain in my chest was too much. Placing her on the ground, I took a handful of deep breaths to shake the agony. I needed something stronger than the alcohol to dull the sensation.

"Are you okay?" she asked, tracing her fingers over my back.

Bent over and trying to breathe, I shook my head. "Just need a minute."

"Dec, are you sure . . ." She trailed off, but the way her eyes glanced over my body before settling on my hard-on suggested that she was asking whether I wanted to continue.

Straightening, I nodded. "I'm fucking positive about this." I needed her more than I needed the oxygen in my lungs. When I met her eyes, the emotions hidden within nearly fucking slayed me. There was so much hurt, so much . . . doubt. "Are you?"

She nodded, but ended it with a shake of her head. "I just . . . I need a minute."

I frowned as I felt her pulling away. She stepped closer to me, placed her hand over my heart and kissed me like she meant it.

"Just one minute. Please?"

With a nod, I granted her the time she needed. I wanted her to come to me willing and ready. When she did, I wasn't sure I'd be able to let her go again. Not easily.

"Thanks." She kissed my mouth, dragging her tongue across my bottom lip. "You go ahead. I'll be up shortly."

I walked up the rest of the stairs, my head full of promises of better fucking tomorrows.

Alyssa was back in my life. My head finally acknowledged what my heart and body always knew: she was the one thing I wanted. The one thing that I needed to make my dreams complete. All the denials were just ways to convince myself that I didn't need her. How could it get any better than what we had?

CHAPTER TWELVE

NO STRINGS

FOR FIVE MINUTES, I waited on the king-sized bed upstairs, wondering what kept Alyssa. I'd expected her to be in the room almost instantly—or maybe *hoped* was the better word—but she wasn't. With each second that passed without her coming to finish what we'd started downstairs, I grew more and more impatient. Just as I was climbing from the bed to check on Alyssa, she came into the bedroom wearing only a smile. In each hand, she held a fresh glass of whiskey.

"You are so fucking beautiful, Lys," I said, holding my arms out for her.

She put the glasses on the bedside table and climbed onto my lap. With the look of the devil in her eyes, she opened her mouth and showed me the cube of ice that was already sitting between her teeth. Before I could even begin to fantasise what she planned with it, she pushed me onto the bed and helped free me of my boxers. Even though it was tempting to just lie back with my eyes closed and take whatever pleasure she dished out—like I would have if it had been anyone else in my bed—it wasn't enough for me. I wanted to watch her, to study her every movement, so I propped myself up so I was resting on my elbows. Even though the position renewed the ache in my chest, it was worth it for the view.

My breathing sped as she fell to her knees at the side of the bed. With her gaze locked on mine, she wrapped her mouth around my erection, rubbing the ice from the base to the tip with her tongue, repaying my actions in the kitchen with her own version of the sweet torture. The contrast between the ice and the warm cavern of her mouth was fucking unbelievable. It was a hundred times better than my little fantasy earlier. A thousand.

In long movements, clearly designed for pleasure but not release, she traced her mouth, tongue, and that blasted, blessed ice cube over my cock. She fucking knew what she was doing and I grew harder than I'd ever thought possible. I longed for her to move faster, suck harder, but I also wanted her to keep going at the same steady pace so that I could enjoy the sensation for as long as possible.

When I tangled my fingers in her hair, desperate to speed her motion, she pulled away completely. An audible protest escaped me. I didn't want her to stop—I never wanted her to stop. Before I could argue too much though, she climbed up my body, dragging her lips, tongue, and the ice cube over the skin of my hips, stomach, and chest. Bucking my hips, desperate for contact, I grabbed at any part of her I could reach. Hair. Waist. Back. Side. Breast. My hands were in constant motion over her warm body.

With soft movements, she touched the bruise on my side, kissing each of my injured ribs with tender affection. Gentle fingers rubbed another ice cube over the area. I fell back against the bed as a moan fell from my lips.

She straddled my hips and her lips pressed to mine. She pushed the ice cube in her mouth against my tongue and I brushed it back against hers. The heat and the cold fused with her taste and I was in heaven. When I grew overwhelmed by the sight of her lust-filled eyes staring straight into me—no doubt providing a new image to be burned into my mind as I raced around the track—my eyelids sank closed. Her hand found my cock, trailing from base to tip before she rubbed the head against her slick skin.

"Jesus Christ," I groaned at the sensation.

With her hand and a twist of her hips, she guided me into her warm, wet centre.

"Holy fuck, Alyssa!" I cried out, as my eyes flew open, startled but oh-so-aroused.

I could barely breathe as the feeling of being bareback inside her took over my every function. It was just as enjoyable as it had been the last time. Her flesh was soft and tender and warm. Utterly unlike the clinical feel of a condom and utterly fucking enjoyable. I didn't want a kid though, or an STD, so I tried to pull out and away. It wasn't that I thought she'd be unprotected or have an infection, but I couldn't know for sure—we hadn't exactly had the "are you safe and clean" talk. "Shouldn't you wait until I get some protection on?"

With a breathless moan, she lifted her hips before shifting down tight against me again. My fingers found her hips and I bit the inside of my cheek to stop from crying out from the pure, unadulterated pleasure

"You usually wear one don't you?" It was a question but held an edge which indicated she already knew the answer.

Clutching her hips, I nodded. "Always."

"Then it doesn't matter. I'm clean and I've got a Mirena."

"A what?"

"Do you want all the gory details or do you want to keep going?" she asked, a look halfway between indignation and amusement on her face. Without waiting for an answer, she rocked her hips over me again.

"I just . . ."

She raised herself off me before sliding back down again.

". . . oh fuck . . ."

With a moan escaping her, she bucked her hips.

". . . don't . . ."

Twisting her body slightly, she shifted the angle and allowed me deeper inside of her.

". . . oh shit . . ."

She placed her hands on my chest, before leaning forward to kiss my skin. My hands found her hair and she looked down at me with a devilish grin.

What the fuck was I saying?

It took me a moment to recover my equilibrium while she fucked me and nipped at my skin with that sexy-arse smirk on her lips.

". . . want kids," I finished my thought finally.

She stopped moving, and her smile fell. I wondered why she paused, but could only think it was the reminder of our one other night together—the night after the formal. Knowing I needed to bring her back to the moment, I pulled myself up into a seated position and wrapped my arms around her waist. Her face was impassive, and I was certain she was seconds from walking away from me—which would just leave me with my hand and a headful of her to keep me company. Desperate to avoid that situation, I kissed her neck and shoulders, trying to draw her attention back to me. I clutched at her hips and used the hold to move them over mine.

Alyssa wrapped her arms around my neck and leaned her weight away from me, giving me full control. Her back was arched and her neck extended as she leaned back, tipping her head, allowing her erect nipples to point to the ceiling.

Despite the fact that I was buried so deep inside her, I wanted more. Holding her tightly, I rolled us both over so that her back was on the bed. One at a time, I lifted her legs and rested them on my shoulders, tilting her hips off the bed. I leaned over her, pinning her beneath me. In long slow strokes, I took her over and over, rubbing my pelvic bone deliberately along hers. She moaned in ecstasy underneath me. Grabbing her hips, I set a perfect, relentless pace, burying every inch of myself inside of her. I pulled almost all of the way out before thrusting hard into her again. Caressing her body, I kissed her greedily, wanting to get my fill but knowing it would never, ever be enough.

I pushed harder and faster, adding my fingers into the mix to press against her clit until she was writhing in ecstasy beneath me.

When she came, her walls tightened around my length and drove me to release too.

"Holy fucking hell!" I cried out as my body convulsed against hers. My arms gave way a little and I fell onto her. She wrapped her arms and legs tightly around me and held me in place.

It was perfection.

The sensation of releasing inside her with no barriers was just fucking bizarre. More sticky and wet than I would have imagined, but somehow that made it all the more sexy. When I regained some control over my body, I pushed myself up just enough to look at her. "So, what's a Mirena?"

She laughed loudly, her body shaking against me, tightening the hold she had on my cock and causing my body to quiver. I captured her mouth with mine and moved my tongue passionately against hers.

I love you, my mind screamed. And I knew without doubt the sentiment was the truth. As much as I'd denied it over the years, I was one hundred percent in love with Alyssa Dawson. I just couldn't force my mouth to make the words. Not in that moment at least. It seemed contrite, as if I were saying it out of some weird obligation because I'd just fucked her. As if love had anything to do with fucking.

Pulling out slowly, I stood and offered her my hand. When she was standing, I wrapped my arm around her and pulled her into a tight embrace. I let her presence wash over me and relished in its calming effect.

"Thank heavens for fucking without complications," she said after a beat. Her voice shook slightly and her breathing was still irregular. It almost sounded like she was on the verge of tears. "I *really* needed that."

She kissed my cheek and pulled out of the embrace before making a hasty retreat from the room. Confused, I watched as she pulled the door closed behind her. At first, I figured she must have been going to clean herself up, but then I heard her bedroom door close.

What the actual fuck?

My stomach sank down to my feet as I replayed what I could remember of our conversation in the kitchen before we'd started. She'd asked me if I *could* fuck without complications. She'd asked me if I would do it again. She *toasted* to fucking without complications.

Oh God.

No strings.

Oh fuck.

Just fucking.

Oh hell.

I ran to the toilet and vomited up all the alcohol I'd had.

Oh Christ.

My stomach twisted. I hurled again. Palpitations stole my heartbeat. The symptoms of a new panic attack washed over me, rendering me almost helpless. I grabbed the edge of the sink and dragged myself to my feet. I flushed the toilet and rinsed out my mouth. I couldn't break down there. Not just then. Alyssa could come out and find me, and I couldn't let her see how much she fucking affected me. Not when there were no strings attached for her. Fucking without consequences.

How could I be so fucking stupid?

While I tried to focus and think of anything but the wave of panic and fear rising within me, I stood with my grip firm again the sides of the sink, desperate for oxygen. I pushed myself forward, back toward the safety of the bedroom. Sanctuary. Where I could let go and let the panic take me away. Maybe this time it wouldn't let me come back. Maybe this time I would be lost forever. I felt sure of it, and the certainty grew with every laden step back to the bedroom.

Holy fucking heaven in hell.

I couldn't move. I couldn't breathe. Pressure constricted my chest. I couldn't walk. My knees buckled weakly beneath me.

Fucking hell.

I crawled the last of the distance, inch by agonising inch past her bedroom door. It was closed.

Just like her fucking heart.

Sounds echoed out from beneath the door. It might have been sobbing, but it could have just as easily been laughter. Either way, I couldn't face her.

Finally, I was in my bedroom, but it smelled of sex, and of Alyssa. I saw the two untouched glasses of whiskey in the corner. I crawled over to them, picking them up and downing them one after the other. I shrugged into a pair of pyjama pants and staggered back out of the room, my head spinning in vicious circles the whole time. When I reached the stairs, I stumbled down trying to ensure I didn't make too much noise and disturb *her*—the fucking harpy who'd decided to completely fucking ruin my life. She'd tricked me and brought me back to life with her magical touch, just to leave me dead inside once more.

I wanted to be angry with her. To hate her. But I couldn't. Even though she'd ripped my heart out and stomped it into the carpet, I couldn't hate her. She didn't know how madly in love with her I was. Fuck, I didn't even know until a few minutes earlier. I pushed myself into the kitchen, yanked the bottle of whiskey off the bench, and slumped to the floor.

To wipe away the pain, I drank deeply straight from the bottle. I barely acknowledged the tears running down my cheeks. Whenever I felt the need to try to breathe, I drank instead. I didn't even realise that I'd emptied the bottle; instead I continued to try to drain it further. Hugging the empty bottle tightly to my chest, I began to sob. Once the sobs started, and the lack of oxygen really kicked in, the full throes of my panic hit me. My heart raced and I was utterly breathless. My palms were sweaty and I was both too hot and too cold all at the same time.

I was going to die.

It was a simple, inescapable fact.

My heart was going to stop beating at any second because it was beating much too fast, I was certain of it. I tried to breathe in, but all I managed were weak, wheezing gasps. I tried to stand, even though I didn't know where I was planning on going. All I knew was that I had to get the fuck away from there. Away from *her*. I pulled myself up along the counter, desperate for something undefinable.

I took a tentative step away from the counter, relying on my own legs to carry my weight. It was a monumental error. My head whirled from the alcohol I'd downed—easily over half a litre. My chest ached from my struggles to breathe.

The floor slipped away underneath my feet and I heard a loud smash an instant before my face impacted on the hard surface.

CHAPTER THIRTEEN

A BIG EFFING COMPLICATION

WHEN I CAME to I had no idea where I was or even when I was. I assumed my head was pressed to the floor, but it didn't make sense because it was too soft.

Much too soft . . .

My head pounded.

Not just pounded. There was a fucking jackhammer attached to the inside of my skull. It wasn't the normal hangover pounding though, which gave the feeling of too much blood pulsating against my temples in a regular, thudding rhythm. Instead, my whole brain felt swollen and at least two sizes too big. My face ached and burned; the whole right side tingled with non-existent flames. My tongue was swollen and my teeth felt loose inside my jaw.

I tilted my head to one side and instantly regretted it. The pounding wasn't just confined to my head; it ran down the length of my body too. Every inch of my right side throbbed with a blinding agony similar to the one I'd experienced after Alyssa's brother beat the shit out of me.

What happened?

Bits of memory filtered back in, as well as a feeling that this was all too familiar.

Ice.

Whiskey.

No consequences or complications.

Oh fuck!

Alyssa . . .

She was what happened.

I raised my hand to run it through my hair, but felt a tugging sensation when I tried to move it, which stopped me. My other hand was wrapped in something warm, someone's hand maybe. I would have to open my eyes to figure it out—together with finding out where the fuck I was, because I sure as fuck wasn't still in the kitchen at Danny's flat—but doing so would allow reality in. And pain. With the throbbing in my head, even the smallest amount of light would only increase the agony. All of that would come when I opened my eyes, as well as awareness and the need to face Alyssa before she left. A groan left my throat, scorching the dry surface, before sticking to my parched tongue.

"Oh, Declan, thank God." Alyssa's strained voice was beside me, yet all around me. It came from the side of the bed with the warm, possibly enclosed, hand. The volume of her voice sent a new ache through me and my head pounded harder than before. The words, and the way she made it sound like she actually gave a shit about me, made my heart throb with an agony ten thousand times worse than the one which held my body captive.

When I risked opening my eyelids for half a second, light flooded into my eyes. The fucking pain ramped up and my assessment of the situation started all over again. I slammed my eyes shut again and issued another groan. Despite my sticky mouth, I tried to slick my lips with my tongue—which was pointless because both were as dry as the other.

"What the fuck did you think you were doing?" Her voice rose higher than before.

I almost felt like smiling at the frustration in her tone. That I recognised. That I could almost understand. At least, it made far more sense than the caring tone from moments before. Only I didn't know what the fuck she could have been angry about.

Opening my eyes completely, I tried my hardest to ignore the light, and the pain, and focus on Alyssa's face.

"Why did you go downstairs and drink the rest of that bottle? There was almost a whole fucking litre left."

The room behind her was wrong. It was so out of place that I couldn't focus on her words. Instead of neutral tones and a warm palette, it was white and expansive. Sterile. I raised my head again, ignoring the throb, and looked left and right.

"Where am I?" I asked, although I recognised the place on some level. My voice croaked and my throat was desiccated. I coughed to clear it, but the action pinched my ribs and sent a new agony rushing through me. I fell back onto the pillow with a fresh groan building in my chest.

"You're in the fucking hospital. Where else would you be?"

With some effort, I focused back on Alyssa's face. She looked like shit. Black bags rested under her eyes and her hair was a mess. Despite that, the sight of her was still enough to twist the knife in my heart and leave it red raw and bleeding. I pushed the agony to the side because there was something I was missing . . . something I needed to find out. "Why?"

"Because you're a fucking idiot."

I tried to sit up. "No. I mean what for? What the fuck happened?"

"I went to bed last night after . . ." She looked away and a blush crept up her cheeks.

Yeah, after you tied my heart up with your fucking strings. I kept my mouth shut even though the thought raced through me.

"Half an hour later, I heard a godawful crash. I ran downstairs to see what it was and found you, unconscious, over a smashed bottle. I was so scared. I . . . I didn't know what to do." Her voice sounded close to tears.

It was the breaking point for me. Biting the inside of my cheek, I closed my eyes so that she wouldn't see the tears threatening me. I wouldn't give her the satisfaction of knowing what she had reduced me to.

"I didn't even realise until after the ambulance came that you'd fucking cut your arm and almost bled out. They had to pump your stomach because of how much you'd drunk. Why would you do that?"

"I want to go home," I murmured without looking at her. I didn't want to be in the hospital anymore. Not with Alyssa at my side pretending that she gave a single fucking shit what happened to me when I knew the truth. Fucking with no complications was the truth. London no longer held any appeal—I just wanted to be home. In Sydney. Alone and coping with everything the best way I knew.

"I'll see what I can get the doctors to do," she said, clearly misunderstanding the meaning of my statement. Whether her lack of understanding was deliberate or not, I couldn't say.

An hour later, after getting some painkillers, a little disgusting food, and a lecture on the dangers of alcohol abuse, I was released into Alyssa's care. As I dragged myself down the hall—the painkillers had only dulled the ache in my body, not destroyed it completely—all I could wonder was what sort of fucking hell was I being forced into by the hospital quacks. I wanted to be away from her, not having her play nurse—despite the fact that my cock sprang to life at the thought of her in a sexy nurse's outfit.

Alyssa hailed a taxi and gave the driver Danny's apartment address. After helping me from the car, she unlocked the front door and led me through. The way she acted, it was almost as if she fucking thought she owned the place. I wondered how long would be polite before I could tell her to fuck off. Knowing her as I once did, she'd probably force me to follow the doctor's advice to the letter, which would see her hanging around for another couple of days.

Just kill me now.

I climbed up the small flight of stairs to the open living area and walked straight to the couch. Folding myself into the seat as carefully as I could with my swollen side, I tried to relax. I stared off into the distance, unsure what I was seeing, or even what I wanted to see. After a moment, Alyssa sat beside me. I wasn't sure if I wanted her to. No, I knew that I wanted her to; I just didn't *want* to want her to.

She didn't want me in her life again. She'd made that perfectly fucking clear the night before. Fucking with no strings. Another nameless, faceless woman to add to my bedpost. Except Alyssa was never that. I'd never *wanted* that of Alyssa. She was my one perfect woman, even if I didn't always admit it, and she'd forced me to use her like any other woman in the world.

Fucking hell, Reede. You've cocked it up again haven't you?

With soft, feather-light caresses, she ran her fingers through my hair. I was sure it was supposed to be a comforting gesture, but I wasn't sure if I was helped by it. Instead of telling her to stop though, I just closed my eyes and leaned into her touch. For a moment, things were quiet, with only the sound of our breaths puncturing the silence.

"Do you know what the worst thing about our break-up was?" she asked in a breathless whisper as her head rested near mine on the back of the couch. Her words carried across my skin in a way that told me she was close. If I opened my eyes again, she would have been within kissing distance.

My heart constricted at the thought. I squeezed my eyes closed tighter to avoid the temptation of checking if I was right.

"That I lost my best friend too." Her tears were clear in her voice "For almost eleven years we hadn't gone more than what, a month, without talking to each other. Then all of a sudden you were gone. Right when I needed you the most."

Even though I didn't want to admit it, I knew *exactly* what she meant. I could still picture the first time I ever saw her. Every moment of our friendship crashed over me and I had to open my eyes to escape the barrage of images.

Even though I'd expected Alyssa to be close to me, I hadn't expected her to be as near as she was. Another centimetre or two and her forehead would have rested against my cheek. Her eyes were closed now, tears staining her eyelids black with moisture and running down her cheeks. It seemed she was as deep in thought as

I'd been, no doubt lost in the past too. I took the chance to examine all the little changes time had wrought on her face. She didn't have wrinkles or anything like that, but the bags under her eyes seemed to have a degree of permanency and her skin was paler than it had been years ago.

She opened her eyes again and captured my gaze. The sorrow and loss buried within almost killed me on the spot. I didn't know what could have caused it, but I couldn't cope with it. My lips pulled down into a frown.

Her eyes darted away, as if embarrassed to have caught my gaze.

"You hungry?" she asked, pushing herself back up off the couch.

I closed my eyes and shrugged. My throat stung like a bitch and my stomach churned. The food they'd tried to force on me at the hospital just didn't cut it, but I didn't want to rely on her to be fed either. I could manage on my own if she would just go away. Even though I wanted her gone, the thought forced my heart into my stomach.

"How about some takeout," she asked.

"Whatever."

I heard her opening a book, no doubt some phone book she'd found on the roll-top desk. Obviously finding something she deemed suitable, she picked up the phone to place an order, walking from the room as she did. She didn't ask me what I wanted, but I didn't care. She knew what I liked. Despite the years that had passed, nothing had changed there. After a few minutes, the springs on the couch shifted as she settled back beside me.

"Did you want me to stay tonight?" she asked. "To look after you?"

Did I? *Yes.*

Should I? *No.*

Opening my eyes to look at her, I shook my head. "You should probably check into your hotel if it's booked anyway."

"Okay, if you think so," she whispered. Then she bit her lip, deep in thought again. She took a deep breath. "Declan . . ."

She stopped. That's what drew my attention. If she'd kept talking, I probably wouldn't have noticed. I might have barely heard what she said after that. When she stopped though, she guaranteed she had my undivided attention. I turned toward her. "What?"

"You know . . ." She trailed off with a sigh. "Why is this so hard?" she added, but I didn't think the words were meant for me.

I narrowed my eyes at her. "What is it?"

"There's so much I need to tell you, and no way to start."

"You open your mouth and let the fucking words out."

A half smile lifted her cheek. "Thank you. For last night. It's been a while for me."

"What's a while?" I asked. She had captured me with her eyes and I felt compelled to continue the conversation.

She looked off into the distance. "About two years. I was with Cain, Flynn's brother, for a while, but I just couldn't . . ." She took a deep breath. "I couldn't commit to him the way he wanted."

"Why?"

She shrugged. "Complications."

"How did you know about the condom thing?" It was a weird, random thought that flew from my mouth long before I'd managed to stifle it. It had just sprung from my lips the moment it entered my head. When she'd said I always wore them, it wasn't a question, she'd known. Somehow.

"Darcy Kinsley," she said as if that name was supposed to explain everything.

"What?"

"You slept with her almost a year ago. She took great pride in telling me all about it, including the little detail that you'd told her about condoms."

"Why?" I tried to remember Darcy. I remembered her from school, trouble-making bitch that she was, but I had nothing more recent than that. It must have been evident on my face because Alyssa laughed at something she saw there.

"Yeah, I figured it was like that. Apparently, it was at a masked ball on New Year's Eve. She recognised you immediately because of your eyes. Such an odd colour blue; not many people have truly turquoise eyes like yours." Alyssa seemed to smile at something unseen, before shaking herself back to attention. "Anyway, apparently you fucked her in the cloakroom. But not until you'd hunted through half the bags looking for a condom to do it, even though she swore she was on the pill."

I swallowed heavily as her words jogged the memory of that night in my head. Truthfully, I had no fucking idea I knew the chick. She was just another blonde. Just another screw. Nothing special or memorable, except for the fact that we never removed our masks.

One thing didn't make sense about Alyssa's admission. "Why would she tell you all that though? It's not like you're friends. Or are you now?" Maybe that was one of the things I'd missed by being away.

Alyssa shook her head, the deep sorrow at the corners of her mouth back in force.

"No, we're not friends. She told me because . . ." She stopped and stared at her hands for a second before bursting into tears "Because I . . . God, Dec, I—I tried to tell you . . . I really did . . . but . . ." She disintegrated into tears and giant, gulping sobs.

My arms were around her, comforting her, before I could even think of all the reasons why I shouldn't.

"Hey, now, what's wrong?" I asked, swiping the fresh tears from her eyes with the pads of my thumbs.

She shook her head and sobbed into my shoulder. "I wanted . . . I tried . . ." She was drawing deep gasps of air. If I didn't know better, I would have thought she was having a panic attack. "You . . . you need—"

There was a knock on the door. I frowned at the interruption before I remembered the food that she'd ordered.

I unwrapped myself from Alyssa and grabbed my wallet. Because I'd left early and the cash exchange wasn't open in Sydney airport, I hadn't had a chance to get any money converted. When we'd landed, I'd been so focused on not letting Alyssa out of my sight the thought to get cash changed hadn't even crossed my mind.

"Do you take Visa?" I asked the delivery boy after I opened the door for him.

He shook his head. "Cash only, sorry."

"There're some pounds in my purse," Alyssa whispered. She was curled up into a ball on the couch. "It's on the counter."

I reached out to grab it, when Alyssa shouted. "No! Shit! Declan, stop!"

Practically flying from the couch, she leapt for me. She was inches from me, hand held out to grab her purse, but it was too late. I'd already found what she was clearly trying to stop me from seeing.

In her purse, in a clear pocket opposite her driver's licence was a photo of a young girl. She easily could have been Alyssa. She had Alyssa's face; the same nose and mouth. She even had the scraggly brown pigtails Alyssa used to wear on either side of her head.

It *could* have been Alyssa.

Except for the eyes.

Alyssa's statement from earlier flooded back into my mind. *"Not many people have truly turquoise eyes."*

Like mine.

I turned to stare at Alyssa. Her face was twisted into a mask of horror. She didn't want me to see the photo. My jaw clenched. She didn't want me to know. How the fuck could she keep it from me? For four fucking years, she'd kept this a fucking secret. Questions ran through my mind in an endless circle.

"Get out," I hissed venomously.

I'd been right in the first place; Alyssa "small town" Dawson was fucking poison.

She looked up at me, her eyes wide and her body shaking. Tears ran freely down her cheeks and dripped to the floor even as her eyes welled over with fresh ones. She opened her mouth to speak, no doubt to spill more lies and bullshit, but I cut her off.

"Get the fuck out of my life!" I pushed past her and stalked up the stairs to the bedroom. The instant I was through, I slammed the door shut behind me and collapsed against it. I couldn't deal with the revelation that had just been thrust upon me. It was likely that

I'd never be able to fucking deal with it. How could I even begin to process something so huge? So monumentally enormous that my life had shifted completely off-axis in one instant.

I listened as Alyssa paid for whatever she'd ordered. There was no doubt in my mind that she would be apologising to the driver about the display—her cheeks probably burning with shame.

Good. She should have fucking told me!

She fucking owed somebody a great big apology, and I wasn't in the mood to hear it. Her footfalls were slow and heavy as she made her way up the stairs and I could hear the sound of her tears, and her steady stream of sobs, but I ignored them. I could almost sense her through the door as her footsteps paused in front of the room. Not long after, they trailed into her room.

A few minutes later, I heard her on the stairs again, along with a thudding that suggested she was dragging her suitcase behind her. My anger must have made my hearing more acute, because I could have sworn I heard the sound of a key being dropped onto stainless steel counters and then the front door being pulled closed. Or maybe I just imagined, and hoped, that I could.

I couldn't believe I hadn't realised earlier. But then Alyssa had been very careful about keeping it hidden since the first time I'd spotted her. As I thought about the secrets and lies, the realisation that, against my better judgement, I'd fucked her with no protection smashed into me like a freight train. My stomach heaved emptily and I wondered if that's what the previous night was for her. The chance for another child. A perfect matching fucking pair to the same unknowing, unwitting, arsehole father. Maybe her boy, Flynn, wasn't gay, just firing blanks and I was nothing more than a ready-made sperm bank she knew was up for anything.

The worst thing was that everything was crystal fucking clear. All the pieces of the jigsaw I hadn't even known existed had clicked into place: the photo, the silences, the pauses, the strange half-completed words, the blow up about town scandals, Josh's words at the airport, even the fucking scar. They all added up to one startling, fucking scary conclusion. That conclusion was Phoebe.

My fucking daughter.

CHAPTER FOURTEEN

REGRET

I HAD NO idea how long I'd sat with my back against the door and my hands tugging through my hair, but eventually I realised that time had passed even though I hadn't felt its passage. It was growing light again when reality eventually crept back in, shifting the bitter blackness that had taken up residence in my brain. When that left, regret steadily filled the gap.

I stood and threw the door open, darting down the staircase. With the new emotion building in my chest, I hoped that what I'd thought I'd heard was wrong; that Alyssa hadn't left after all. Maybe she was just sitting downstairs at the dining table or on the couch. I pictured her like that, suitcase in front of her, tears in her eyes—but *there*. Ready to shout at me for being an arse, or plead with me to understand—but *there*. My hopes were dashed when I hit the bottom of the stairs. The whole space was too dark and too quiet to be occupied.

Even before I'd cleared the last step, I saw the key sitting on the kitchen island. A piece of paper sat next to it. Hoping it was a hotel name or phone number, or something—anything—that would help me get in contact with Alyssa, I grabbed at it. As I pulled the paper off the bench, a photo fluttered to the floor. Not just *a* photo, *the* photo. Of Phoebe.

Once more, I was caught by the oddity of my own blue-green eyes staring out from a miniature Alyssa. Grabbing my wallet, I tucked the photo safely away inside. I turned my attention to the piece of paper. At first I thought it was blank, but then I noticed two words, *I'm sorry*, in small, fine print along the bottom edge. The ink was splotched and leached into the paper around it, making it difficult to read. She'd obviously been crying when she wrote it.

I read the words again. *She* was sorry?

I'd fucking ignored her for years and *she* was sorry.

I was the one who kicked her out onto the street in a fucking foreign country and *she* was sorry.

My mouth went dry as I processed the thought and guilt that accompanied the knowledge that she was alone in London because of me. The image came to me crystal clear: Alyssa walking alone on the streets, dragging her suitcase behind her, tears streaming down her face. Any one of a hundred horrific situations could have happened to her. I leaned over the kitchen island, and tried desperately not to think about those. Instead, I tried to focus on where she would go. She'd said she had a hotel room, but she'd never mentioned where or which hotel.

She'd said something about being in England to check out some law firm that'd offered her a job, but I couldn't remember its name either. I'd been my typical, self-obsessed dick self—too fucking interested in my own issues to even fucking pay an ounce of attention to anyone else. Other than to fuck her like the cock I was, of course.

No fucking strings? Bullshit!

A child would constitute a pretty major fucking string. I wanted to leave the house and run; to scour every inch of London until I found her and spoke to her. It was pointless though. She could be anywhere, and I didn't know London at all.

I was lost and I had no way of contacting her.

She was lost to me.

Think, you idiot! Fucking think! How can I get hold of her?

In an instant, the answer was there.

Her mum! She'd know where she is and Alyssa called her last night.

For half a second, I hoped the number would be on redial.

Shit!

Alyssa had used the phone twice since then. For the ambulance and the food.

I turned on the computer assuming that if the apartment had a phone, it had to have the Internet too.

Fucking wrong! Damn it.

Even though it was a long shot, I decided to try Alyssa's childhood phone number. Those digits were so deeply ingrained into my brain after years of dialling them that I would probably remember them for the rest of my life. I just had no idea if Alyssa's parents had moved or not in the four years since I'd left town. Again, I was reminded just how fucking little I knew about any of the people to whom I'd once been so close. I'd fucking alienated myself from everyone and everything. In fact, I couldn't remember speaking to Ben at all after the fucking formal, and he'd been my best friend, besides Alyssa.

I picked up the phone and dialled but all I got was a recorded message in a high-pitched voice that the phone number had been disconnected. I hung up the phone and growled in frustration.

I *needed* to find her. My anxiety shot through the roof and I was positive I was about to have another fucking panic attack any second. I wasn't sure I would be able to survive another one in my current state.

If *anything* happened to Alyssa, I would forever hold myself personally responsible.

There was only one other number I could possibly ring. It was by far the longest of long shots, but it was the only other number I had. My childhood home. Mum answered the phone on the third ring. She heard the tone to indicate it was an international call and sounded confused when she said, "Hello?"

"Hey, Mum."

"Declan?"

I rolled my eyes. "Seriously, who else would be calling you *mum*?" I was going to ask whether she had a love child I didn't know about, but the words froze on my tongue when they hit too close to home.

"Sorry, it's just a little odd. I mean, getting a call from you."

"Actually, I was calling to ask a question . . ." I hesitated. How could I ask for Ruth's phone number without sounding like a complete fucking lunatic?

"What is it, Declan?" She sounded worried.

I sighed. "Do you have Ruth Dawson's phone number?"

Something dropped and clattered in the background, a pan or pot or something. It clanged loudly when it hit the ground.

"Why?" Her voice was low and harsh.

"I need to speak to her."

"About?"

"About Alyssa."

There was a sharp intake of breath. "Declan, what's going on?"

What is this? *The fucking Spanish inquisition*? I decided to answer with as much of the truth as I thought I could handle speaking aloud. Which wasn't much. I still didn't know if my mouth would work if I tried to form the word "daughter."

Fucking daughter!

Not even a baby, but a ready-grown fucking little lady daughter. I tried to do the math to figure out how old she must be, but my brain just wouldn't fucking work. I wondered if someone had permanently disconnected the fucking thing.

"I ran into Alyssa and got some *news*. I was . . . well, I was a fucking dick to her. Now, I need to find her, but I have no fucking idea where to start. I'm hoping Ruth might be able to give me a fucking clue."

"Declan," Mum admonished. I thought I was going to get a lecture about swearing—God knows it wouldn't be the first—so I was surprised by her next words. "As if that poor girl hasn't had it hard enough. You had to go and make things worse, didn't you?"

"What the fuck do you know about what Alyssa's been going through?" I asked harshly. How the hell was I going to explain to my parents that I had a fucking child running around in the world?

"A whole lot more than you do, I'd be willing to bet. God help me, Declan, if you've hurt her—"

When the words hit my ears, my brain decided to kick in with a painful thud as it recognised the truth in her statement. "You knew?"

She sighed, then whispered, "Yes."

"You fucking *knew* and you never fucking told me?" My fingers formed a fist around the handset.

"It's a bit more complicated than you make it sound."

"Well, then un-fucking-complicate it, Mum, and tell me why you didn't fucking feel the need to tell me I have a fucking kid." The neighbours on both sides of Danny's apartment could probably hear every word I said, but I didn't give a crap.

"I promised Alyssa I wouldn't."

"When?" I was trying very, very hard to keep myself together. It really wasn't working. I drew in measured breaths through gaps in my teeth as my heart thudded against my chest.

"What?"

"*When* did you promise Alyssa you wouldn't tell me?"

"When Alyssa first told me she was pregnant. She came to me and told me everything and then begged me not to tell you. She wanted to do it personally. She was so excited about telling you, but she was never stupid enough to think it would change anything. She was still so scared and happy, but then you wouldn't take her calls and day by day I saw her heart break. And then . . ." She paused, and took a deep breath to calm herself. "Well, I don't know if you'll ever really comprehend just how much you hurt her."

"Why didn't you fucking tell me though? Didn't you think I had a fucking right to know?" I asked again, trying to be demanding, but my voice just didn't have any volume anymore.

"After I realised you weren't going to talk to Alyssa, I told myself I would tell you the next time you asked about her. But you never did. You never even rang home. Alyssa brought Phoebe around to see me at least once a week, and I didn't even get a single phone call from you." It sounded like she was in tears.

"I called," I argued, but it sounded weak even in my own ears, because honestly, I *couldn't* remember calling her. *Had I?* Surely in four years I'd called at least once? I remembered emails and texts, but I couldn't recall ever picking up the phone and calling my parents.

"No," Mum argued. "In the four years you've been gone, the only time I've spoken to you was if I called you, and then I was usually off the phone again within five minutes."

"So you've met her?" I felt hollow.

"Yes. Like I said, Alyssa brings her around regularly. She wanted to make sure I had a chance to get to know my granddaughter."

I didn't want to talk about it anymore. My heart was somehow both in my throat and my feet at the same time. My head and face were starting to pound once more, which was probably a good fucking reminder to take some pain medication for the fucking bruises that now lined my body, not to mention the lovely cut now gracing my arm. All because of Alyssa and her fucking with no complications.

"Whatever," I said dismissively, anxious to get off the phone. "Do you have the fucking number or not?"

She rattled it off from memory and I hastily wrote it down.

"Don't hurt her again, Declan." It almost sounded like she was begging.

The fear in her voice chilled my blood. What sort of monster was I that my own mother was afraid of me on behalf of the woman I'd once loved?

"I think it's too late for that," I admitted in a whisper as I hung up the phone.

I picked up the receiver again. I knew this next call was going to be even worse than the last.

"Hello?" The voice belonged to Alyssa's arsehole brother.

My mind spun with questions. Why was Josh even there? Wasn't he married now? Shouldn't he be out fucking living in his own fucking house by now? I knew I couldn't speak to him about Alyssa. He would probably find some way of reaching down the phone to kill me. Not that I didn't fucking deserve it.

"Would Ruth Dawson be available please?" I asked, hoping

152

with everything I had that he wouldn't recognise my voice. The issue of course was that I was too well known by him, both personally and professionally. Despite the intervening years, there was no way he wouldn't recognise me.

"No, sorry she's out for the day." The new edge to his voice confirmed my fear.

"Can you help me then?" I asked with desperation. Another minute more and I was sure he'd hang up the phone. I just needed to try to appeal to his compassionate side before then.

"No, fucker, I don't think *anyone* can fucking help you." The phone clicked and then beeped. He'd hung up on me.

Shit! I forgot the arsehole didn't have a compassionate side. At least not when it came to me. Maybe he had once, but not anymore.

I picked up the phone and dialled again.

"Hello?" There was no joviality in Josh's voice this time. No doubt he suspected it was me again.

"I need to find her, Josh."

"No. What you need to do is leave her alone, fuckhead. You've done enough fucking damage already."

The phone clicked again. I dialled for the third time. I didn't wait for him to say hello.

"Look, I feel pretty damn shitty about all of this. I just need to fucking know that she's safe, all right?"

"She's safe," said a female voice that I didn't recognise. It was almost soft and caring. Then the phone went dead again.

I wasn't sure if my frustration or defeat was winning when I dialled the number again.

"Please, I just need to speak to her. Tell me the hotel she's at. Anything?" The defeat—and the tears—climbed to the top for the moment.

"I . . ." It was the female voice again, and I hoped she'd help me, but then she paused. "I can't."

"Why not?"

"Because Alyssa asked me not to."

What? "You spoke to her?"

"I told you she was safe didn't I? Did you think I was fucking lying?"

Whoa, the bitch is back. With the comment, and the attitude her voice contained, recognition rammed into me. It was Ruby, Josh's wife.

"Look, I know I fucked up by throwing her out like I did. I know it was a dick move. I fucking know all of that. But it was a bit of a fucking shock to find out that shit like I did."

Ruby chuckled slightly. "Yeah. Although in her defence, she *did* try to tell you earlier. Quite a lot actually."

"I know," I whispered. "I just wish she'd tried harder."

"How exactly?" Ruby snapped. "Turn up at Sinclair Racing with a fucking gift basket saying 'Congrats, Daddy'?"

"I don't fucking know, all right? But she should have found some fucking way to tell me."

I was greeted by a beat of silence. I was sure the click and tone of a hang-up were about to follow. I calmed myself down as best I could, but my frustration was taking over and bursting from me in uncontrollable ways.

"If you won't tell me where she is, can you at least do me a favour? Can you please tell her how fucking sorry I am and let her know I'm ready to listen whenever she's ready to talk?"

"What if she's not ready to talk?"

"Then I'll wait until she is."

I was about to hang up when I heard a small voice. "I wanna talk to Mummy."

"It's not Mummy, sweetheart," Ruby responded to the little girl.

"I wanna *ta-alk*." The voice became demanding and whiny.

My heart hammered in my chest. That was her. That was Phoebe. That was my daughter.

Oh my fucking God!

"Can I speak to her?" I asked tentatively, not knowing what the fuck to say to a child but knowing that I absolutely fucking had to try to find some words.

"No. I don't think that would be best right now."

"I have a right, you know."

She snickered. "Actually, you don't."

"What the hell is that supposed to mean?"

"You need to talk to Alyssa about that."

I growled. "I'm fucking *trying* to talk to Alyssa, but no one will help me."

"I'll let her know that you called. But if you call again, we'll regard it as harassment. I'm sure Curtis will be more than willing to have his mates press charges, or something." Alyssa's Dad, Curtis—*Killer* Curtis—was a prison warden at Wacol. He knew plenty of cops, and just as many criminals. With that threat looming between us, she hung up.

Fuck!

I was no fucking closer to finding Alyssa than I had been before all the fucking phone calls. I didn't feel better about anything either. I felt even worse.

My own fucking mother knew. My mother had known and kept it from me. Because I was too much of a fucking dick to give two shits about anyone but my own fucking life.

My life is just fucking perfect right now, isn't it?

It was daylight but with a murky grey sky that had no warmth at all, I was fucking hungry, and my brain was dancing a fucking conga against my fucking skull. All of that, and I still didn't have a fucking clue where Alyssa could be. At least I knew she was safe though. It was a small consolation, but better than worrying about her lying dead in a gutter because of me.

I grabbed the rest of the duty-free alcohol from my bag. I had another bottle of whiskey, although I wasn't sure I wanted to fucking touch *that* yet. Not with the reminder it was of the previous night. There was also a bottle of vodka. Preferring my vodka chilled, I opened the fridge to put it in, planning to drink as much of it as I fucking could later that night.

What I saw in the fridge was something I hadn't expected. Alyssa had ordered enough takeout—Indian curries—to get me through about four fucking days, all in individual containers. She'd left it all there, nicely stacked in the fridge waiting for me, despite the fact that I'd thrown her out onto the fucking street. There was a moment where I wondered whether it was actually possible to hate myself any more than I already did.

Fucking fuck!

I risked Ruby's ire, and Curtis's possible punishment, and made one more phone call to Alyssa's mother's house.

"Hello?" It was Ruby again.

"Please." My voice was laced with the tears that had sprung to my eyes and were running uninvited down my cheek. "Please. I need to speak to her."

There was a pause and the phone was being handed to someone else. Fuck. Josh was probably going to fucking threaten to rip my balls off or something. Well, fuck him. There was nothing he could fucking say to me that could make me feel any worse than I already did.

One small word, "Hello," in a small fucking voice told me I was wrong.

Ruby had clearly misinterpreted what I'd meant.

That was my fucking daughter. On the phone.

Fuck. Fuck. Fuck. How do I fucking deal with this?

My breathing hitched. More tears flowed and I squeezed out, "Hello?"

"You're not Mummy. Who are you?"

Fuck.

What a loaded fucking question. How the fucking hell was I supposed to answer it? "I'm just a friend of your Mummy's. My name's Declan."

"I'm Phoebe Castor Dawson." Each word was said with such gusto and enthusiasm, I couldn't help but smile.

"It's nice to talk to you, Phoebe Castor Dawson." I was surprised she could even hear me over the beating of my heart. "How old are you?"

"I'm three and on my next birthday I'll be four, and I'll have a yellow birthday party with a yellow chocolate cake and my friends will be coming to my house."

My lip twitched. I had no idea what to say to her. "That sounds fun," I said eventually.

"It's time to go now, sweetie. Say goodbye." I heard Ruby say in the background.

"Okay, bye-bye, see you later."

I hung up the phone and sank to the floor trying to breathe around the lump in my throat. That was *my fucking daughter*.

I knew in that instant, no matter what else happened, my life had irreversibly changed. I was a father now. A fucking father. Nothing could change that. I would always be a father. Now I just needed to figure out if I was ready to be a dad.

I thought about the photo that was sitting in my wallet and the voice over the phone line. Two pieces of irrefutable evidence that she was real, that she actually existed.

What a fucked-up ride the last few days had been. If the trip to London had done nothing else, it helped to confirm in my own mind just how fucked up I really was—much more than I'd ever admitted to anyone else, or even myself. I grabbed some of the painkillers the hospital had given me, washed them down with a mouthful of vodka, and then threw one of the meals into the microwave. I had no idea how to work the damn thing so the food was blistering hot in some places and ice cold in others, but it was edible. I wondered if it was just the luck of the draw that Alyssa had ordered a beef vindaloo, one of my favourites.

After finishing the food, I grabbed the bottle of vodka and headed up to bed. I figured if I drank myself into oblivion there at least I wouldn't have far to fall. As soon as I hit the bedroom, the events of the previous twenty-four hours crashed down on me—hard—and I couldn't breathe. I skulled as much of the vodka as I could and took another painkiller. Then I closed my eyes and let the panic take me away, stealing my breath and exploding my heart.

Maybe it wouldn't bring me back. At least then I wouldn't have to deal with any of the shit I faced.

The last thoughts I had before unconsciousness took me was that I was fucked-up. Too fucked-up to inflict myself on an innocent child. She didn't deserve to be stuck with a fuck-up like me in her life in any capacity, not even watching from the sidelines.

She deserved better than that. She deserved Alyssa, who could do this a hundred times better on her own than she ever could having to put up with my shit. A thousand. I decided I would call the airline first thing in the morning and book my return flight. There was no fucking point staying in London any longer than I already had. There was nothing there for me. Maybe there was nothing for me anywhere. Not anymore.

Not long after that thought, I blacked out.

CHAPTER FIFTEEN

WAKE-UP CALL

ALYSSA STOOD IN front of me, her face lined with tears. She held her hand protectively over her stomach. Her eyes were downcast, staring at my feet. I followed her line of sight and saw a gaping chasm between us. As soon as I saw it, the distance seemed to grow exponentially until I could barely see her features anymore. Except her eyes — they were clear as day to me.

"Alyssa, I want to talk to you!" I shouted to her. "Is there any way to cross?"

I couldn't look for myself, I was completely immobile.

She shook her head.

"Please, Alyssa? I need to make this right!"

She raised her eyes and they locked on to mine. I expected to see them full of pain, or anger, or something. But they were dead. Flat lifeless pools of golden brown stared back at me. I cried out in strangled agony.

"Please, Alyssa! I need to talk to you!"

She shook her head and then turned away, walking slowly into the distance.

"Come back!"

She stopped but didn't look back at me.

"Please?"

She shook her head slightly.

"I love you!"

She turned back toward me and opened her mouth to speak, but all that came was a shrill ringing.

Waking with a gasp, I opened my eyes. My heart raced in my chest as I tried to calm myself. Just a fucking dream, I realised, only the ringing from within it continued.

I sat up in bed, and regretted it the instant that I did. My head swam and my stomach churned. I didn't know if the pain was because I needed more painkillers for the bruising on my face and cut on my arm, or if it was a result of the—*oh fuck*—bottle of vodka I'd drunk the night before. I really couldn't start with that shit again—it was a slippery slope that I'd climbed to the top of not that long before, and I didn't want to end up back at the bottom. The drinking needed to stop.

The ringing still continued. Rubbing my temples to try to clear some of the cobwebs and cottonwool that seemed to have taken up residence overnight, I wondered what the fuck it could be. Where the fuck was that ringing coming from?

I climbed—*fell*—out of bed and staggered toward the stairs. Whatever the fuck was ringing, the noise definitely came from downstairs. I held tightly on to the railing; my head was spinning too much to risk trying to pick my way down safely without the support. When I saw the desk, I worked out what was making the sound. The fucking phone.

Who the fuck has this number?

I debated ignoring it, but it had been ringing persistently for a while now—more than just a casual caller would try for. I walked over to it and stared at it for a few seconds, daring it to stop ringing before I could pick it up. It didn't, so I cradled the handset to my ear.

"Hello?" My voice sounded like I'd downed a cup of bleach. Although I supposed downing a whole bottle of vodka probably wasn't far off that.

"Declan." I recognised Danny's voice of calm authority immediately. Fuck. I really didn't want to talk to him while I had the hangover from hell and my body ached.

"Danny." I responded. I couldn't think of anything more appropriate to say.

"I trust you had a productive flight."

What the fuck was that supposed to mean? Productive flight—not safe flight, not easy flight, fucking productive flight. Who the fuck talks like that? Oh yeah, fucking multibillionaire team bosses obviously do. Who the fuck am I, the hired fucking wheelman, to argue?

"It was very interesting," I countered.

"How are you going with our little agreement? Are you getting yourself together?"

Fuck no. I'm more fucking shaken apart now than I have ever been in my entire fucking existence, and I don't know which fucking way is up anymore. "Sure, or at least, I'm working on it."

"I just wanted to let you know we've decided to run you in the new car next season, so I'll need you back a month earlier for fitment and testing."

Fuck me. The *new* fucking car. He was really hanging his balls out there on this one. Actually no, fuck it—he was hanging *my* balls out there.

"Why?" I managed to force the solitary word out around the lump in my throat. I really shouldn't have felt as terrified about it all as I did.

"Morgan's stoked with the way his car has been running lately and wants to stay in it. And I decided it was more beneficial to spend the dollars on the new car than to repair yours after Bathurst."

Fuck me. "So when do you need me back?"

"January. So get your shit together by then."

"Uh huh." *Fuck me.*

I hung up the phone and grabbed some more painkillers. This time, I washed them down with water. For a moment, I thanked my lucky stars that I'd had the fall and the hospital grade painkillers because normal paracetamol wouldn't have done shit all for the fucking roaring ache in my head.

After the pain slowly lulled to a dull throb, I realised I was famished again. I wondered if it was too early in the morning for curry, but then figured fuck it, because there was nothing else in the apartment anyway. I'd have to go get some normal fucking groceries soon if I was going to stay. And that was the kicker: despite my moment of "clarity" the night before, I couldn't fucking decide whether to stay or go.

If I stayed, I could only hope that Ruby spoke to Alyssa and that by some fucking miracle she could convince her to come talk to me. I still didn't know if I wanted to inflict my fucked-uppedness on Phoebe, but I did know that I needed to talk to Alyssa before I made any definite choices. If only to find out what Ruby had meant by her statement that I didn't actually have any rights.

Rubbing my eyelids, I thought about the phone conversations I'd had. I wanted to know what the fuck had happened. Everyone seemed to hint about there being more to the story, but no one was willing to spill their guts on exactly what that might be. They all just told me to fucking ask Alyssa. Too bad Alyssa was the one person in the fucking world I couldn't fucking find.

I heated the curry in the microwave for longer than the previous night. This time none of it was cold. Instead, it varied from lukewarm to molten lava. I'd really have to fucking learn how to use that shit properly if I was staying. Fucking *if*.

While I ate, I tried to remember what Alyssa had said on the plane. I was certain she'd told me how long she was in the country for, but as I ran through what I could remember of our conversation, I came up blank.

After a moment, I remembered she was staying for a week, but she hadn't told me while we were on the plane. No, she'd imparted that information while she was standing over her fucking vibrator.

Oh God!

The thought of her using that on herself took over my mind and made me instantly fucking hard. The image was clear in my head—her hand sliding the silicone dick in and out of her body. Her moans would grow louder with each thrust. Her other hand would massage her breasts or her clit. Her mouth might scream my name as her orgasm took her away.

A boy can fucking dream can't he?

Had it really been just a little over thirty-six hours ago that we'd had that conversation? My whole fucking world was different then.

My mind was rebelling, picturing her the way I wanted to, rather than figuring out the problem at hand. *Fuck, what was I trying to work out?*

How long she was in London for, and how long I wanted to stay myself. I jumped on the phone and booked my return flight. If Alyssa was only there for a week, I wasn't going to stay any longer than that. I figured Danny would probably be pissed that I used his fucking expensive-arse seats for a week-long holiday, but I honestly didn't give a flying fuck. I was doing what he told me to do—I was getting this fucking shit out of my head so I could race. Or at least, I was trying to.

With that organised, I raced upstairs. When I hit the bedroom, I was lost in memories of Alyssa and me in that space. Part of me wanted to just sit and relive the images, but I couldn't. I needed a fucking shower. It had been far, far too long since I'd had one.

It was only when I reached the bathroom that I recalled Alyssa was the last one in there. With that thought, her naked body was back in my head. She would have been all wet and hot from the steam. I could almost see her sliding her hands up into her hair to brush the water off her face. *Fuck me.* I shouldn't be thinking about her like that.

The small tattoo on her chest raced into my mind. For the first time ever, I wished I knew which constellation was which. Maybe the stars and lines had something to do with the story everyone kept mentioning—the one they said was Alyssa's to tell me.

Knowing there was nothing else to it, I turned on the water and stood under the stream while images of Alyssa assaulted me relentlessly.

The trip wasn't supposed to go that fucking way. I was supposed to get Alyssa *out* of my head—not lodged even more permanently inside. Standing under the water, the images of our fun-filled night raced into my head again. I couldn't stop my hand making a quick downstairs visit. I needed to think clearly and as long as my cock was in charge, I wouldn't be able to.

Stroking up and down in rapid succession, I brought myself to the edge as fast as I could. I needed relief, not love. Closing my eyes, I didn't even need to try to fantasise—Alyssa was already there. I saw her as she had been that night, lying on the floor underneath me, her legs wrapped around my neck. *Oh fuck*. I leaned against the bathroom wall as my orgasm hit me almost painfully, providing only a fraction of a moment of brain-emptying, mind-numbing relief before everything flooded back in. *Fuck*!

I climbed out of the shower and dried myself off. For the first time since before I'd jumped on the plane, I looked at myself in the mirror. Fuck, I was fucked-up. I still had the black eye, although it was more yellow, green, and brown now. Along the right side of my head was a long, deep black bruise from where I'd smashed into the floor and passed out. I shuddered to think what the fuck might have happened to me if Alyssa hadn't been there to call the ambulance. Especially with the cut on my arm. I looked at the waterproof covering. Fucking five stiches they'd told me I had. I looked at myself in the mirror again, meeting my own gaze. I saw Phoebe's face staring back at me. Did she deserve that sort of fuck-up as a father?

The answer was a resounding no, but what exactly did that mean? Did it mean I couldn't—shouldn't—even bother? Maybe it just meant I needed to try to be less of a fuck-up.

The first step was going out and facing the fucking world. If I hid away in the apartment, I would go fucking crazy. I would drink the other bottle of whiskey, and I couldn't do that. I couldn't return to that fucking lifestyle. A shudder ran through me at the thought. I *wouldn't*. I wouldn't submit to it and live like I did just after I joined the team, between the November I arrived and the February before the first race of the season.

Now *that* was fucked up. I was only lucky that Danny had never found out about how badly I'd fucked things up then. If he had, I wouldn't still be on the fucking team. I was fucking thankful that I was just driving production cars then. Their drug testing wasn't nearly as rigorous and preseason activities were much more limited.

I could still remember the first time I'd given in to the temptation of the lifestyle Morgan had introduced me to.

The spiral had escalated pretty quickly after that night.

CHAPTER SIXTEEN

IT'S IN THE PAST

"COME HERE, SQUIRT," Morgan called over the pounding music.

He'd given me the nickname on my first day with the team, even though he was only six years older than me. Because he was already in a ProV8 car, and I was only a production car driver, he thought he was king fucking shit.

Truthfully—he was.

That was just the ranking in the team. Morgan was *it*. He couldn't shit without fifteen people knowing about it. Me, on the other hand . . . I got to skulk around doing whatever fucking shit I wanted to most days. So long as I was in the car on race day, and ideally on podium at the end of the event, I was left alone.

Even though it meant losing my anonymity, I wanted what he had. The thrill of the fucking V8, the roar of the engine, the bonus money for every win, and the fucking women coming at him from all angles—if only as a way of getting rid of the one who haunted my dreams. I hadn't admitted it to anyone, but I hadn't been with anyone since my one night with Alyssa. In Morgan's eyes that left me practically still a virgin. The thing was that I wasn't sure whether I even wanted to be with anyone else. The thought of it hurt my chest and made it hard to breathe.

To make things worse, she'd called me practically every day since I'd first moved to Sydney. It was all I could do to ignore her. A big part of me wanted to call her back and beg for forgiveness, but she deserved more than I could ever give her. She was due to start uni around the same time that the racing season kicked off so it would never work between us. I was better off not returning her calls at all. Calling her would start me down the path of getting back together with her.

It was easier to try to forget about her and go out on the town when Morgan had invited me. The thought raced through me that maybe he was right. Maybe I just needed to get over myself and get my dick wet.

"See those sweet-arse honeys over there?" He tipped his head toward a gaggle of girls wearing nothing more than thin slips of clothing.

I nodded. Moments earlier, the three had been dancing with him in a very seductive fashion while I minded the booth and drank anything that Morgan ordered for me. I was definitely a third—or possibly fifth—wheel. With his wavy blond hair, ice-blue eyes and boisterous personality, he'd been centre of attention at every venue and could have taken any number of girls home—maybe even had some of them on the spot.

While I wasn't bad on the eyes, I didn't have the confidence he had either—especially not when I knew I wasn't even supposed to be in the club. I wasn't even eighteen, and yet Morgan had dragged me along with him from nightclub to nightclub all night long. None of the bouncers had questioned him or even batted an eyelash at me, but I still didn't want to draw extra attention to myself.

"What about them?" I asked.

"They're coming home with us."

I didn't see any point in arguing.

"Betty and Veronica are coming with me." He pointed out two of the girls. I knew Morgan enough to know the names weren't real names. He often came into work telling stories of his conquests, always giving them names from comics. *Betty* and *Veronica* had obviously been duelling for his affections, like most of the other girls, and he'd obviously convinced them to do a double act. The things I'd learned from the periphery of his life would probably have made my mother's hair turn grey. "I'll toss the third your way. Trust me, she'll be an easy catch. She's ready and waiting for it."

I did a double-take at his words. "W-what?"

"C'mon, squirt, it's time we made a man of you." He slapped my back.

My breathing came in fast bursts. At that moment, I couldn't even remember why I'd gone along at all, except I didn't have anything else to do but mope around my apartment and try not to think of Alyssa. "But . . . I . . ."

He laughed. "Seriously man, you are far too uptight. Maybe getting fucked by a woman who knows what she's doing is exactly what you need."

Before I could argue, he moved away—back toward the group of girls. He whispered something in the ear of the one he'd designated for me and she'd laughed before casting a sneaky glance at me with a smirk on her face.

It was a little after two in the morning when we left the club. My head spun with whatever alcohol Morgan had funnelled down my throat all night. It was the first time I'd ever been truly drunk. Like really fucking-smashed-off-my-face drunk.

We stumbled into a maxi taxi. Inside the cab, Morgan had started his night with Betty and Veronica. The three of them were going hard at it right then and there. I tried to look away as he pressed his hands against the breast of one of the women as the two girls kissed each other but I had to admit that the sight was making me so fucking hard.

The girl who sat next to me looked a bit more timid up close than she had in the club. A bit younger too maybe—although she still had a couple of years on me. I smiled shyly at her in apology for the way Morgan was acting. As soon as we got back to his place, he disappeared into the bedroom with the two girls, only to come out minutes later and grab a can of whipped cream and a bottle of chocolate sauce from the fridge. He threw a couple of condoms at me and winked.

I sat next to the girl he had graciously "tossed my way" as he'd fucking put it, and wasn't sure what to do. The moans and sounds of sex had started in earnest from the bedroom and I was fucking hard as a rock. I didn't want to do anything the girl didn't want though, especially when I still didn't even know if *I* wanted it.

"Is there another bedroom?" she whispered in my ear after a minute.

I nodded and pointed in the direction of Morgan's guest bedroom where I'd stayed during my first month in Sydney and still did from time to time.

"Let's go then." She stood and gave me what I guessed was supposed to be a seductive smile. It had nothing on Alyssa's though. The thought was enough to push me into action—however long my ex danced in my head, I would never be able to enjoy my life.

I allowed her to pull me to my feet. Once we reached the bedroom, she pushed me down onto the bed. She grabbed something out of her purse and popped it into her mouth. Then she climbed over onto me, straddling my waist and kissed my mouth deeply. Her tongue pushed a small tablet into my mouth, and it fell to the back of my throat. Before I could protest or ask what it was, it was gone; washed away as I'd swallowed. I moved to sit, to question what the hell she'd done, but she silenced me with a finger pressed to my lips. Sitting up, and brushing her fingers through her hair, she moved her hips against mine. The sensation of her hips rocking against my cock distracted me and sent thoughts of the tablet rushing from my mind.

While she writhed above me, she peeled her shirt off to reveal a lace and diamante bra. It occurred to me that she wasn't quite as shy and reserved as I'd assumed. She grabbed my hands from the bed, where they were lying prostrate at my side, and pressed my palms against her breasts. I massaged them in small circles over the cups as she tipped her head back and moaned a little. Although the sound was a little off, and very different from the sexy little moans my ex had offered when I'd been with her, it was enough to keep me moving. I slid my hands around to her back and unfastened her bra. Quickest hands in the west I was—I'd taken off my ex's bra more than enough times to have perfected it to a fucking art form. The constant thoughts of Alyssa made me harder, and the girl above me took it as a sign of interest.

The chick leaned over and dropped the tip of one of her breasts into my mouth. I sucked it as deep into my mouth as I could, and held her sides as I licked and nipped at her skin. It felt wrong, because it wasn't like Alyssa's. It didn't fit the same way, or even feel or taste the same. It just wasn't what the sensation was supposed to be like. Nothing about the situation was right.

I tried to push her off, but whatever she had given me started to take effect on top of the alcohol. I felt dizzy and woozy and wanted to be fucking sick. Obviously she'd taken one herself because her eyes had grown glassy and she started to giggle. She pulled my pants down just far enough to pull out my dick before rolling a condom over me. She pushed her panties to the side and holding my shaft tightly in her grip, slid herself over the top of me. Just like that, I was fucking someone else. Someone who wasn't Alyssa. That's all it was though—fucking.

Throughout it all, my mind was disconnected from my body. I could have been watching a porno for all I accepted the actions as happening to me. A complete fucking stranger bounced on top of me and although my balls grew tighter and tighter until they finally released into the latex wrapped around my cock, I felt nothing. Not even when the fucking whore who straddled me had licked my neck to entice me to come.

No joy, no love, no *anything* except a vague sensation of release. It was fucked-up, pure and simple. I was empty and wasn't sure if I was even capable of feeling anything outside of the hole which had opened up inside of me and sucked the joy from me like a giant fucking black hole.

My head spun and even though Alyssa and I had well and truly broken up—even though I didn't plan on ever seeing her again—I still felt like I'd just cheated on her.

Once I was done, the chick slid the condom off my cock before taking my shaft into her mouth to lick me clean. The move was too much for me to fucking stand. It seemed far too intimate and left me disgusted.

"Fuck off," I said to her, pushing her head away.

"What?"

"I said *fuck off*, slut."

At first, she looked shocked. A moment later, she went fucking nuts, launching herself at me. She beat at my chest with her fists and called me every name under the sun. I endured it for a minute before her words, the alcohol, and whatever the hell it was that she'd given me pushed me to the edge.

In less than a second, I went from irritated at her actions to pissed off. I just wanted her to get the fuck off me. I screamed and shouted, telling her to fuck off, but when that did nothing to stop her attack, I grabbed her arms and shoved her away. I pulled myself to a sitting position and scrambled backward on the bed to escape her. She came at me again, swinging her arms wildly. One of her hands connected with my cheek, and her nails raked the skin like talons. Not even trying to be gentle anymore, I pushed her again. She smashed into the wall near the door with a loud thud. For a moment, she appeared dazed and disorientated.

When she looked back at me, she spat in my direction. "Fuck you, arsehole."

ONLY CERTAIN things of the following three months stayed in my memory. I remembered the races, the track tests, and the days when I was at the team offices. Around those times, my days and nights were a fucking blur of alcohol, bongs, pills, and women—anything that could offer even a semblance of relief from the pain I felt constantly. Without fail, my trysts all ended the same way: me having my fill—not giving a shit about what the bitches wanted—then angrily throwing them out on the street. Somehow in my mind, it was always their fault. In every case, I threw them out for one simple reason—they weren't and never could be Alyssa. That fact alone was enough to piss me off, especially when I was high.

Eden had been the one to help me wake up to myself. There'd been a moment when I was at a true crossroads between straightening up and fucking up. Every day after, I thanked my lucky stars that she'd been there just as I was starting to slip even further into the clutches of drugs and alcohol abuse.

On my absolute worst day, I'd turned up to work stoned. Eden had grabbed me just as I was about to walk into the offices.

Danny would've had my arse ripped to pieces if he'd seen me. The one thing he'd demanded was clean drivers.

"DECLAN!" EDEN'S voice was shrill and as sharp as her nails, but neither were enough to pierce my mellow. The only thing that surprised me was that she knew my name. She was the strategist for the ProV8s and didn't have anything to do with my class. We'd probably had four conversations in total since I'd started.

"What?" I asked with a lazy smile.

"You go in there," she pointed to the offices, "like that," she pointed to my eyes, "you will be given your marching orders quick smart."

I went to shrug away from the hold she had on my arm, but she just gripped more tightly. My mellow dissolved and my lips curled into a snarl. "What does it fucking matter to you?"

"It matters because you're fucking talented. You'll be a fantastic driver one day and I would love to work with you on the ProV8 team. In fact, I'd be willing to bet it'll be sooner rather than later that you're given a chance in one of those cars. That will never happen if you get kicked off the team though. You think anyone else wants to touch Danny's trash? They all know Danny's regulations. The simple fact is you fuck up here, you're fucked everywhere."

It was easiest to pretend I didn't care, so I shrugged.

She wasn't buying it. She squared up her six foot frame and, despite her slender build, somehow managed to be fucking intimidating as she stared into my eyes. "Why'd you come here?"

"What do you mean?"

"Why'd you move here? To Sydney. Why are you here at Sinclair? What is it that you want to do?"

My brows knitted into a frown. "I want to race. Why the fuck else would I come here?"

She sighed. "If that's what you want, then you have to do yourself a favour and listen to me. Go home, get yourself sorted, and come back in tomorrow clean. Then get off the fucking drugs for good." She paused for a second to let her advice sink in. "If you don't, I will tell Danny everything you've been doing in your spare time."

"And how the fuck would you know what I've been doing?"

"Morgan."

I snarled at her. I'd forgotten that she'd straightened him out a few weeks prior and they'd been fucking each other exclusively ever since. Honestly, I could threaten to expose *them* to Danny, but it wasn't worth making enemies, especially when she was just trying to look out for me.

"Fucking whatever," I said, but I still took her advice and turned away.

"Oh, and Declan?" she called after me.

"What?"

"Give this guy a call." She handed me a card for a fucking shrink, a Dr. Henrikson. "He's discreet, he'll help, and it won't get back to Danny."

AFTER EDEN had straightened me out and put me onto Dr. Henrikson, I didn't actually stop drinking, but I'd never touched illegal drugs again. Since that day, I'd known it was a fucking fine line for me to end up back there whenever my life went to shit.

The thought made my guilt over my actions spike. Drinking a whole bottle of alcohol in one fucking night, two nights in a row, was a damn scary start.

I grabbed the apartment key and my wallet, sparing a second to glance at the photo that now resided in there. With the image of my daughter firm in my mind, I swept out of the apartment, unsure what to expect of the rest of my day.

Unsure what to expect from the rest of my fucking life.

CHAPTER SEVENTEEN
LONDON

FOR FOUR DAYS I'd been alone in London.

Four fucking days.

For that time, I'd been petrified to venture any farther than the corner store half a kilometre from the apartment. A lingering dread filled me whenever I thought about going out and exploring anything else. I was certain that the one time I went any farther than that would be the time Alyssa chose to visit me. It was stupid that I felt that way even though it was pretty fucking clear to me that she wasn't coming. Four days of absence and silence had proven that. Still, I was trapped like a prisoner in Danny's apartment.

In two more days, I was due to be on a plane flying back home, which left just one day of prison. I had absolutely no clue what the fuck I was going to do after I got home though. I'd half debated going back to Browns Plains to confront her, but that would only have landed me squarely in the lion's den. I'd have to deal with too many fucking crazy people, most of whom were all kinds of pissed at me. Not that I blamed them. I just didn't want to be forced to deal with them.

Frankly, I was fucking terrified of some of them—Josh and

Curtis in particular. If I faced either of them, I'd been surprised if I ever walked again—let alone drove—for the dick manoeuvre of throwing Alyssa out on the street after I'd learned about Phoebe. True, Alyssa already had a hotel room she was able to go to, but it was still a fucking dick move. I knew that and tortured myself mentally—her family's torture would be physical and would ensure my agony was complete.

Even without the thought of the hate I was certain I would face, I didn't think it would be a good idea to follow Alyssa home for another reason: I wanted to talk to her alone because I needed to know the truth and I was sure that was the only way I would get it. If I wanted to know what she was thinking, and to try to figure out what the fuck she'd been through, it had to be just her and me. The fact that there was much less chance of my face being mangled was just an added fucking bonus.

Although, truthfully, there was no guarantee no mangling would occur with me alone with Alyssa. She could be a fucking wildcat when cornered. A memory from school came to me unbidden, something I hadn't thought about in years. I snickered to myself as I recalled the time she'd caught Darcy Kinsley trying to pretend she'd received a valentine from me.

Thinking about Darcy dredged up Alyssa's confession of her reason for knowing I always used condoms when I fucked random chicks. She only knew because Darcy had been one of the masses and she'd wanted to make damn sure Alyssa knew it, the fucking scrag. I hadn't been physically violent with a woman since putting the drugs behind me, but fuck if it didn't sound like a good idea where Darcy was concerned. Maybe she'd be a little less likely to fuck with Alyssa then. I should have made her take her mask off; maybe then I would have known who she was and told her to fuck off. Although, it was just as likely I wouldn't have made her leave—and that fact made me feel like shit.

Recalling the things I'd done to distract myself made me feel a hundred times worse about myself than I already did. I'd been the one who'd stuck my fucking dick into Darcy. Ultimately, I was responsible for the ammunition she'd used to hurt Alyssa. Every fucking day we'd been apart, I'd fucking hurt Alyssa in some way, even when I didn't allow her to cross into my thoughts.

I was such a fucking arsehole.

The guilt that ate me slowly from the inside out was the ultimate reason I sat on the kerb in front of Danny's apartment every day until at least nine at night. Then I would go inside and ring her parents' house in Australia and get chewed out by whoever answered the phone, all while begging them to let me know where she was staying, or give me a contact phone number, or fucking *something*. That was what my fucking life had been reduced to.

A fucking dog waiting to be either kicked again, or given a fucking treat, depending on the whims of one fucking woman. A woman who clearly didn't want anything to do with me despite the bombshell she'd unwittingly dropped.

Fuck this shit!

I needed a night out. One good night to forget it all, to go out and get myself completely fucking wasted, and hopefully get laid. All I could think was four days and that fucking bitch hadn't even bothered to call, even though I'd left the apartment number with her family every time I called them.

Why should I wait for her anymore?

Standing from my position on the kerb, I brushed myself off before walking back into the apartment. Before jumping in the shower, I pulled my black slacks and the formal grey team shirt from my suitcase. Whether the grey formal one, or the casual orange, the team shirts always guaranteed me a screw in Australia. They might not have quite the same pull in the UK but one could only hope. I was getting sick of my own fucking hand being the only thing that came near me, and four fucking days for me was like a year. Especially with all of the shit going on inside my head. I needed some fucking tension relief; the sort that only a wet pussy or willing mouth could provide.

After I'd finished in the shower, I pulled on my boxers and grabbed my electric razor. The blade was already set to just the right length to allow a little of the rough stubble that seemed to drive women crazy. When I was about halfway through the job, the phone rang. Stopping the razor, I headed down the stairs to answer the phone. It stopped ringing just before I answered it.

I was almost at the top of the stairs when it started ringing again. Whoever it was they must have really wanted to talk to me. I figured it was probably Danny again. He was the only one who had the number—at least the only one who was actually likely to call. When I answered it, I was surprised that I didn't hear the usual beeps indicating that it was an international call.

"Hello?"

There was silence on the other end of the line.

"*Hello?*"

The line was still almost silent, but I could hear faint sounds, like barely contained sobbing or possibly someone hyperventilating.

"Who is this?"

I heard a sigh. Then I had a thought and my heart did the strange throat/feet combo thing again.

"Alyssa? Is that you?"

The phone line clicked and the call was disconnected.

Fuck. Was it her? It was the only thing that made a lick of sense. Who else would call the apartment number from within the UK? Someone dialling a wrong number wouldn't have remained silent for so long. Grabbing the phone directory, I leafed through it to find the number I needed to dial in order to call back the last missed call. I waited anxiously as it rang once . . . twice. It was answered on the third ring by a pleasant female voice.

Pleasant, but not Alyssa.

"Suncrest London, Caroline speaking."

"Hi, I . . . um, I just had a missed call from this number."

"All of our rooms dial out over this number, sir, so I won't be able to put you through unless you know the room number or name of the person who called you."

It was a long shot. "I think there's an Alyssa Dawson staying there. She's the only one I can think of who'd have called me."

There was a pause and tapping on a computer. "I'm sorry, we have no record of any rooms registered in that name."

Fuck.

Maybe I was wrong. Maybe it hadn't been Alyssa. There was no one else who would ring me from a hotel in London though. Maybe she was staying there under another name, which could be fucking anything. It was a long shot, but it was also a possible lead. I knew it would sound suspicious if I asked Caroline for the address when I'd just admitted to not knowing who was there, so I finished the call with her with a polite, "Thank you for your help."

I hung up and then pressed redial, hoping I got someone different.

"Suncrest London, this is Suzette."

"Suzette, would you be able to give me your street address please?"

She gave it to me. It was too late to be making a polite visit to the hotel, but I had a plan to go first thing in the morning. It was my last hope. My only hope. I climbed back up the stairs, set the alarm beside the bed for five the following morning, dressed in just a pair of sweats ready for bed, and then grabbed a towel from the bathroom. Fuck the randoms; my hand would just have to do the trick again for another night.

FIVE A.M. was far too fucking early.

There should be no reason in the world to be up at this time of the morning unless it was a fucking race day. Then again, it almost felt like a race day. It felt like I was racing toward Alyssa. Toward answers. I still didn't know what I would do once I got those answers, but I knew I fucking needed them if I wanted any semblance of sanity. Realistically, going to the Suncrest was my last chance at finding her while I was still in London. In thirty-six hours' time, I would be on a plane and heading back to the fuckery that was my normal life. At some point during the night, I'd decided for certain that I wouldn't chase Alyssa to Brisbane. I couldn't. If she tried to contact me again, I'd be willing to listen, but part of me still thought both she and Phoebe would be better off without me forcing my way back into their lives.

The hotel was my only chance for answers. I decided that if Alyssa was trying out a law firm, she would presumably leave the hotel early. With that in mind, I was ready and waiting near the front by six thirty.

My location of choice was a bus stop about fifty metres away from the hotel entrance. I watched the face and body of every woman with dark hair, keeping an intent eye out for Alyssa. Everyone was so rugged up against the cold as they stepped outside that it was hard to see much of anyone. I did see one potential candidate and followed her halfway down the road before she disappeared. I'd been calling Alyssa's name, but the girl didn't turn around. Of course, that didn't mean it wasn't Alyssa. She might have just been deliberately ignoring me.

I slid the photo of Phoebe in and out of my wallet as I waited and watched. I couldn't decide whether to confront Alyssa with it or without it. I wondered if she'd want it back eventually. If that was the case though, why had she left it with me in the first place? Was it designed to seep away the last fucking remnants of my sanity? Was that the reason she'd given it to me? I wondered if Alyssa honestly enjoyed fucking with my mind. Having me sit patiently waiting for her like a fucking lap dog must have been a heady drug.

For the entire fucking day, I sat at the bus stop and never saw another prospect. No one else that looked even remotely like the one I wanted to see. I finally returned to the apartment at a little after nine that night. My entire being was completely shattered, and I was fucking exhausted. I was due to leave on a fucking flight at eight the next morning, so once more I'd need to be up at five. Only it wouldn't be to get answers. It would be to leave, most likely leaving any chance at peace behind.

I set the alarm and grabbed the remaining bottle of whiskey, swallowing a big swig. I threw everything I had back into my suitcase and then took it downstairs to the living room. When I was set, I glanced around the empty apartment. The first day I'd arrived, the place had felt like home. For the last five days, it had felt like an empty fucking prison cell. Nothing there drew me in, nothing fucking called to me. I couldn't fucking figure out what the difference was.

It was a little after ten when I decided that I was going to go out. If Alyssa wouldn't even fucking talk to me when I'd dragged my arse all the way up town to see her, then she could go fucking fuck herself. She had the equipment. On that thought my fucking dick stood firmly to attention.

Fuck, I need to get laid.

I would get some fucking sleep on the plane.

THE TAXI beeped out the front. I raced downstairs in the outfit I'd planned to wear the previous evening—my black slacks and grey team shirt. I climbed into the cab and—once I realised the driver was a young, red-blooded man like myself—asked him where was the best place to go for an Aussie to score a root. He drove me to the nearest Uluru Inn. Apparently they were *the* Aussie bar in the UK. I found it mildly amusing that in Sydney every second fucking pub was Irish, and yet the UK seemed flooded with Aussie bars.

We hadn't gone very far when he pulled up, maybe three kilometres. I could fucking walk home, provided I was lucid. That was good. It gave me a fucking exit strategy that didn't rely on waiting for a taxi.

After tossing the cab driver some cash, I went into the bar and ordered a beer. When I took my first sip, I thanked my fucking lucky stars that it was cold. There was nothing worse than drinking warm beer. Settling in to a stool at the bar, I scoped around at the talent in the place. As was habit, my gaze immediately brushed over every brunette in the place. They weren't going to cut it for me. I couldn't do that shit, not with my brain supplying constant fresh images of Alyssa fucking herself.

In one corner, taking up two tables, there was a large party of pretentious fucking snobs. All of them dolled up in power suits, even the fucking women. I ignored them. Women in power suits don't do random fucking against club walls, and that was all I needed at that point. I wasn't going to fucking take anyone home after all. I needed a screw—that's it.

I saw a possible candidate alone in the back of the bar. She was a bit plain, but then everyone was in comparison to Alyssa. Her short-cropped jet-black hair was just different enough to please me. Surrendering my seat, I moved to sit on the stool next to hers. Once I had her attention, I flagged down the bartender and ordered another of whatever she was drinking. She gave him her order and I heard the unmistakeable twang in her accent that told me she was an Aussie too.

She smiled shyly at me, then she glanced up again and her recognition was clear as day. Her eyes widened into saucers and her face flushed.

"Holy fuck!" she shouted. "You're fucking Declan Reede!" So she was an Aussie, and a fan apparently.

"You could be too, if you play your cards right." I winked at her before giving her a panty-dropping grin and waiting for my statement to settle into her alcohol-addled brain.

Her gaze settled on mine, the light brown colour a little too close to the one I really wanted. Why did that one simple thing have to remind me so much of Alyssa? I was about to turn away when her hand came onto my thigh and quickly grazed over my dick. God it felt good for someone else to touch me again. It was the wrong sort of touch, not exactly the way I liked it, but it was enough to distract my focus from her gaze.

I shot her a wicked grin and then asked her name. Not that I cared or it even mattered; I wouldn't remember it in the morning. However, I knew from experience that women were more likely to fuck you if you at least knew their name.

She whispered it into my ear, taking the opportunity to lick the lobe as her mouth was close. Talk about fucking shooting fish in a barrel.

"It must be amazing to drive a V8?"

My grin became a smirk. I fucking loved it when women knew what I did, because it gave me the chance to pull out the usual shit about the power of the car, the roar of the engine, the vibration of the seat—that one usually got chicks hot.

Her fingers stroked long lines up and down the length of my thigh as I spoke, and I was ready to go. I didn't want to make small talk with this random stranger any longer. I put my hand to her face and caressed her cheek for half a second, pretending to hesitate in anticipation of the kiss. Girls went fucking nuts for that shit. I'd done the whole routine enough to know precisely what to do to have them eating out of my hand, or more precisely sucking on my dick.

I pressed my lips to hers, slipping my tongue straight into her mouth without any hesitation. If she had any qualms about moving fast, she definitely didn't show it. After humming into the kiss, she moved off her stool to straddle my lap. I brushed my fingers into her hair, and she moaned. It was easy, but it was wrong. The taste was off, the feeling wasn't there.

With the recent reunion with Alyssa branded onto my brain, all the things that usually made the encounters less than perfect were magnified to make it almost a turn-off. With just one night, Alyssa had ruined me. Instead of letting it destroy my night, I tried to push her out of my head. It might not have been exactly what I needed, or wanted, but it was just a chance for a random screw, just like it always had been. A chance to find momentary relief and nothing more.

The air around us shifted as someone came up to the bar to order a drink, but I didn't open my eyes or break off the kiss. Why should I? If the fucker had never seen kissing before, well, maybe they could learn a fucking thing or two. My hands slid up the inside of the random's shirt and played with the straps on her bra. A promise of things to come.

A warm breath brushed my earlobe and a thrill ran through me. The right kind of thrill. My eyes snapped open and I broke off the kiss with . . . whatever the fuck her name was.

"Well, I see some things never change," an icy voice that sounded desperately close to tears whispered in my ear.

I turned to see one of the women from the group of pretentious bitches in the power suits running for the door. Her dark hair was swept up into a bun and her hands covered her face, but there was no doubting who it was.

Fuck.

Miss Random, who was still straddling my lap, peppered small kisses all over my face, even though I was clearly no longer into it. She probably figured she could draw my attention back to her by grinding her hips against my dick. Pulling my face away from her, I tried to push her off gently, but she didn't move.

"Get off," I said, glancing back at her without feeling.

She stopped her kissing. "What?"

"I said get the fuck off me."

She slid from my lap and the instant I was free, I raced to the door. Bursting out onto the street, I looked side to side, but it was empty both ways.

Fucking hell!

"Alyssa!"

I ran to each corner and looked up every street in the vicinity, but she was gone.

God, you've fucked it up royally this time, Reede!

CHAPTER EIGHTEEN

MURPHY'S LAW

JUST AS I'D planned before my night out, I didn't go to sleep that night, but for entirely different reasons than I'd hoped.

Instead, I crawled into my last bottle of whiskey and took up residence there. I sat on the couch and drank swig after swig until the bottle was dry. Like I always did when I took comfort in a bottle, I tried to make my head as empty as the bottle. Only, it didn't work. I just kept seeing image after image of Alyssa's pain: her hands over her face as she fled from the bar; her terror as I shouted at her to get out of the apartment; her tears when I'd told her goodbye before I left Brisbane. There was no point going to bed while these images danced in my head. I'd learned that lesson the hard way years earlier. It was always useless. Even if I could silence my mind long enough to fall to sleep, I would just be haunted by the twisted arsehole that was my psyche.

There were only three ways I could possibly get a restful sleep: tablets, a sufficient quantity of alcohol to make me black out, or a combination of the two. The fucking alcohol hadn't worked, and I didn't have any sleeping tablets. Hadn't for so long.

It was a relief when I finally heard the alarm going off upstairs. It meant it was time to do something. Action meant that for a brief moment, I could push all of the thoughts out of my mind and focus on what I needed to do. Dragging myself to my feet, I staggered up the stairs to turn the alarm off. Then I jumped into a quick cold shower to shake off the sleepless lethargy that had settled over me. I hoped it would also sober me up a little, but I worried that it failed on both counts. I gathered all the used towels and sheets, throwing them in the hamper for Danny's year-round maid service to deal with. At least it meant washing and cleaning was one less thing I had to worry about before I left.

For the trip home, I dressed in a t-shirt and a pair of sweats—nothing fancy. It wasn't like I had anyone to impress, and I didn't really care to try. Once I was dressed, I threw some essentials, including my sunnies and hat, into my carry-on bag and roughly shoved everything else back into my already packed suitcase.

By the time the taxi arrived, I was ready and waiting out the front of the apartment. The driver joked that people usually looked like shit when they got *off* the plane, not on the way to the airport. In a trial of patience worthy of Mother Theresa, I bit back the "fuck you very much," that rose in my throat. Once we'd arrived at the airport, I slumped my carry-on over my shoulder and rolled my suitcase toward the check-in counter.

"Window or aisle?" I was asked. Outside of that, the clerk didn't seem interested in conversation—which I was incredibly fucking thankful for.

The only thing that ran through my mind when the question came up was that Alyssa had been in the window seat on our last journey. The thought sent my mind wandering. Did she prefer a window seat or was she just placed there by sheer luck? What would our return trip have been like if we'd been able to take it together? If I hadn't reacted the way I had to the photo, would I know the full story now?

"Sir?"

I glanced up at the clerk. "Aisle," I coughed out. My voice was hoarse and sounded like I'd spent the whole week puffing down on cigarettes.

The clerk nodded and finished checking me in before handing me my boarding pass. "Have a nice flight."

Fucking doubt it. "Thanks."

Just like I had in Sydney and Hong Kong, I had some time to kill between check-in and needing to get through security so I found a cafe and crawled inside a coffee. I fucking needed it like oxygen. My brain was already starting to tick with the beginnings of a hangover, or possibly a fatigue headache. Either way, caffeine would help it, at least temporarily.

Sipping my latte, I heard an unfamiliar female voice at the counter ordering a caramel macchiato. Even though I knew it wasn't Alyssa, my gaze travelled in that direction as wishful thinking overtook me. A red-haired woman, whose clothes were practically painted on, was the offending orderer. I fought the urge to scowl at her for not being the person I wanted her to be. Instead, I picked roughly at the chocolate doughnut that had seemed like such a good idea when I'd been at the counter, but was currently making me nauseous.

While I sat finishing my coffee, I tried not to think about anything. Especially not Alyssa, and double especially not Phoebe. Most of all, I was trying desperately to avoid thinking about the last flight I'd had—the one shared with Alyssa—and the evening that followed it. Even as I tried not to think about it, I felt myself harden at the memories and the image that my own mind had conjured up that had been haunting me since. The one of Alyssa using her vibrator to fuck herself silly with my name on her lips.

Fuck, I was so hard. I wondered if I had time to knock off a quick one in the airport toilets. Even though I was completely disgusted, as I adjusted myself I realised I had little choice. My cock had a hair trigger and the sweats weren't designed for the concealment of large objects.

I moved to stand, but the redhead who'd ordered the caramel macchiato slid into the booth beside me. Her hands were empty and her drink was nowhere to be seen. The tiny silver top she wore captured the light, and practically hung from her nipples. Almost nothing was left to the imagination, and I figured if I looked under the table it would *all* be on show. She tilted her body toward me, grazing my arm with her tits. Once, that might have excited me, but I was too filled to the brim with thoughts of Alyssa.

"I think you and I have some unfinished business," the red-haired stranger purred at me from across the table.

"How's that?" I asked, frowning in confusion.

She smiled wickedly and giggled a little. "It's Tillie. From the club. Remember?"

I looked at her blankly. Was I supposed to know who the fuck Tillie-from-the-club was?

"You made me famous. I mean, how often do people like me get on the *Gossip Weekly* cover?"

Oh fuck me.

She giggled. Straight-up schoolgirl giggled. Once, I would have found that shit sexy but it just made me realise how much I didn't want to deal with games and random hook-ups.

"We could finish it now if you like?" She raised her eyebrow at me in what I guessed was supposed to be a seductive way but just ended up looking a little pathetic.

Oh God!

Her hand dropped under the table and she pushed it up the length of my thigh and into my already hardened crotch. I pressed myself back into the seat a little. I needed to think before my head became too clouded with . . .

Oh Christ, what is she doing?

She slid from the seat, her whole body lowering under the table. Glancing up at me, she licked her lips in promise before her head disappeared out of sight. Not that long ago, I would have jumped at the chance. At that point, I couldn't think of anything I wanted less.

Holy fuck.

Her hands brushed across the top of my dick through my pants. She gripped it firmly before her fingers played with the waistband, trying to get inside. I quickly pulled myself onto the seat and climbed over the table, grabbing onto my sweats as I went to make sure I didn't lose them.

"I'm sorry, Tillie, I just can't." I reached under the table and grabbed my carry-on from beside her disappointed face. Once I had it, I turned and fled out of the cafe as quickly as I could. My erection rubbed painfully against my sweats as I walked as quickly as possible without drawing attention to myself. I was probably pitching a tent out front if any wandering eyes cared to look down there, but there was fuck all I could do about it. Making a beeline for the men's toilets, I jumped in a cubicle and ground one out to get rid of the bulge in my pants.

Wanking in a toilet — what have I been fucking reduced to?

I felt no relief when I was finished, just nausea. Just fucking hungover and sick. Ignoring my reflection in the mirror, I washed up and moved on to security.

As I was putting my things on the conveyer, I saw a woman ahead with hair the exact same dark shade of brown as Alyssa's. At first, I thought I was seeing things, but the more I watched the girl, the more convinced I became that it had to be Alyssa. I just wanted to make the fucker doing security hurry the hell up, but he pulled me to the side, saying something about random fucking bag searches or some shit. Wasn't that what the fucking X-ray machines were for? I kept my eyes on the back of the girl's head for as long as I could, but realised my mistake fairly quickly when she walked into the first class lounge. Even if by some miracle Alyssa was on the flight, she'd be in premium economy class like me. I laughed at myself for being such a fucking idiot to think we could possibly be on the same flight together twice. It was purely wishful thinking on my part.

I boarded the plane on the first boarding call. Then I waited restlessly in my seat. I wasn't sure why, but I couldn't shake the feeling that maybe I wasn't being a *total* fucking idiot to think that Alyssa could be on this flight. She was only staying a week after all, and I had stayed a week. It wasn't like there were hundreds of flights to Australia every day.

Perhaps the feeling was nothing more than a desire to see her again. To speak to her. Fuck knows what I wanted to say to her though. I didn't have a single fucking clue what I wanted to say or what she wanted to hear. I just had a burning desire to be close to her again and to talk to her. It felt like anticipation hummed around the plane; as if my body just fucking *knew* she was nearby. I glanced anxiously toward the door every time a new passenger climbed on board. Not one of them was the one I wanted.

After the cabin crew started giving me strange looks—obviously trying to decide whether I was up to no good or just a nervous flyer—I decided to try to calm myself down. I closed my eyes, leaned my head back against the headrest and pinched the bridge of my nose—relieved that the action was finally pain-free again. I wondered vaguely just how big a hobo I looked at that point. I felt faint, dizzy, and nauseated. My sleepless night—or maybe the alcohol—was catching up with me.

I figured that perhaps it would be better for me to forget my fantasy of Alyssa being on the plane. She wasn't, and even if she was, seeing me like this would probably be a major turnoff for her. I was in sweats for Christ's sake. Just as I'd given up all hope, I felt a shift in the air beside me as someone reached up and put a bag in the overhead compartment. Opening my eyes, I saw brown hair and my heart skipped a beat.

If I'd been paying any kind of attention, I would have instantly noticed the little things that made it clear it wasn't Alyssa. The shade of her hair was the wrong colour, and her skin was a little more tanned. I wasn't paying attention though, and as her hair danced in front of me for one second as she climbed over me to her seat hope bubbled up in my chest. For that one split second, I believed it was Alyssa and my heart grew in size so rapidly that it stopped my breath. I was convinced that we would be able to talk again, and start on the path of being friends—just like the last flight. That hope was pricked and burst like a balloon when the girl took her seat beside me.

The reality of the last week crashed on top of me and I fucking broke down. Tears and sobbing and all that shit men weren't supposed to do. It was going to be a long fucking flight.

The woman who'd just sat next to me seemed to regard me for

a few minutes, no doubt wondering whether to fear or pity me. At some point in her assessment, she obviously settled on pity because she twisted in her seat, patted my arm and asked what was wrong. Before I could control my tongue enough to stop, the verbal diarrhoea hit and I was telling her everything about the fact that I was going crazy—that I had been so certain Alyssa was on the plane. After I finished, I asked, "So do you think I'm fucking crazy or what?"

She just patted my back and comforted me silently.

I sat with my head pressed against this stranger's shoulder for far longer than circumstance and decorum would probably dictate. Strangely though, the non-Alyssa offered me some small semblance of comfort that I'd only ever been able to get from Alyssa, Ruth, or my own mother before. She calmed me and eventually I was able to pull myself together and sit up away from her shoulder. After so long in her embrace, it was a little awkward to know how to move the conversation. In the end, I held my hand out to her and said the only thing I could think of.

"Hi, I'm Declan."

She laughed in reply. When she spoke her voice was traced with a thick Irish accent. It reminded me of my grandmother, and I couldn't help but reminisce. "Well, that was certainly the most interesting introduction I've ever had. I'm Siobhan." She shook my hand in hello.

Trying to put the awkwardness behind us, I asked her about her trip. As she explained that she was backpacking around the countryside for a few months, talking with a familiarity that shouldn't have existed between two people who were still strangers, it made me think that maybe it wouldn't be such a bad flight after all.

WHEN I woke from a dream about Alyssa—filled with memories of our time together—my first reaction was to adjust my newfound erection. I grabbed my cock through my sweats to shift it a little to the left. Someone nearby cleared their throat and I looked toward the sound to see Siobhan staring out the window with the start of a smile at the corner of her lips.

I released the hold I had on my dick. "Oh, shit, sorry. Just . . . oh, fuck. Sorry."

Raising her hand, no doubt to silence me before I disintegrated into a blubbering mess again, she looked back toward me. "So why did you let this fantastic girl go anyway?"

I didn't understand where the question had come from.

"You were talking in your sleep. You said something about having a fantastic girl at home. I assume you were talking about . . . Alyssa, wasn't it?"

I nodded.

"Well, from your tears and your dreams, I'm guessing she's still important to you. So why did you let her go?"

"It's a long story."

Siobhan smiled at me. "It's a long flight."

WHEN WE climbed off the plane I gave her my number and told her to call me if she was ever passing through town. Somehow over the course of the twenty-four hour flight we had come pretty close to friendship. I'd certainly felt better for having been in her company. She made me think that maybe, just maybe, I could fix this. That I did deserve to have Alyssa in my life, as a friend at the very least.

The problem was that the feeling of hope she inspired, the thoughts that maybe I wasn't a complete and utter nut job, only carried me as far as the baggage collection area. Then the truth smashed back into me with no remorse. I really was too screwed up to function. For a long time, I'd been fucked-up, but functional. In the last few months, I couldn't even do my day job properly. Worse, I was starting to see reminders of Alyssa everywhere I went. I could have sworn the chick who grabbed her luggage from the carousel just before I got there was Alyssa, but when I double-checked, there

194

was a blonde in her place.

It was clear to me that I needed to go home, have a shower and get settled back into whatever sort of life I could carve for myself. If nothing else, I needed to try to push this trip out of my head. I needed to forget about the little girl whose image was seared into my mind, but who was far better off without me in her life.

Most of all, I needed to forget about any chance of having any kind of relationship with Alyssa. I'd fucked up too much, and hurt her too many times. It was no fucking wonder she didn't even want to talk to me. Just when she'd maybe considered it, I'd fucked it all up again.

It was almost seven at night by the time I got a taxi home. Before I even reached my door, I found something out of place. Resting on my doorstep was a letter, which should have been impossible. I never gave my address to anyone. The team had a post box for fan mail and all of my bills and shit went to a post box that my accountant had a key for. It was easier that way; I didn't have to do mail. Usually anyone who wanted to contact me direct did so through email or text. There was no stamp on the envelope either, which was another oddity. It meant someone had hand delivered it. I spun on the spot, just in case whoever had left the letter was still hanging around—even though realistically it could have been left at any stage over the last week.

After I flicked on the light in the entryway, I ripped open the top of the envelope and yanked out the paper inside. There was nothing extra written on it, but I realised it was a photocopy of a birth certificate. Phoebe's birth certificate.

My jaw snapped shut and my teeth ground together when I saw the name printed under "name of father," but then something else caught my eye and my blood froze in my veins.

I raced inside, hunted down my mobile phone, and grabbed my car keys. It was a twelve-hour drive to Brisbane, but it would still be quicker than ringing the airline and trying to get a flight. Especially considering by the time I made it back to the airport the last flight for the day would have already left. Without stopping to get any new clothes, I threw my suitcase into the backseat of my Monaro.

My heart was pounding in my chest and tears pricked at my eyes as I turned the ignition.

I took two deep breaths to try to steady myself and then I put my foot to the floor.

When I hit the highway, I brushed away the tears that had started to form and floored it past the speed limit. My mind rebelled against what I'd read, refusing to acknowledge it, but it still fucking hurt.

All the while my mother's voice rang in my mind. *"As if that poor girl hasn't had it hard enough. I don't know if you'll ever really comprehend just how much you hurt her."*

Message received loud and fucking clear.

CHAPTER NINETEEN
DESTINATION

THE HOURS DRAGGED by as I forced my car through the dark of night up the M1 toward Brisbane as fast as I dared. Despite the weight of sleep on my eyes and the sorrow in my heart, each holding me in a tight embrace, I only stopped for fuel. The only time I slowed was when I came to the stretch of road with a number of fixed speed cameras because the last thing I needed on top of everything else was to have my licence suspended. Not that it mattered anymore. Nothing mattered anymore.

My heart ached for Alyssa, for Phoebe, and selfishly, even for myself.

How did I not know?

My mind was still stuck on the details of the birth certificate, and I was thankful for the lack of cars on the road. The fact that the name, Flynn Olson, was listed under father's name had pissed me off when I'd first seen it, but even that wasn't what compelled me forward. It wasn't the reason I drove my car as fast as I possibly could in the direction of the one place I'd sworn I'd never return to.

For so many years, I'd felt as if going back would somehow

signal failure. Failure to stay away from Alyssa. Failure to live my dreams to the full. Staring at the moonless night, with the darkness completely circling both around the car outside and within my soul, it was crystal fucking clear that the true failure had been *not* going back. Not fucking being there for Alyssa when she'd needed me the most. She'd said those very words before I'd thrown her out in London and in the messages she left on my answering machine. Now, I'd learned the precise meaning of them, and hated myself for letting her down so fucking badly. After hours of being stuck on the plane, and then squeezing myself into the car, every inch of me hurt. The ache that blossomed on the outside of my body was nothing compared to the agony trapped inside though.

For the first time since learning about Phoebe, I tried to put myself in Alyssa's shoes. She'd been left not only without the father of her child, but without her best friend. How did she cope with that, pregnant and alone?

"Fuck!" I smacked the steering wheel.

Even though I guessed she was never completely alone, because her family would have supported her, it still had to be tough. It was more than I'd ever had to cope with.

I am such a fucking arsehole.

And then to fucking have to cope with . . . with . . .

My mind shut down, refusing to allow me to think about it. I swiped the tears away again. For the moment, I had to fight the sorrow off. It wasn't doing shit to help me stay focused on the road. Eventually though, I would have to let the sorrow win—no fucking person in their right mind would be able to cope with shit like this without tears.

More than ever, I longed to talk to Alyssa, if only to understand what happened and why. More than anything, I had to know if it was my fault. If I could have somehow prevented it by being around. If things would have been different.

THE SUN was just cresting the horizon when I crossed the border between Queensland and New South Wales. It was climbing higher in the sky as I drove past the Gold Coast and up through Yatala. I couldn't believe how much everything had changed and yet somehow nothing had. So much of the highway had moved and shifted, stomping through in a mass of concrete and cutting off so many corners and twists to be just one big expanse of road. Yet all the landmarks I remembered remained unchanged. I wondered if I would find the same thing when I returned home—that somehow everything would be different and yet nothing would.

When I saw the sign for a travel centre along the side of the highway, I pulled in to wash up and change. I really didn't want to stop until I reached my destination, but it didn't feel right turning up in my current attire either. I pulled on my team shirt and black pants—it was the nicest outfit I had. It was crushed to buggery having been forced into my suitcase after my failed night out, but it was at least cleaner and more presentable than sweats and a tee.

After dressing, I splashed my face with cold water. When I glanced up, I saw my reflection. Behind the stubble and the bags under my eyes, I looked haunted. The fact remained that I was.

My eyes were still filled with unshed tears. I wondered if they would ever leave, but I wasn't sure I even wanted them to. The birth certificate had shattered my heart into a million pieces and each piece wanted to have its turn at expressing the grief etched into my very being. Meeting the failure and fear in my own gaze, I was sorely tempted to let go then and there. With another splash of water, I beat the tears back into submission. Turning away, I raked a wet hand through my hair and decided I was as presentable as I could hope to be under the circumstances.

At the attached cafe, I grabbed a coffee and then I was back on the road. My heart pulled me in, dragging me to Browns Plains faster even as I closed the distance. It was almost as if it knew some part of it had been left behind. A fucking bigger piece than I could have ever believed possible.

Finally, after a little over twelve hours on the road, I was within the borders of my home town. The place where I had spent my entire life, save the last four years. The place that would now forever hold a wretched chunk of my heart.

Biting my cheek to hold back the tears that threatened, I moved onward with my mission. I was too late to be useful, too late to change anything, but I wouldn't budge from my course until it had been run.

I DROVE past the street that would take me to my old house—my parents' house. My hands started to shake as I edged closer to my destination.

Too late, and yet also far too soon, I arrived.

Parking the car, I tried to take a few deep breaths to steady myself. I didn't know how I was going to do it. Wasn't sure I could. I knew I needed to though. There was nothing that could stop me from seeing the evidence of my failure. Not after all this time, not with all my regrets laid bare in my soul. For all I knew, he could have been in a hundred other places, but somehow I knew he wouldn't. He'd be close to my family; Mum would have insisted. It would have been easier for Alyssa that way too.

Willing my legs to carry me over the final distance, I moved to find my nana's grave. It was near the back of the cemetery and she'd been buried with plenty of room around her. Mum and Dad had bought a number of plots when Nana had passed, just so that they could all be together in death. My legs were on autopilot as I stepped forward, the line from the birth certificate rolling on repeat through my mind.

As prepared as I was, my heart shattered when I saw what I'd come in search of.

The first thing that captured my eye was the cold, white marble cherub. So tiny. No bigger than the size of a newborn baby. The cherub had his head buried in his hands and white wings extended out from each shoulder—reaching up for the sky.

Carved onto the stone plinth beneath the little angel were two horses. Each the mirror image of the other, they faced inward with their forelegs reared. Each had a name engraved beneath: "Castor," and "Pollux."

Underneath the horses was an inscription that made the line of the birth certificate achingly real. I fell to my knees as I saw the words.

"No." The word was barely a breath. I shook my head as my chest tightened. The grief I'd experienced during the drive was nothing compared to the cold chill freezing my body and stopping my heart.

Even though nothing was different in the world compared to the day before, the little monolith, with the angel perched on top, changed everything. The day before, I hadn't known about him. I'd been living in a state of oblivion as fucked-up as it had been blissful. I'd had no knowledge of the levels of pain that a heart could endure and yet still continue to beat. Had the keen sting of the agony of truth not been twisted around my body, tightening like a tourniquet, I wouldn't have thought it was even possible to hurt so much and still be alive.

The twenty-nine words and two dates on the plinth were tangible proof of just how badly I had let everyone down. Of just how badly Alyssa had needed me when I refused to talk to her.

A name: Emmanuel Pollux Reede Dawson.

Two dates: 11th June and 14th June.

And an epitaph: *An angel opened the book of life and wrote down my baby's birth. Then she whispered as she closed the book, "too beautiful for earth."*

They were all that was needed to make everything final.

They were what marked the grave of my son.

I fell to the ground with a wail as each of the million pieces of my heart let loose their agony in a simultaneous release, rendering me helpless to the waves of grief that battered upon my soul.

My fingers raked at the grass, gripping hard and trying to ground me. Trying to hold myself in place—to stop myself from floating away. I crawled over and placed my hand on the cold marble of the tiny angel. I bent toward it and rested my forehead against the top of his petite head, baptising him with my tears.

"I'm so sorry," I whispered, as I moved to kneel at his side.

They were words I owed him, Emmanuel, a thousand times over. Words I owed Alyssa and Phoebe.

"I'll tell them too," I promised. "I swear to you, I'll tell them until they know how fucking sorry I am."

Even though I'd never met him, had never even dreamed he'd existed, the agony of having lost my child was unbearable. I had no doubt that my pain was only a fraction of what Alyssa would have suffered.

Had suffered.

Alone.

A sob ripped from me and I fell to the ground again.

"I'm so, so fucking sorry, Lys," I murmured, wishing the words would find their way to her ears.

They will. I'll tell her. I'll make her see how truly sorry I am. Somehow.

My gaze lifted back up to the stone angel. *But it won't fix this.*

All the physical torture in the world would be preferable to the pain ravaging my soul. I would have faced a hundred of Josh's beatings to avoid the pain. A thousand. Being burned alive at the stake would have been preferable to the fire that consumed my lungs and left me unable to breathe around the ashes in my throat.

Anything would have been preferable to the absolute agony that twisted inside my stomach as I looked at my son's tombstone. That one line from Phoebe's birth certificate, "Siblings: Emmanuel Pollux Reede Dawson 11th June (Dec'd)," would be burned into my brain forever.

CHAPTER TWENTY

HOMECOMING

I HAD NO way of knowing exactly how long I'd sat beside Emmanuel's grave. All I knew was that it had been midmorning when I'd arrived, and it was almost dark again when I heard footsteps behind me. By then, I was practically curled around the cool marble of the headstone, taking comfort from the pain of the sharp edges digging into my body. It drew my attention away from the fog that had taken residence in my brain.

Raising my head, I glanced up to see who had arrived. The outline was unfamiliar. Although the guy was tall and muscled, it wasn't Josh. This guy was a little bit shorter and a little less bulky, but not by much. His jet-black hair was short and spiked. When my eyes adjusted to the low light, I could see that it was the fucker from Queensland Raceway, Flynn. The fucking arsehole who'd claimed paternity of my daughter, and no doubt my son too.

A small voice inside my head, the one I usually drowned in alcohol, reminded me that he'd claimed that place only because I hadn't. Because I wouldn't answer the phone when Alyssa called. Because I'd been so damn scared that she would drag me back into a suburban life—where I would have to settle for a dead-end job rather than doing something I loved—that I didn't even consider she might have her own shit going on.

Another sob escaped my lips. I didn't know how many that was; I'd lost count long ago.

My tears were long since dried though. Not because I didn't want to cry or anything like that but because there were just no more tears left inside me. All that remained was an empty husk filled with bitter remorse and empty regret. I wanted nothing more than to fill the void with half a bottle of whatever sleeping pills I could lay my hands on and a bottle of whiskey.

If I could have, I would've just lain on the spot and let the earth fucking swallow me. I knew I couldn't though, and the reasons were multiple and complex. First and foremost was the fucker still staring at me through eyes narrowed into thin slits.

When I met his gaze his face brightened just a little. "I hoped I might find you here."

I grunted at him, but didn't move to stand. I wasn't sure if I even could. Instead, I pulled myself into a seated position and rested my head against the side of the headstone. Flynn sat next to me and passed me a beer. I debated whether it was too fucking morbid to be sucking back on a beer in the middle of a cemetery at twilight, but decided I fucking needed it too much to care. I snatched it from his hand before popping it open and sliding the bottle cap into my pocket. I may have been an arse to even consider drinking at the side of Emmanuel's grave, but I wasn't going to desecrate it with litter on top of that.

"I'm Flynn, by the way." The fucker held his hand out for me to shake.

I didn't take it. "Declan."

"Yeah, I know." He fucking smiled. How the fucker could smile when my world had just crashed into tiny fucking pieces was beyond me. He seemed to understand my thoughts because in my peripheral vision, I saw his face flick to Emmanuel's tombstone before returning to my direction.

"Sorry about the fucked-up way you had to find out about this.

I just . . ." He sighed and then brushed his hands through his hair. "I knew that if it was left to Alyssa you might not have found out the whole story for a while longer. And I thought it'd be better for her if you knew."

"You left me the birth certificate." I wished my voice would be something other than flat and lifeless. It held no emotion, not even anger or sorrow. I couldn't even ask it as a question. The words came out as a bland, monotonous statement. My gaze remained focused on the grass in front of me.

He nodded. "I was in Sydney yesterday to meet Alyssa. I flew down a little earlier, so I paid your house a quick visit."

I glanced over at him.

"She told me about the near misses you two had on the flight back. She managed to get herself bumped to first class just because she didn't want to talk to you."

I nodded. Although I should have been surprised, or shocked, or angry, or well, *something*, it all just seemed too much to manage. Anything beyond hollow, empty, and filled with agony was too much.

"She will speak to you again, man, she's just . . . afraid."

She was afraid of me. Again, I supposed I should have felt something about that revelation, but I didn't. I closed my eyes and exhaled everything that was left in me; it wasn't a lot. I went to ask a question, but once more it left me as a hard, uncaring statement. "She really suffered."

I opened my eyes again to see his reaction. His eyes flicked back to the tombstone again. He nodded. "I think you might be beginning to see just how much. The most fucked up thing is she never said a bad thing about you. In the almost four fucking years that I've known her, she has never once said anything negative about you. She's always made excuses for you, man. Even after what happened in London, she tried to justify the arsehole things you did."

"What happened?" I touched the horses on the tombstone. Castor and Pollux. I vaguely wondered what the significance was supposed to be. Considering Emmanuel's middle name, there had to be one.

He shook his head. "Sorry, *that* is Alyssa's story to tell. I just wanted you to get your arse up here so she could tell it."

I buried my head in my hands. "If she ever talks to me again."

"I told you, she will . . . eventually."

"Why the fuck do you even care?" I could feel some semblance of emotion filtering back into my body. That emotion was anger — which probably wasn't a good emotion to take out on somebody who could very likely beat me to a pulp. It couldn't hurt more than the gaping wound torn into my heart though.

"I care because I care about Alyssa. I care about Phoebe. They've been a pretty fucking permanent feature in my life for the last few years, and she's my best friend. I hate that this is fucking hurting her. That *you* are hurting her. The sooner you two figure this shit out, the sooner she can move on."

I shook my head, but I didn't know what I was denying. I knew what he said was the truth. Hearing him use the words that once belonged to me hurt though—there was a time when I'd been Alyssa's best friend. Then I'd broken her heart. Then she'd moved on. Or so I'd thought. And now, she really did want to move on but needed to sort shit out with me first.

"Denial isn't just a river in Egypt you know," he said as he sucked back deeply on his beer.

"How did you even know I was here?"

He laughed. "Browns Plains isn't exactly known for its prevalence of hundred-thousand-dollar Monaros, especially ones with Sinclair Racing on the back."

"But why—"

He cut me off and stood up. "My house is about fifteen minutes that way"—he pointed to the left—"Alyssa lives that way"—he pointed to the right—"I was driving past and saw the car. I figured it would be you. At least, I hoped it would be."

"You live here?"

"Sure. I moved here from Chermside to be closer to Alyssa after the twins were born. To help her out, you know. It's what *friends* do. They're there for each other. They answer calls and they don't run away."

Was the fucker *trying* to infuriate me? What was his fucking game? Did he want me to fucking attack him so that he could play the innocent card with Alyssa? I stood up and got in his face. Apparently my emptiness had been completely filled with stupidity and rage. "You just want to fucking get in her pants don't you, fucker!"

He rolled his eyes at me but didn't react in any other way. "First, if I wanted to get in anyone's pants, they'd be yours and not Alyssa's."

My mouth fell open.

Before I could think of a response to that, he continued, "Second, I would've had my chance at her many times if I really wanted it. Third, and most important, as much as it might surprise *you* to learn this, there are people in the world who want to do things for other people just because they fucking care. They care about other people and not only themselves."

I didn't want to listen to him. All I wanted to do was fucking smash his smug fucking face into the ground. I didn't want to hear the truths that were coming from his mouth. Instead, I said, "Just fuck off and leave me alone."

He shrugged. "I don't really give a shit about you, man. It's Alyssa I care about. Right now, she needs you to know about this. To deal with it. That's the only reason you're here. If you fucking hurt her again—"

"Yeah, yeah, I fucking know. Like I haven't heard it before." I walked straight past him, shoulder checking him on the way to my car.

I'd just turned the key in the ignition when he walked slowly out through the gates of the cemetery. He folded his arms and narrowed his eyes in what was clearly supposed to be a threatening manoeuvre. His thoughts were clear. *If you hurt Alyssa, I will hurt you.* Well, he could get in fucking line.

Instead of making me afraid, the sight pissed me off. Every fucking person acted like I *wanted* to hurt her. I revved the engine in defiance. Fucker.

Throwing the car into reverse, I kept my eyes trained on him as I pulled out of the park, only stopping when I was less than half a metre in front of him. Then I deliberately dropped the clutch and sent the wheels spinning. I fishtailed up the street and flipped up my middle finger at him. As I drove, I had no destination in mind. I just needed to be moving again. Now that the loss and emptiness had burned into anger, I needed an outlet for the burn. It may have been completely irrational, but it was potent enough that I could explode at any fucking second.

For a while, I drove aimlessly. Then I saw a pub and my stomach snarled at me. Aside from the coffee I'd had on the road, and the airline food on the plane, I'd had nothing to eat for two days. Hoping the food inside would be decent, and not a pile of greasy crap, I pulled into a parking spot. For a moment, I wondered whether I would have been better off just having a liquid dinner. If nothing else, it would dull the agony. I couldn't though—I needed to think straight as I worked out my next step. I needed to see Alyssa, but I didn't even know where she lived aside from the vague direction Flynn had offered. For half a second, I debated swinging back to the cemetery to beg him to give me her address, but I didn't want to owe the fucker any more than I already did.

I slipped my sunnies and hat on before I slid from the car. In that moment, I didn't care how much of a tosser I might have looked wearing sunglasses at night, not if it stopped even one person from approaching me. I was beyond my capacity to deal with people. Agony and rage burned through my veins like fire, searing me and giving me the feeling of superhuman strength.

When I entered the pub, I headed straight to the counter and ordered the first halfway healthy thing on the menu. Then I headed to a secluded corner to wait for my meal. Sitting at the table, I slumped my head forward against the hard surface and tried not to think about or feel anything.

"Oh my God! Look who fucking decided to slum it with the little people." I heard the voice shout from across the bar and my heart sank. I didn't recognise the owner, but whoever it was I just fucking hoped that they weren't talking about me, even though I was almost certain they were.

"It's fucking Declan Reede!"

Fucking hell. The voice was closer.

"Dec! It's me, Blake!"

I kept my head down.

"Blake Cooper? We were at school together."

Without waiting to be invited, he sat in the seat across from me at the table. I raised my head and nodded to acknowledge his presence. Knowing I'd been recognised anyway, I slipped off my sunglasses. What else could I do? Tell him to fuck off? As tempting as it was, I didn't really want to establish those words as my standard greeting.

"So, what are you doing back here?" he asked.

I shrugged. "Just visiting."

"You catching up with anyone while you're here?"

I shrugged again before glancing in the direction of the kitchen, wishing my food would make an appearance already. It couldn't be that hard to make a steak sandwich with the lot, could it?

"So, we all know what you've been doing since you left school, talk of the fucking town and all that."

It took a mammoth effort, but I managed to resist rolling my eyes.

He seemed to be getting frustrated with my nonverbal communication. "Yeah, there's been lots of stuff happen here since you left."

Leaning back on my chair, I crossed my arms and stared wordlessly at him.

"I got married."

I tried to feign interest.

"To Darcy Kinsley. Remember her? Blonde with a smoking hot body."

That little titbit piqued my interest. "How long ago was that?"

He fished a gaudy, tarnished bronze ring from his pants pocket and twisted it in his hands. "We've been happily married for two years now."

I refrained from raising my eyebrow and asking why, if they

were so fucking happy, he was alone in a pub with his ring in his pocket rather than on his finger, and she'd been out screwing me on New Year's Eve not even a year ago.

"Did you hear Alyssa got herself knocked up after you left?"

I set my jaw and tried to warn him silently that he did not want to continue on that path. Not if he wanted to keep his fucking face intact. He was not big and muscled like Josh or Flynn. He was exactly the right size for me to pummel into fucking shit. And if he said one more fucking word about Alyssa . . .

"Yeah, I mean after you left, I kinda thought she was fair game and asked her out."

I closed my eyes and pinched the bridge of my nose with one hand. The other was clenching in and out of a fist under the table. The force I exerted on my knuckles echoed up my arm into the strained muscles around my ribs.

"She always refused and I realised why pretty quickly when she started getting fat."

My hand was no longer pinching the bridge of my nose. At his words, both my hands were under the table clenched into tight fists and my whole body coiled as I tried to stop myself from leaping across the table at him.

"And when it was obvious she was pregnant, I stopped chasing her and went for Darcy. No one wants sloppy seconds after all."

Blake started to laugh at his own joke but his face fell as I tipped the table between us over with a primal cry on my lips. His drink and the rest of the contents went flying and seconds later, the sound of smashing glass echoed around us. Without stopping, or slowing at all, I launched myself at his throat with one hand. The other rounded quickly and connected with his cheek. He backed away almost as fast as I pushed forward, but after a handful of steps found himself trapped between me and the wall.

"If I *ever* hear about you saying one more thing against Alyssa, I will fucking hunt you down and gut you." I shoved him against the wall before pinning him in place with the hand around his neck. "And if I were you, I'd stop my wife from going to masked balls. You never know who might *bang* into her." I made sure my voice was dripping with innuendo. With one final shove, I pushed away from him and left the pub. The kitchen staff could keep my fucking sandwich.

I hadn't heard Blake following me until he grabbed my shoulder when I was near my car. He pulled me around roughly and opened his mouth to speak. The anger that was simmering in me burned into a raging fire with his touch and the memory of his words. I turned and swung at him, knocking him to the ground. Then I fell over him, pinning him beneath me and pouring my anger at the world and at myself into him. My fists rained down on him over and over, pounding into him again and again, even as he lay on the ground trying to shield himself with his arms. I kept going until three guys came out of the pub and forcibly pulled me off of him.

CHAPTER TWENTY-ONE

CASTOR AND POLLUX

IT WAS ONLY when I climbed into the car that sense flooded back into me. My whole body shook with tremors of rage and regret, each new spasm like twisting a knife in my already aching side. My knuckles were bloodied and sore. The cut on my arm felt like I'd been torn open all over again.

I welcomed it all.

The physical pain gave me an outlet to focus on so that I didn't have to feel the emotional scars as deeply.

Glancing down at my bloodied hands, I didn't know how much of the blood was mine and how much was Blake's. My knuckles had burst from connecting with the concrete during my frenzy, so it must have been at least a little of each. After a handful of breaths, the anger leached out of me, leaving me unfeeling and emotionless again. With shaking fingers, I started the car and drove from the car park before the police arrived—if they'd been called. For the second time that night, I drove without thinking and with no set destination in mind.

When I stopped the car, I was at my mother's house. I blinked, trying to remember how I got there but I drew a blank. There was no way I could leave again though, not until I'd had a chance to stop and process.

Leaving the car parked at a skewed angle to the kerb, half on Mum's front lawn, I stumbled to her front door. My brain refused to process anything; my body was numb. The only thing I could feel was the painful throb of my heart. That was obviously enough to compel me to return to a place of familiarity. I hadn't seen my mum face to face in almost eleven months, not since the previous Christmas, when we'd met for coffee while I was in Brisbane. Of course I'd stayed in a hotel then, not wanting to return to Browns Plains. At the time, I hadn't wanted to risk seeing Alyssa.

How could I have been so stupid?

I banged on the door with my open palm because my knuckles were too badly scraped to use. I didn't know what the time was and I only hoped it wasn't too late. The door pulled open to reveal my mother's shocked face. She was still dressed in her normal clothes so I couldn't have been disturbing her too much.

"Declan?" She looked out into the darkness at me.

Even though I towered over her, I'd never felt more like a little boy in all my adult life. I'd never before wanted so badly to be pulled into an embrace and reassured that everything would be all right, even though I knew it wouldn't be. *Couldn't* be. I just wanted to feel like maybe, just maybe, I could find a way past the pain. I wanted to hear from someone on my side that maybe Alyssa would talk to me soon and we could at least try to be friends again. With those thoughts in my head, I collapsed into my mother's arms, rested my head on her shoulder and began to sob again.

She held me like she used to when I was a child, gently brushing her fingers through my hair. She didn't ask what was wrong—no doubt she suspected the reason. She just stood there and comforted me until I felt able to move. When I could, I headed for the living room but stopped dead at what I saw there.

Alyssa was curled on my mother's armchair. A coffee mug sat abandoned beside her on the small side table. She looked like a deer in headlights, a gasp frozen on her lips.

At the sight of the shocked expression, I remembered what Flynn had said. She was afraid of me.

I didn't want her to feel that.

After taking two steps to cover the distance between us, I fell to my knees at her feet. I ducked my head and pressed my fists into my eyes. Gut-wrenching dry sobs tore from my chest and I couldn't get the breath to say what I wanted—*needed*—to say. I could feel the blood from my fists ooze from between my fingers and rub into my eyes, but I didn't care. Couldn't care. After a moment, the blood mixed with the moisture in my eyes and dripped down my face in small tear-like drops.

In a gentle gesture of comfort, fingertips brushed hesitantly through my hair. Even though I couldn't look to confirm my suspicious, I realised they were Alyssa's by the sensation of rightness that raced down my spine. One of my hands was gently coaxed away from my face. Cool, wet material ran over the knuckles and wrapped softly between my fingers. I kept my eyes pressed tightly together, not wanting to break the spell of the touch—*her* touch.

If I opened my eyes, she would see how broken I was. The one who'd been too scared of her hold to pick up the damn phone, leaving her alone in her time of need. Before I understood what she was doing, she'd wrapped dry material around my knuckles. I relished the contact and didn't do or say anything that might risk her stopping.

She let go of my hand, and I let it fall to my side. With a gentle touch, she coaxed my other hand toward her and repeated the process. Once she'd finished wrapping it too, her hands gingerly touched my face, just on the either side of my jaw. When she used her hold to tilt my head from side to side, I followed her desire without words or resistance. The wet rag ran over my eyes and down my cheeks, washing away the blood and the salt tracks that remained on my face.

She ran a finger along my arm, just to the side of the covering over the cut my arm. Taking obvious being care not to hurt me, she pulled the dressing off, checked over the wound, and then re-covered it with something new.

Throughout the whole thing, we were both silent. I couldn't

find the words I needed, because I was too concerned they'd only drive her away. That I would.

Slowly, I opened my eyes, and fresh tears sprang up from God knows where when I met the honey-gold depths of her gaze. There seemed to be a knowledge buried within them, an instinct to care and protect. In that moment, I wanted to be cared for. I wanted to be protected. I was selfish enough to take everything she offered me. I leaned over her lap, clutching her hips between my hands and pressing my face against her thighs as I sobbed. Her hand traced small circles on my back.

"I'm sorry you had to find out like this, Declan," she whispered to me. "You don't know how many times I tried to tell you when we were on the plane and in London. It's just . . . it's not very easy to talk about. Especially not to you."

I shook my head. I wanted to tell her that I was the one who should have been apologising. I was the one who hadn't returned her calls. I was the one who'd thrown her out on the streets rather than listen to her story. All of it was my fault. I couldn't get anything out other than, "I'm sorry," so I whispered that into her lap again and again. The soft denim of her jeans brushed my cheek as I clutched her hips to keep myself grounded.

Eventually, I found other words.

I whispered them in the same hushed tones as my apologies. "What happened?"

"Do you know the story of Castor and Pollux?" she asked in response.

The names were from the tombstone, but I didn't really know more than that. I shook my head.

"In Greek mythology, Castor and Pollux were the twin sons of Lēda and Zeus. In the myth, the twins shared the same mother but had different fathers, so Pollux was immortal while Castor was mortal. At one time, they were involved in a dispute with their cousins, and Castor was mortally wounded. Pollux begged Zeus to save Castor's life. Zeus agreed, but on one condition: Pollux would have to give up half of his own immortality in order to save Castor. Pollux agreed and so they spent their days alternating between

Hades and Mount Olympus. Eventually, they were cast into the heavens and form part of the Gemini constellation."

My eyes flicked to her chest, just beneath her heart. Although she had a shirt on, I could still picture the small tattoo hidden beneath it. From her words, it was obvious that the stars were shaped into the Gemini constellation—the twins. My heart sank to the floor at the thought.

She stopped rubbing the circles on my back, presumably to wipe away her tears. Her voice was full of them. I wished I could do more, but I was struck by grief and wound so tightly under her spell that I couldn't move an inch. I waited for her to continue. The story she'd told obviously had some greater relevance, but she needed to tell it all in her own time.

She took a deep breath and then the circles on my back started again. When she spoke again, her voice sounded far off, as if she was allowing someone else to take control of her body or reading a story from a script. "When I was a little less than eight months pregnant, Phoebe's placenta detached from my womb. She started to suffocate and I was rushed for an emergency caesarean. They delivered both her and Emmanuel."

I waited for the impact of her telling me he'd already passed by the time they got the babies out.

"Despite being so early, Emmanuel was a fighter. I can still see him in his humidicrib. He was so strong and so healthy despite his tiny size. Although they got to us in time to save Phoebe, not long after delivery, they found she'd had issues which had irreparably damaged her kidneys and liver. She probably would have been stillborn if I'd gone to term. As it was, she was on dialysis from the hour she was born."

I couldn't understand what she was saying. Emmanuel had been the healthy one? *But then why . . .*

I started to sob again as my thoughts turned to him—to the son I'd never met and never could.

Alyssa's voice continued with the same ghost-like quality as before. "Then, when they were three days old, Phoebe was getting worse. The doctors said that if she didn't get a transplant, she would die. It's next to impossible to get a matching donor organ for a baby though. An adult's organs are just too big. Then Emmanuel—" She choked back a sob. "The doctor said it was SIDS—Sudden Infant Death Syndrome. They couldn't give us a reason for it other than that. I knew though. I knew exactly what had happened. He'd given up his life to save his sister's. He protected her and saved her, the way a big brother should." She said it with such conviction and certainty. "The operation was so difficult they still could have lost her. It took hours and hours." Her voice was thick with tears, and I found myself drawing less comfort from her and trying to provide it instead. "The next few days and weeks were touch and go to see if it worked. Transplants in ones so little are so rare they are practically non-existent. We were just so blessed that it did."

I wanted to say that I was sorry again—over and over until everything was back to the way it should have been—but I didn't want to stop her story. I needed to hear it all—even though every word was a dagger to my heart.

"I named Phoebe for the moon. I'd always thought of her that way. From the first moment I knew I was pregnant. She helped give light to the empty night my life had become without you in it. Emmanuel's sacrifice helped me to see that sometimes there's a plan for things and even though that plan isn't always what you think it should be, you need to have faith, so I named him for that faith. While he was trying to comfort me in the hospital, Flynn told me about Gemini and the legend of Castor and Pollux. They just seemed like the perfect middle names after what happened."

I pulled back into a kneeling position and was finally courageous enough to meet Alyssa's gaze. Her eyes were brimming with tears, but surprisingly none fell. It was then that I remembered she'd been dealing with the heartache for almost three and a half years. Although it was clear she still ached and grieved, the wounds weren't as raw for her as they were for me.

In that instant, looking deep into her eyes, I saw the depth of the heartbreak she'd endured. At my hand.

I didn't break eye contact as I whispered. "I'm sorry."

She broke.

Then I did.

I climbed onto the seat next to her and we both sat wrapped in each other's arms.

Each broken in our own way.

CHAPTER TWENTY-TWO

JUST A FACT

I DIDN'T KNOW how it happened.

I didn't know who initiated it.

I didn't even really know why.

All I knew was that one second Alyssa and I were in each other's arms, sharing our sorrow over our joint loss, and the next our lips were pressed together. Our kiss was slow and soft. It was warm and welcoming. In some ways, it was like the first kiss we'd ever shared, with one exception: our shared tears wet our cheeks and coated our skin. She tasted of sorrow, heartbreak, and broken promises.

She hummed against my mouth as her hands found their way into my hair. I reciprocated as best as I could with my bandaged hands, running them up the side of her face, cupping it and pulling it to mine. My eyes were closed as I felt my world become completely immersed in her.

She made no move to stop the kiss, and neither did I.

She made no move to take the kiss any further, and neither did I.

Even though our lips dragged slowly across each other's, our tongues didn't meet. The kiss wasn't passionate or fuelled by desire.

It was just about comfort. About sharing with each other the love we both felt—that we always had felt and would always feel. It wasn't about the fevered love shared between lovers, but the peaceful love shared between best friends—the type of love that distance, barriers, and problems couldn't break. An innocent and pure love that reached between our souls, transcending all the crap that had gone on between us.

The kiss was a perfect salve for my fucked-up soul and utterly unlike anything I'd ever experienced before.

At some point, my mother must have returned from giving us our space to talk because I heard the audible gasp when she re-entered the room to offer me a drink. What had started as a question became an admonishment.

"Declan!"

I pulled back from the kiss to meet Alyssa's gaze. The sorrow was still there and so was the fear. I closed my eyes and rested my forehead against hers. I didn't want to move. Moving would mean talking, which would mean getting to the fucked-up part of the evening where the little progress we'd made would be wiped away with one wrong word. To the moment we would shout at each other, and hurl barbed insults, and would probably end with one of us walking out the door forever.

Most likely me.

In the imperfectly perfect moment we'd shared, I could feel the connection that ran between us. The same connection that had scared the shit out of me and sent me running when I was seventeen, but that I now wanted to cling to in order to pull myself out of the mire of my life. When I was with her, I could pass half of my pain and suffering on to her and take half of hers in return. Somehow that made it easier to deal with the agony.

Alyssa's hands fell away from me and she moved her body as far away from mine as she could in the armchair. I followed her lead and pulled farther away too, even though the action threatened to shatter me anew.

Then Alyssa spoke. "I'm sorry. I've got to go. I . . . I can't do this. Not now. You need to deal with this yourself first."

I nodded and slumped forward under the weight of my own grief returning in full.

"Kelly, thanks for the talk before." I watched impassively as Alyssa walked across to my mother and pulled her into an embrace. "I'll talk to you soon, okay?"

Alyssa moved to the front door, opened it, and then she was gone. Out into the dark night.

No! *Fuck that shit*! There was no way I was letting her just walk away from me again.

I leapt from the chair and rushed to the front door and sprinted up behind her. "Alyssa, wait!"

She stopped for a second and then took another step toward the car in the driveway that was obviously hers.

"Please?"

She turned slowly toward me. "Declan, I—"

"Marry me," I cut her off.

Her jaw dropped and her face fell into a frown. It didn't seem like the usual reaction to a marriage proposal, but who the fuck was I to know? I'd never done this shit before. Never planned on doing it either.

"What?" she asked. Her voice held no joy or even sorrow, only indignation.

"I want to fix this," I explained. "I want to make it right."

"And you think getting married will somehow magically make everything better?" Her voice pitched higher and higher as she spoke.

Taken aback, I retreated from her rage. "No, but it's what I should have done four years ago. Instead of running, I should have married you."

She stared at me with her jaw slack and the same frown still marring her features. As I watched her, I could see her anger slowly melt away, leaving her with nothing but a pained expression. I wanted to do everything I could to wipe away her agony.

"I love you, Lys."

She closed her eyes and took a few deep breaths. When she opened her eyes again and spoke, it was as if she was explaining something simple to a three-year-old. "No, you don't."

"Of course I do," I argued. I'd discovered just how much when we were in London and I'd learned that apparently all she'd wanted was a casual fuck. "I always have. I know that now."

"You love who I was, maybe, but you don't know me, Dec. Not anymore. I . . . I'm a different person now. And so are you."

I shook my head. Didn't she feel the same way as I did? Didn't she feel the thrill when we kissed? Didn't her heart race from something as simple as holding hands with me?

"We've both changed," she continued. "Four years is a long time, and a lot has happened. To both of us."

Her refusal to even acknowledge the way I might feel was too much. "Then what the fuck do you want from me?"

A tear slipped down her cheek. "Nothing. Remember you're the one who came here, Declan. I haven't turned up on your doorstep begging you for anything."

At the sight of her fresh tears, of the sorrow I was responsible for, my anger left me. I stepped closer to her, reaching out to caress her tear-soaked cheek. She jerked away from my touch.

"I want to fix it," I whispered. "What can I do to fix this?"

"I don't know what to tell you." Her voice was strained.

"Tell me how to make this right," I begged.

"I don't know how!" Her voice came as a shouted cry. "All right? If I knew how to make it right I would have done that by now. But nothing is going to change the fact that you left four years ago and nothing is going to change the fact that Emmie is dead. Those are facts, Declan. Facts don't change, but they do change people."

"Please, Lys, even if you don't believe that I love you, you have to believe that I care about you. I don't want to just leave it like this between us."

She sighed and stepped away from me, closer to her car. "We won't. At least . . . well, what I mean is, it's your choice. If you're still here tomorrow, maybe we can talk again then."

I nodded. "Tomorrow it is then, Alyssa, because I'm not going anywhere. I'll prove it to you."

Covering the distance between us, I went to pull her into an embrace, but she jerked backward at my touch once again. I dropped my arms and my head before turning and stalking back into the house without a second glance behind me. Her little leap away from me had torn out the last little part of me that had been left unharmed.

MY MOTHER was waiting for me in the living room when I came back inside. "Declan, what are you doing here?"

"I didn't know where else to go."

"I don't mean why are you *here*, because of course you're always welcome home. I mean, why are you in Browns Plains in general? You've made your opinion of the town very clear in the past."

"Flynn. He left a copy of Phoebe's birth certificate at my house. When I saw . . . I . . ." I couldn't finish the sentence, because a lump had spontaneously grown in my throat and I couldn't manage to breathe around it.

"You found out about Emmanuel?" Her voice was soft but not surprised.

I nodded and fresh tears sprung to my eyes as the pain Alyssa had kept at bay came flooding back in.

Mum patted the seat next to her on the couch. Without even thinking about it, I walked over and sat beside her. I couldn't remember the last time we'd been close like this. We'd probably seen each other face to face two or three times since I'd left for Sydney, each time over coffee and each time discussing nothing but me and my career. Mum had been as reluctant to talk about Browns Plains as I always was, but I'd never really understood the reason until now. It wasn't good enough though—she should have found a way to make me see the truth.

"Why didn't you tell me?" I said in the most demanding voice I could muster, which honestly wasn't very demanding. More . . . broken. Defeated.

"I told you, it's complicated."

I rolled my eyes at her. "This whole fucking situation is complicated, Mum. I know you said you promised Alyssa, and I get that, but it's not the only reason is it? How could you not have told me I had two kids, for fuck's sake?"

Her brows pinched together as I swore at her, but I could also see her biting back on her desire to tell me off for it. She looked away from me and out the living room window. "You really don't remember do you?"

"Remember what?"

"The phone call we had during the first Christmas you had in Sydney or the meeting that February?"

I frowned as her words brought up nothing; I had no memory of either event. Then I froze. Both of the times she mentioned were during my *troubled* time. I scoffed at myself for using that term, as if I wasn't still troubled. Shaking my head, I turned to follow her gaze out the window. I didn't want her seeing the guilt in my eyes over what I'd done to myself—and to other innocent people—during that time.

"On Christmas morning, I rang you and wished you a merry Christmas. You weren't interested in talking, and when I tried to keep the conversation going, and steer it toward Alyssa—trying to hint that you should call her, because I knew she missed you so much—you told me you were getting your Christmas present as we spoke so you weren't interested in talking to me anymore. You made it pretty clear there was a woman with you. Of course, none of us knew about the babies then."

There was so much I'd done wrong to everyone I loved, and I could sense from the growing tension in my mother's body that whatever she said next was only going to be worse.

"Then in the February, about a week before you were due to start your first season with the production cars, your father and I flew down to Sydney to surprise you. We knew you were settling into the team and everything, but we wanted to see you before you got really busy. Alyssa had been trying for months to get a hold of you. She even tried sending an email. The reply she got had her in tears for hours. I don't know why though, because she never let anyone see it."

I tried to remember an email or the visit Mum was talking about. Honestly, I struggled to remember any fucking thing from those few months, but unless it involved the hours I spent at Sinclair Racing I had nothing. I drew a complete fucking mental blank—or maybe blur was the better word.

"We stayed in a hotel in Sydney and arranged for a table at a restaurant nearby. That lovely girl, Eden, from your work arranged for you to meet us there. We didn't want to spoil the surprise so she told you that you were meeting a couple of fans."

I turned back to look at her again because her voice was quiet. She was watching her hands and wringing them together.

"When you arrived, you were already drunk. Instead of being happy or even surprised to see us, you were furious. You started yelling about how you thought we were going to be an easy score for you and how we'd ruined your plan for the evening. You just didn't stop. You went on for ages, tearing the place apart. We were kicked out of the restaurant, and I was so worried for your safety and sanity. I was so close to taking you back home then and there.

"Finally, your father managed to settle you down and we asked to meet up for breakfast the next morning to give you some time to calm down and sober up. You agreed. The next morning you turned up with a strange woman practically attached to your hip. You still seemed drunk or something."

Or something was right. I could have taken any number of drugs that night. Fuck knows what I'd been on.

"You sent the girl on her way pretty quickly though and I thought that maybe we could have a talk. I tried to raise the issue of Alyssa. I wasn't going to go back on my promise to her as such, but I just wanted to give you another gentle push to call her so that you would find out."

She had tears running down her face. I wanted to comfort her, but I was so disgusted with myself that I couldn't.

"When I mentioned Alyssa's name you went crazy again. You threw every piece of furniture you could get hold of and told me that you were happy with your lifestyle of having, and I quote, a different chick on your dick every night, and that if I ever mentioned Alyssa's name to you again, you would slit my throat."

She sobbed openly.

"Mum, I am so sorry. I wasn't myself those few months. I had a difficult time adjusting."

She held up her hand to stop me, she took a few steadying breaths and then continued. "That afternoon Eden called to find out how it went, and I couldn't help it. I told her everything that had happened with you. I just wanted to help you, to take you home and save you from whatever was causing you to act like that.

"Eden said that she would sort you out and because she had some distance you would be more likely to listen to her than to me. She promised that if she couldn't help you, she would let me know. The next time I spoke to you after that you seemed better, but still anxious to get off the phone. I never knew whether it was safe to mention Alyssa or not. Not that I thought your threat was serious as such, but I'd just never seen you fly off the handle like that before. It terrified me."

"Did Eden know too then? About Alyssa?" *Did the whole fucking world know but me*?

Mum shook her head. "I never told her that. Not even when we spoke afterward and she let me know of your progress. It didn't seem right to tell her if you didn't know."

"But why didn't you tell me after . . ." I didn't think I would be able to say the words. At least not yet. But I hoped she knew what I meant. There was only one *after* anymore, after all.

After Emmanuel.

"The day Alyssa gave birth, I tried calling you, but there was a meet on and you refused to come to the phone because of a drivers' meeting. I left messages for you to call me urgently. I tried to call you so many times that whole weekend, but I never got a single call back. After Emmie passed, it just became a blur of arranging birth certificates and death certificates, funeral arrangements and birth announcements. Everyone's hearts were broken. There wasn't any joy except when we were told that Phoebe had survived her surgery. We all wanted time to stop, to stand still so that we could grieve properly, but there was too much to do. Alyssa had piles of paperwork that needed to be signed by the father, including the two birth certificates. There were ways around it, but they would have all taken time—time we didn't have and didn't want to waste. Until everything was signed, we weren't going to be able to bury Emmie.

"She came over here and begged for permission to put Flynn as the father because she knew he would be around for them and would be willing to sign any paperwork she required. He helped her so much during her pregnancy. She cried with me for hours about how we both wished you would just call so we could explain.

"Then days turned into weeks, turned into months and you still never showed any interest in Alyssa. Whenever I rang you and raised the topic of what was happening at home you'd change the subject or hang up. The problem was the more time that passed, the harder it was to just come out and say the words."

I nodded, unsure what to do with this information. I figured my brain was AWOL and I had no idea when it might decide to return. Until it did I just needed food, a shower, and a bed. "Thank you for telling me this."

"I'm sorry. I know you've been hurt by this too, but you isolated yourself from everything so effectively I just . . . I didn't know how to get you back. Your father wouldn't let me fly down by myself just in case you got violent again, and you know what his hours are like."

I nodded, but wasn't willing to offer anything more. I knew I should apologise for my side of the issues, but I couldn't. I couldn't even find it in my heart to tell her it was okay or that she was forgiven. I just didn't know anything anymore. "I need to get my suitcase from the car."

Stumbling up from the couch, I headed into the cool night air once more. Needing a moment to myself, I climbed into the driver's seat of my car. I was so fucking tired. I hadn't slept since the plane, and that was twenty-four hours earlier. My brain was numbed by grief in a way that was far more effective than alcohol or sleeping tablets had ever achieved. I sat in the car pinching the bridge of my nose until I felt like I was ready to go back inside. Then I pulled my suitcase from the backseat and headed back for the house. I looked at the clock on the wall. It was later than I'd thought.

"Where's Dad?" I asked, surprised. Between seeing Alyssa and Mum's revelations I hadn't noticed his absence until now.

Mum looked away. "He had a business meeting to attend."

"Until ten thirty?"

She shrugged. "You know the crazy hours they keep. It's to speak to people all over the world you know." She wouldn't meet my eye.

I put my finger on her chin and guided her face toward mine. "Is there something you're not telling me still?"

Her eyes flittered away before settling back on my face. "Of course not, everything's fine. Your dad's always worked strange hours."

I nodded, partly because there was some truth in her words but mostly I didn't have the energy to drill her for more information just then.

"You can sleep in your old room if you like? I think there are some old clothes still in the wardrobe if you want to change."

"Thanks, Mum," I said. Then I smiled at her, or at least gave her the closest thing to a smile that I could manage. "It's nice to be home."

She smiled back. "It's nice having you back."

When she pulled me into her embrace I could feel her silent sobs wracking her body. I stood there with my arms around her until I felt the tears stop and then carried my suitcase to the bedroom door at the end of the hall. For a moment, I paused and took stock. Just like everything else I'd encountered since being back home, I had no idea what the closed door kept hidden. It was possible I could find a shrine, untouched in the years I'd been away, or a blank canvas, a spare bedroom with every bit of my personality stripped away. I wasn't sure which would be worse. After a deep breath to settle myself, I opened the door.

It was the former. The only thing that had been moved was the dust. It was clean and tidy but exactly as I had left it, including the

Holden posters plastered on every surface. Back in high school, I'd never had girly posters because Alyssa came by too frequently, and I thought it was in bad taste to have other chicks on the wall while I made out with her.

It was with thoughts of her in my mind that I noticed the one change in the room. A photo of Alyssa and me. After Josh's attack, I'd torn it from the wall and ripped it to shreds. Someone—Mum or possibly even Alyssa—had lovingly taped it back together and put it back in its rightful spot.

I traced my finger over the Alyssa in the photo and realised that she'd been right when she said I didn't know her anymore. The Alyssa I'd known was probably buried alongside our son. I vowed then and there that I would get to know her, and if she'd let me, I'd get to know our daughter too.

I changed into an old pair of pyjamas, ignoring the shower because I knew that would only wake me up more, and settled into my old bed. Even with my stomach churning I fell asleep in record time.

It turned out to be the best night's sleep I'd had since the plane ride to London.

CHAPTER  TWENTY-THREE
TOMORROW

IMAGES OF MY night with Alyssa in London haunted me while I slept. Every sight, smell, and taste echoed through my mind on repeat. The feel of her hair brushing over my skin, the sensation of taking her bareback. Over and over, her moans and sighs filled my mind. It wasn't like the normal dreams I'd had of her, where I was shaken awake in a cold sweat. Instead, I relaxed further into the dream until it encompassed every part of me.

I woke up from the highly erotic dream with a start. Without thought, my hand crept down to adjust the erection I was sure to have, but instead hit a sticky mess. *Fuck.* Just the thought of Alyssa had given me a wet dream.

Am I fucking thirteen?

Climbing from bed, I went in search of my suitcase and a fresh set of clothes. It was gone though. I looked around to see if maybe Mum had moved it somewhere else in the room, but I couldn't see it anywhere.

Fucking great.

Remembering what Mum said about the clothes, I pulled open my closet. When I saw a pair of baggy-arse jeans hanging in the closest, I had to laugh at the memory of how cool I'd thought I was when I'd got them. Alyssa had loved them, but only because they were so easy to pull down for quick access. Reaching for the hanger, I pulled them from the shelf. They were likely the only thing in there that even had a hope of fitting me, and that was only because they were so baggy. My time with the team, and the fitness regime Danny had us drivers on, had left me bulked in a way I hadn't been when I was seventeen. It was more than likely that none of my old underwear or shirts would fit so I figured I'd be going commando and topless until I could figure out what happened to my suitcase. First, I needed to clean up though because there was no way in hell I was going to face Mum in pants full of jizz.

I grabbed the jeans and a towel and headed straight into the shower. With careful attention, I unwrapped the bandages on my hands—worried what I might find beneath. Aside from a few scrapes and a couple of swollen joints though, they actually weren't too bad. Between the almost faded bruises on my face and chest, the stitched wound on my arm and the new litany of scrapes on my knuckles, I was a fucking sight. As well as all the visual reminders of my injuries, my body hurt whenever I moved. My ribs protested, my fingers ached. Despite the job I had, and how many times I'd crashed in six months, there was only one other time in my life when I felt so fucking sore all the time, and that was after Josh beat my arse.

Turning away from the banged-up version of myself in the mirror, I climbed into the shower. The water ran down my back and washed away the dirt and grime from the past few days. It felt . . . not great, because I didn't know if *great* even existed anymore now that I knew about Emmanuel, but better. Like I could actually face the day and not just hide out in my bedroom in an alcoholic daze. I had no clue what caused the difference, but I suspected it was the fact that Alyssa had said we'd speak again. She hadn't shut me out completely.

Climbing out of the shower, I realised I had no fucking idea what the time was. The sun was bright and the day was hot, but it was summer so the sun was pretty much fucking bright and the day was fucking hot almost constantly after five a.m, so that didn't mean much. Drying off as fast as I could, I pulled on my old jeans, taking care not to catch anything vital as I pulled up the zip. They actually fit better than I'd expected them to, still hanging slightly from my waist as was their style. I walked out from the bathroom toward the dining room, ducking my head and drying my hair as I went. I dropped the towel just as I arrived in the room.

Oh fuck me.

Flynn and Alyssa were sitting at the dining table. Both of them wore matching expressions with their eyes as wide as their mouths. My mind raced. What the fuck were the two of them doing there? Surely it was too early for visitors? I looked at the clock. It was eleven a.m.

"Um . . . hi?" I offered, not sure what else was adequate.

Both Alyssa and Flynn mumbled "Hi," in response. Even as my gaze fell onto Alyssa, hers raked over my body again, bringing my near-nakedness back to my attention. When she met my gaze, her face burned bright red—no doubt from being caught out. I turned away from her, feeling my desire grow at the thought that my body excited her so much. Still, I needed to find some fucking clothes. There was no way I could sit and have a conversation with Alyssa with nothing on but a pair of jeans. I'd be sporting a raging hard-on the whole time, which wouldn't be appropriate for the type of conversation we needed to have. I walked into the kitchen where I could hear my mum fussing around.

"Did you move my suitcase?"

"I put all your clothes in the wash."

Ah, mothers. I might have been twenty-one but to her I would always be her baby boy who couldn't wash his own clothes. I was just fucking thankful that I hadn't packed anything too embarrassing. The thought reminded me of Alyssa's vibrator, which reminded me that she was sitting at the table just metres away. I peeked out through the gap in the door to look at her. She had her head buried in her hands and was laughing about something with Flynn. It killed me to watch their obvious comfort around one another.

"They're in the dryer at the moment. I put them on early this morning, so they won't be too much longer. Do you want something to eat?"

Fuck yes. I was famished, especially after not getting to eat my meal the night before because of Blake fucking Cooper. "Yeah. What is there?"

"I made some pancakes this morning and there's some batter left over. I can cook that up for you if you like."

"That'd be great. Um, do you think Alyssa or Flynn will want some?"

She chuckled. "Who do you think I cooked them for originally?"

"Oh." I nodded before attempting to ask the most vital question. "So, is . . . um . . . is . . ."

I couldn't manage to force the words out and ended up standing there making odd gestures with my hands instead.

Thankfully, Mum seemed to understand and answered me as she pulled the frying pan down to cook the pancakes. "No, dear, Phoebe's with Ruth for today."

I nodded, relieved. I was still unsure what to do about Phoebe, especially seeing as though Alyssa and I still needed to have our talk. I did know I wasn't quite ready to meet my daughter yet, even if that did make me an arsehole. The truth was, I didn't know how to deal with kids—especially not my own. While Mum started cooking, I took a deep breath to steady myself and walked back out to greet the two people in the dining room again. I sat down across from them. With the table blocking my pants from view I somehow felt even more exposed. Especially with the way both Flynn's and Alyssa's gazes kept dropping to stare at my naked chest.

"Excuse me for another second," I said.

I raced back into my room and tore around trying to find a shirt or something, anything that would cover my nakedness. I finally found something in the bottom drawer—my pyjama drawer. It was an oversized boy band t-shirt that Alyssa used to wear at night when she'd stay over, always in the spare room of course—or at least so our parents believed. The tee was the only thing from my old room that might fit. Wearing a too-tight shirt would be just as bad as wearing none at all. When I pulled the t-shirt on, I felt like I'd stepped five or six years back in time.

Mum was just putting the pancakes down on the table when I arrived. I offered Flynn and Alyssa some more, but they just politely refused. It was obvious Alyssa was trying hard to hold in her laughter at the sight of me. She had to remember the shirt just as well as I did. The boy band tee was given to me on Christmas by an aunt who was told that they were *the* band for the kids. She'd bought the XL because she wanted to make sure it would definitely fit me. As such, it had swum on me and Alyssa had claimed it as a nightshirt. No doubt me wearing it was as vivid reminder for Alyssa of our time together as it was for me. It was obviously too much for her because she grabbed Flynn's hand and pulled him into the living room. Although I wasn't entirely sure whether it was to get away from me and my ghastly outfit or because she thought I would want some privacy while I ate.

I spread butter and sugar over the pancakes and quickly tucked in. Fuck it felt good to have something in my stomach after so long. The more I ate, the more I felt ready to face the day. To face Alyssa. I didn't know why the fuck Flynn was there, but I was sure I would be able to convince Alyssa to talk to me alone without too much coaxing.

First I needed clothes though. Proper clothes. *My* clothes.

Once I'd finished eating, I took my dishes into the kitchen and cleaned them off before heading into the laundry. Mum was just pulling my clothes from the dryer.

Thank fuck.

I could hear the sound of Alyssa and Flynn talking in the living room as I grabbed the thinnest shirt and pants I could find in the pile of clothing. Unfortunately, I had packed for winter in London, not summer in Brisbane, so my choices were limited. If I was going to stay in Brisbane for any length of time, I would need to go shopping or risk dying of heat stroke.

While I changed, I heard the front door open and close and then a car drive off. The sound sent my heart racing as I worried Alyssa had grown impatient waiting for me to get my shit together and talk to her. I cursed myself for fucking around so much worrying about what fucking clothes I had on. I threw the old jeans and t-shirt back onto my bed and then walked to the living room, fearful I would find it empty.

Thankfully, it wasn't.

The fucker, Flynn, had left, but Alyssa sat there staring down at her lap. I walked over to her and offered her my hand and what I hoped was a winning smile. "Walk with me?"

She didn't answer, but did put her hand in mine, which I took as an acceptance.

"Mum, we're going out for a bit," I called, leading Alyssa out the door before Mum had a chance to respond.

Alyssa and I walked in silence. I held her hand in mine, refusing to let go unless she pulled away. She seemed almost as reluctant to break the contact as I was though. Without words, we both headed straight to our table. For so many years, the park—and specifically the table in the middle of it—was our spot to go to after school when we couldn't decide whose house to go to, or when we preferred a general lack of parental supervision. The park was where we'd shared our first kiss, and also where I'd said goodbye to her. It seemed fitting to continue our history there.

Alyssa didn't drop my hand until we were only a few metres away from the table. She led the way over to it and sat sideways against the table, curling one leg underneath her. I sat next to her, turning into her and mimicking her position. Then I sighed.

Last night, I had been terrified of her walking away and not talking to me and now, with her right in front of me and us alone, I just couldn't think of anything to say. She rested her hand on the seat in front of her and once again, I copied her position. Our hands linked between us—even though I hadn't specifically planned on touching her. I wanted to ask why she was waiting at Mum's house for me and why Flynn had been there. I wanted the answers to so many questions and yet now that she was in front of me only one thing mattered. Her.

"Are you okay?" I asked, knowing how grossly inadequate the question was, but it was a start.

She looked away from me for a second. When she looked back,

she had a question rather than an answer on her lips. "Are you?"

I laughed darkly and then shook my head. "Not really, I don't think."

She nodded. "It's a lot to take in, to understand. Even after almost three and a half years, I still find there are days when I just don't get why it had to happen the way it did."

"Will you tell me about him?"

She smiled and her eyes developed a faraway gaze. "He looked just like you. A perfect miniature Declan. It's strange because when I was pregnant that was one thing I dreaded most. I had no idea how I would react, how I would cope, if the babies looked like you. Once he was in my arms, though, it didn't matter what he looked like." She dropped her eyes. "Of course, he was already gone by then, so he was just my little sleeping angel."

"You didn't get to hold him while . . ." The lump had grown inextricably in my throat again.

She shook her head. "No. Because they were premmie, they were in humidicribs. I didn't get to hold him until after, when I had to make the decision about donation." A tear ran down her cheek. Unthinkingly I raised my hand and brushed it away.

"I'm such a huge fucking arse," I said. "It's no wonder you hate me."

She shook her head. "I don't hate you, Dec. I just don't know you anymore, not the real you."

"I'm still the same though, Lys. Just a little bit more fucked-up."

She chuckled but there was no humour in the sound.

"I think you were right when you said that I don't know you anymore," I admitted.

She dropped her head and nodded.

Touching my fingers to her chin, I guided her to look at me. "But I'd like to get to know you again. If you'll let me."

"I'd like that too, Declan. I just . . ." She trailed off, uncertain how to word her feelings.

"You're afraid?" I guessed.

She nodded as fresh tears sprung to her eyes.

"Of me?"

She seemed to struggle with her composure for a second. "Not *of* you as such. I know you'd never hurt me physically or anything. I just . . . I can't trust you. I don't know if I can survive what we had before. Not anymore. Not with someone else to think about."

"I want to fix that. How can I?"

She shrugged. "Honestly? I don't know. But I guess time will be one way."

Time? I thought about that. I had another month and a half or so before I was due back in Sydney. But I knew that wasn't the sort of *time* Alyssa was talking about. Then I remembered Alyssa's words on the plane. She was leaving Australia for good. She was only in Australia for another couple of months. A fissure ripped open in my chest and my breathing sped as a panic attack gripped me in its icy claws.

They'd never been as frequent as they were now. I turned so that I was sitting with my back to the table and leaned forward to put my head between my knees. I cupped my hands against the back of my head and tugged on the hair there. I tried to calm myself down but it wasn't working. The thought of Alyssa leaving for good in just a few months, of never seeing her again, tore at me. Once again, she rubbed small, calming circles on my back.

"Tell me what you've been doing," I panted, trying to get her to talk about something that would hopefully stop the panic.

"I've pretty much been full-time at uni. Between that, a part-time job down at the local shop and Phoebe, I've been pretty busy. And then I got the job offer from Pembletons."

Fuck, that wasn't helping. My breathing hitched again and Alyssa seemed to sense that because she shifted her body a little closer. I was treated to the scent of her, and that did help calm me a little.

"I'm not taking the London offer," she whispered.

My breath left my body in one exhausted, but relieved, sigh. "Why not?"

"I can't be that far away from my family. Or from Emmanuel."

I nodded. Which meant she'd never move to Sydney. Which

meant if I wanted to be with her I had to give up what could be a promising fucking career or at least one that could be promising again if I could get my head back in the game. And that meant we were right back where we'd started.

Something inside me screamed at me to run again. Run as far away as I could as fast as I could. Get the fuck away from Alyssa and all the drama she was sure to bring into my life.

No! I thought in response. *Fuck that.*

Sydney wasn't that far from Brisbane, a little over an hour by plane. If I could be fucking man enough to pick up the phone, maybe we could at least be friends again. Although, I wasn't sure whether *friends* would work when I was getting hard as a fucking stone just from her rubbing comforting circles on my back. This smallest amount of contact from her did more for me than being balls-deep in any of the whores from the clubs.

I didn't understand why she had so much sway over me, but it had always been that way. That's what made me run initially and had kept me running since. I didn't want to be tied down and unhappy in my job like my father was. He'd worked crazy hours for as long as I could remember and he'd told me so many times how he'd had his dreams and maybe he could have achieved them if he hadn't married so young and fucked up his chances.

As always, I was torn between what half of me wanted and what the other half feared. Alyssa and the fucking perfect connection that made me want to bury myself in her.

Finally, I was able to gather control over my breathing and the panic subsided. I turned back toward her, resting my arm on the table and putting my fingers in my hair instead of linking them with hers again.

"Where does that leave *us* though?" My heart hammered my ribs, trying to break free as I asked the question.

"Is there an us?"

I thought about it for a minute. "I'd like there to be. Would you?"

She shrugged. "Yes and no. I don't want to get hurt again, Dec. It nearly tore me in two when I saw you—" Her words died on her lips. She met my eye and seemed to have an internal debate. "In the hospital," she added in a hushed whisper.

I frowned. The hospital was after so much other stuff between us. Unless . . .

"You were there? After Morgan . . ." I trailed off.

She closed her eyes and her tears wet the lashes. She didn't confirm it, but she didn't have to. Her reaction made it clear that I hadn't been having visions. She'd actually visited me in the hospital, but obviously hadn't wanted me to know.

"Then when you got on the plane beside me, I cursed fate. How could I be so unlucky? And then we . . . " She tailed off, but I didn't need her to elaborate. I knew exactly what she meant.

Fucking without complications. *Yeah, fucking right.*

"Do you know the real fucked-up thing about that night?" I asked.

She shook her head.

"I wanted to tell you that I loved you before you bolted from the room."

With a frown, she narrowed her eyes at me.

"I didn't even realise you meant sex without strings until after you'd left. I was so fucking drunk when you found me, I just didn't know what was happening. It ripped my heart apart when you walked out of the room."

I thought she might see the truth in my words, and realise that I'd been changing since that night. But instead her face was set with anger.

"Is that why you went back downstairs? To the bottle of whiskey?"

I nodded. "It was the only thing that made sense." I wasn't trying to make her feel guilty, I just wanted her to know the truth. Her reaction, however, startled the fuck out me.

She started to scream at me. "You thought the best way to deal with that apparent pain was to drink a fucking litre of alcohol?"

I was shocked and sat blinking at her, unsure of what she wanted me to say. She seemed to be demanding a response though so I nodded again.

"Fucking hell, Declan. You really haven't grown up a fucking bit have you?"

I just stared at her, uncertain of what I was being blasted about, but unwilling to add to it by saying the wrong thing.

"This is what I fucking mean about trust. One thing goes wrong and you fucking drink yourself into oblivion and end up in hospital. I mean Christ, what if I'd left for the night or didn't hear that bottle smash. You could have been fucking dead. How would I explain that to Phoebe? How could I tell her that her father died in a fucking alcohol binge session because one thing didn't go his fucking way?" She'd started her rant in shouts but ended it in tears. As soon as the crying started, I felt emotion return to me. I pulled her tightly into my chest. She sobbed against me for a few minutes before her breathing settled.

"This is what I mean, Dec. I can't trust you to make decisions if that's the sort of place they lead you to. And if I can't trust you to make responsible decisions, how can I trust you with Phoebe? How can I trust you with *me*? I think you need therapy."

I scoffed. "Been there, done that."

When she pulled away, her face was set into a mask of determination. "You need to talk to a psychiatrist. If you genuinely want me to try to trust you again, that's what I need you to do. Before we can ever have a hope of there being an *us* you need to sort yourself out. I won't allow Phoebe's life to be ruined just because you don't have yourself together."

"So let me get this straight. You'll only allow me into my own fucking daughter's life if I see a shrink? And I don't get a fucking say in that shit?"

Her eyes flashed. "Legally, she's not your daughter."

"Fuck that. You and I both know she is. I don't give a flying fuck about legal. If I want to see her, I fucking should be able to see her."

"Do you want to see her?"

Alyssa's question startled me with its frankness. "Um . . . I don't know."

"You don't know?" she asked incredulously. "Are you kidding

me?"

"Look, fuck, I'm trying to be honest here. I've known for all of a fucking week that I'm a father. I don't fucking know how to deal with that shit. What I want to do though is what's right."

"What's right is sorting yourself out and then seeing her."

A dark chuckle escaped me. She had no fucking idea. "Sorting me out could take fucking years."

Alyssa's response was a genuine laugh. She either didn't realise just how fucking serious I was or she was trying to lighten the now tense atmosphere. "At least start trying, that's all I'm asking."

"What do I get in return?"

She raised her eyebrow at me. "Besides being less fucked-up you mean?"

A scoffed exclamation left me. "Yeah, besides that."

"What do you want in return?"

"Will you agree to let me take you on a date?"

She thought about it for a second and then nodded. Then she smiled slyly. "One date for every session."

It was clear she thought she'd outfoxed me. "How will you know if I'm actually going?"

"It's about trust, Declan. I will *try* to trust you again. Part of that will be you earning my trust by showing me you are worthy of it. If you lie to me about something as simple as whether you've had a therapy session or not, how can I ever trust you on anything else?"

I nodded. It made sense. "Do phone sessions count? If I have to see a fucking shrink, I'd at least like to go to one close to home but"—I dropped my voice and broke eye contact because it was hard to admit to my feelings after hiding from them for so long—"I don't want to wait until I go back to try *us* again."

I didn't voice my greater concern that by going back to Sydney there would be no more us.

"I'm not just going to jump into bed with you," she said.

"Is that what you think I want? Fucking nice vote of confidence, Lys."

"Just going off recent evidence."

"Gossip mags and fucking innuendo."

"Are you saying they're wrong?"

Fuck. "No."

"Then you can understand why I would think that."

"Fuck, Lys, you should know you've always been more than that to me. It's why I can't do brunettes."

She rolled her eyes and huffed. "Nice. You draw the line at fucking brunettes. I guess I should be glad that you believe at least some part of the population to be off limits."

"Shit, Lys. I didn't mean it like that. I meant . . . Fuck. I'm sorry I said that, okay? I just, well, fuck, I just want to be honest with you."

She closed her eyes and took a few deep breaths. "I have a few more conditions on the dating thing."

"What?"

"First, you do so exclusively. No screwing random chicks. You wait until I'm ready and have a relationship with me alone. Even if that takes six months or more."

It's fucking disgusting to admit, but I did have to consider it for a few seconds. I was already so fucking wound up that I needed stress relief and my hand just didn't fucking cut it. The promised land at the end was Alyssa, though. She was worth the serious case of blue balls I would no doubt encounter. I nodded.

"Thank you."

"What else?"

"You stop drinking, and drugs if you are on any."

I shook my head. "I'm not on anything illegal."

She cast me a doubtful stare.

"I'm not," I reassured her. "Not anymore," I added in a quiet voice.

"And the alcohol?"

"C'mon, Lys, it's not like I'm a fucking alcoholic."

She considered me for a second. "Fine, not completely then. But you've got to stop drinking to excess and definitely not as a solution to your problems."

"I can try. All of what you are saying. Everything you're

asking, I promise I'll try."

"I would say that's all I can ask, but instead I'll say this: whenever you think you are trying your best, then try just a little harder. Make yourself someone who is worthy of that little girl. As much as it will kill me if you fuck up, she's the one I really need to protect here."

"Some people would say I'm a pretty fucking good catch."

She smiled slightly. "And they'd probably be right."

I preened a little.

"Once you've sorted yourself out, that is," she added before pressing a kiss to my cheek.

Without another word, she walked off.

For a dazed moment, I sat, unsure whether I should follow her or not.

CHAPTER TWENTY-FOUR

LET'S RIDE

WHEN I CAME to my senses, I jumped from the table and chased after Alyssa. I wanted to show her that I would follow her lead in things for the moment, but that I wasn't going to back away. That I wouldn't run again. I would go as fast or as slow as she wanted to, but I also wanted to take the chance to show her that we could be friends again. All things considered, we'd actually gotten along fairly well. It was a reminder of what we'd shared before lust and heartbreak had interfered with us.

"Alyssa, wait!" I called.

She stopped and then turned back to face me. When she did, the small smile from before had disappeared. "What is it, Declan?"

My steps slowed and my confidence faltered. Maybe I'd misread the signs and she wanted space. "I, uh, just wanted to ask you if you wanted to hang for a while, and maybe go shopping."

She burst out laughing. When she collected herself, she raised an eyebrow at me. "Shopping? Seriously?"

"Um, yeah."

"Why on God's green earth would *I* want to go shopping with you?"

My face fell as fast as my hopes. I hadn't expected a rejection quite so harsh, especially to an offer which was only one of friendship.

A look of horror crossed Alyssa's features. "No. I—I didn't mean it like that, Dec. I'm not saying I don't want to spend time with you. As a friend." She gave me a pointed look. "I just don't understand why that has to be spent *shopping*."

"Oh, fuck, sorry, I should have fucking explained better." I chuckled as relief flooded through me that her words hadn't been intended as a flat-out rejection. "I *need* to go shopping. Because I left home so quickly"—I left the reason for my speed hanging in the air for a moment—"all I brought with me was winter stuff I already had packed for London. I just thought you might . . . I don't fucking know. Oh fuck it."

I couldn't seem to form any fucking words for some reason, especially not any that could be misconstrued or twisted away from their intended meaning. With a frown forming, I turned to walk back to the table thinking that chasing after Alyssa had been a fucking mistake. I should have just sat still and shut up until she was gone so that I didn't fuck up the progress we had made.

Alyssa's hand closed around my arm to stop me, and my gaze shot to it, unbelievingly.

"It's okay," she said with a cautious smile. "I'd like to go shopping with you."

"Good 'cause I've got no fucking clue when it comes to this shit."

She chuckled darkly. "And you think I do? Obviously you don't remember me very well."

Despite regular visits to the Grand Plaza when we were younger, we'd very rarely actually shopped. I found myself laughing along with her. She was always far more focused on textbooks and texting than designer Dior.

"If you want style advice, Flynn's probably a better companion," she teased.

I decided two could play at that game so I trailed my eyes up and down over her body in a mock appraisal. "Yeah, probably. Do you have his number?"

She laughed. "So you don't want to take me now?"

I pretended to sigh. "Well, I mean, you're obviously no Flynn, but I guess you'll do."

She slapped my chest and smiled, not one of those half-hearted small smiles she'd been giving me before, but a true fucking light-up-the-room type of smile. It made my heart clench with something as close to joy as I could feel.

"You're so fucking beautiful when you smile," I said before I'd had a chance to consider the possible ramifications.

The smile fell straight away and she looked away from me and sighed. The she stepped away from me, locking her emotions away.

"What is it?" I asked.

"I'm willing to try and be friends. I'm even willing to try dating with the conditions we've discussed. But I can't have you saying shit like that to me; it's just not fair."

I mumbled an apology even though I didn't want to apologise because it was just the fucking truth. After a moment, I said, "Alyssa, you're going to have to tell me what to do, all right? I have no fucking clue how to handle any of this shit. I just know I wanna try. If I step over the mark, just fucking tell me to shut up or something. Don't push me away, okay?"

She nodded and a hint of a smile crept back onto her face. She held out her hand to me. "I guess *this* is okay."

With a grin, I grabbed her hand and led her back to Mum's house to get my car. Truthfully, we could have walked to the Plaza, but I didn't want to have to lug home a pile of heavy fucking bags if I actually managed to find some clothes that I wanted to buy. I fucking hated shopping. Most of my wardrobe consisted of gifts from corporate sponsors, so I rarely had to actually step foot inside a shop. They generally loved it if you were caught out and about in public wearing one of their shirts. It's what they paid for after all.

The walk back to the house was just as silent as the walk to the bench, and again our hands didn't break contact the whole way. I pulled my car keys out of my pocket and unlocked the Monaro. Heading for the passenger side, I held the door open for Alyssa. She climbed in and took a deep breath. My car may have been a few years old—it was the last CV8 Monaro off the production line and I had wanted to buy that shit for posterity—but I kept it pristine, so it still had the lingering new car smell. The smell of the leather seats was fucking intoxicating. I smiled to myself that Alyssa noticed that shit too.

"Nice car," she said after I'd climbed into the driver's seat.

"Thanks." I smiled at her as I started the engine. "I didn't think you liked cars though?"

Shifting into first, I checked the road and then squealed the tyres as I left the kerb. Showing off for Alyssa a little, I revelled in the sounds that issued from my baby. I always loved the fucking soft purr of the engine. It was the only music I needed, and the rhythm of my life. I'd even put a new exhaust system on the beast to get the note just right.

Alyssa laughed, but I wasn't sure what at and when I looked at her she shook her head to indicate she wasn't going to tell me. "I guess between you and Flynn I didn't really have much choice."

"He's into cars too?"

"Yeah. He's more into fours though. He's got a Silvia."

"Fucking ricer."

"I don't know . . ." Her voice held a quiet challenge, as though daring me to react to her next words. "He gets that thing to do some crazy shit. He got a fourteen eight at the drags."

Although I wasn't going to admit it, I couldn't help but be slightly impressed by the numbers. Despite the fact that he was gay, he was still my rival for her attention. I couldn't help but be jealous that he was the one who got her into cars when all of my attempts had failed. She'd never once shown any interest in that shit before I'd left for Sydney four years ago. Instead of saying anything complimentary toward the fucker, I turned to Alyssa and raised one brow. "You wanna see how a real fucking car handles?"

She shrugged but the corners of her mouth turned up slightly. "I can't be gone too long. I need to pick Phoebe up from Mum's in a few hours."

I shook my head. "This won't fucking take long."

Then I had a thought. "Actually, why don't we go to Garden

City for shopping instead? Kill two birds and all that."

"That should be okay." I took that as an acceptance and headed toward the motorway. When I hit the on ramp, I slowed right down. After ensuring there was no one behind me, I pulled to a complete stop. Then, when the motorway ahead was clear enough, I dropped the clutch and floored the accelerator, slamming through each gear and pinning Alyssa back in her seat with the G-force of my take-off.

It felt good and right. It was what I was made to do. When I tore past one-twenty, I hesitated because I wasn't sure about Alyssa's reaction. I honestly thought she would scream or get pissed with me like she used to when I pulled this shit after first getting my licence. She fucking surprised the shit out of me by giggling and fuck if it didn't sound terrific. It made me forget everything that had happened in the last four years. I was simply a fucking boy taking his girl for a drive. I flicked it into sixth as we sailed past one-fifty kilometres per hour before finally slowing back down to the speed limit.

"So, will—" I cut myself off. I was going to ask whether she'd tell me a little about Phoebe, but wasn't sure I was ready to hear it or broach any topic that wasn't completely and certifiably safe. "Why don't you tell me about uni?"

Alyssa told me all about her course, her studies, and what she'd been doing. I listened with rapt attention as I headed in the general direction of Garden City, hoping it wasn't a wasted trip. For all I fucking knew the place had been torn down or whatever in the years I'd been gone, but I assumed Alyssa would have said something if it had been. Back when we were kids, it was always bigger than the Grand Plaza, so I figured it still would be.

IT TURNED out my instinct was right and the shopping centre was fucking huge. It was the sort of place you could easily get fucking lost in. After parking the car, I walked to Alyssa's side and offered her my hand. I pushed the lock on the remote and prayed to high fucking heaven that no one touched it. For their own sake.

When I walked into the shopping centre and saw an expanse of white marble and flashy shopfronts, I freaked the fuck out.

"Where the hell am I supposed to go to get clothes from?" I thought out loud.

I didn't really expect a response, but Alyssa laughed and pulled my hand, tugging me away from the food court and in the direction of some shops. We passed a surf shop and I pulled her inside. Grabbing a few pairs of boardies and a couple of surf tees, I headed straight into the change rooms. Usually I wouldn't have given a shit whether they fit or not, or even what they looked like on me, but I wanted to prolong the time I spent with Alyssa. The fact that it meant she had to look at my body to see whether the clothes looked any good was just an added fucking bonus.

We spent the next hour going from shop to shop, but I only found two pairs of shorts and three fucking shirts that Alyssa said looked good. I refused to buy anything that she didn't like. The few items we'd got weren't going to be enough to get me through for long. Which meant that I had a ready-made good fucking excuse for another day of shopping with her. Internally, I celebrated, but outwardly, I sighed. "I guess we should head back?"

I glanced up and noticed we were back where we started from, near the food court.

Alyssa looked at her watch and nodded. "Do you mind getting something to eat first?"

Fuck no. I shrugged. "What do you feel like?"

She shrugged. "Sushi?"

"Okay, my treat."

She looked like she was going to argue. I put my finger on her lips, partly to stop her argument, but mostly because it gave me an excuse to fucking touch her lips again. "For dragging you around against your will."

She laughed and muttered something about it not being totally against her will, but relented.

ON THE way back to Browns Plains, Alyssa's phone rang. She had a quick discussion with whoever it was and then hung up.

"We'll go straight to my house, if that's all right?" she asked.

"Of course, but what about Phoebe? Isn't she at your mum's house?"

"Flynn picked her up and took her home after her nap."

I felt my eyebrows scrunch reflexively, but tried not to let it show to Alyssa. There was no way I was going to screw up our decent day. "Are those two close?"

"I guess. I mean he's practically been a father to her since she was born. So she's comfortable around him at least."

"Does she love him?" *Do I really want to know?*

Alyssa shrugged. "Yeah. I mean as much as a three-year-old truly loves anyone. He dotes on her though."

I wanted to say that it was all right, that I understood, but I couldn't. My fucking chest burned too much. Even though I knew I had no right to be angry about it, and that I only had myself to blame, I couldn't get over the fact that some other fucker was playing dad to my daughter. I fumed.

"She takes after you so much," Alyssa said. I could tell it was a distraction. I wondered how she knew exactly the right moments to fucking distract me—especially when she claimed to not know me anymore. "She's a little hothead too. And so stubborn."

"Stubborn?" I asked, my eyebrow raised. "I seem to recall you had the market cornered on stubborn."

In my peripheral view, I saw her open her mouth to say something, but then she shut it again almost immediately and her expression fell.

"What?" I asked.

She shook her head.

"Tell me what you were going to say, please?"

"Uh-uh. No way."

"What were you saying about stubbornness being my trait?" I laughed.

Her replying chuckle made me smile. "Okay, maybe you have a point, but you still out-stubborn me."

"What makes you say that?" I asked. Then I glanced at her and groaned. Sorrow filled her eyes, forcing me to see exactly what made her say that. Despite the news she'd had to impact, she'd given up calling me long before I would have ever accepted her call. In fact, even if she'd called every fucking day for the past four years, I probably wouldn't have answered the phone. It was only a pure fucking coincidence that threw us together on that plane. If it hadn't, I'd still be ignorant to everything and ignoring the pull to return home—to return to her.

Some say ignorance is bliss; I say fuck that shit. Despite the pain and heartbreak I'd experienced, I was glad I'd learned the truth. If not for the plane ride with Alyssa, and everything after it, I'd still be fucking around through life wondering exactly what the fuck was wrong with me. Now, at least I knew what was causing me to crash: regret.

I regretted leaving Alyssa. If I'd stayed with her, I would have regretted not going to Sinclair Racing and probably grown to resent what I had. My life was destined to be filled with regrets whichever path I took. And apparently it made me whinge like a bitch.

"Forget I asked," I said, acknowledging her pain without voicing the words.

Alyssa gave a small nod—either of gratitude or acceptance, I didn't know which. Except for Alyssa's whispered directions to her house as we drew closer, we were quiet the rest of the trip home.

I pulled the car up to the kerb near her house. Despite the silence between us, she seemed as reluctant to leave the car as I was for her to go.

"Thank you," I said. "For coming today. I think you saved me from a few fashion disasters."

She stared steadfastly at her hands. "I don't know about that. I just told you what I preferred. Nothing really looks bad on you."

"That sounded dangerously close to a compliment," I teased.

She raised her eyes to mine and then lifted one eyebrow. "Why are you fishing for one?"

"Would I have to fish hard?"

She sighed. "Of course you're hot, Dec. But you know it, you know? That does take away some of the appeal."

"Is that why you came on to me in London?" As soon as the words left me, I felt a surge of regret. It was the first time either of us had mentioned what had happened on the plane, and I was certain I'd just fucked up what had been a mostly decent day.

She cast her eyes down. "That was . . ."

When she trailed off, I wondered how her sentence was going to end. A mistake. Nostalgia. Desperation. *Perfection*.

She met my eyes again and shrugged. "Well, it was what it was, and perhaps it's better if it's left at that."

Even though my heart plummeted at her words, I nodded with the best smile I could. When the air between us grew awkward, I decided I couldn't let the moment hang. "I don't know if I'm going to get in trouble again for this shit, Alyssa, but I was telling the truth before when I said you were beautiful. I mean you were always fucking beautiful but now you're just stunning."

She blushed and her eyes dropped back to her hands. I wasn't sure what to expect, especially after being shut down over the London thing, but when she raised her gaze again she simply whispered, "Thank you."

"It's just the truth." I brushed a loose strand of hair behind her ear. The atmosphere between us shifted again, and the sensation of touching her ran from my fingers straight down into the pit of my stomach. She closed her eyes and leaned ever so slightly into my touch. The urge to reach across and kiss her burned in the pit of my stomach like a fucking desperate need.

Instead, I dropped my hand and leaned back, feeling a little breathless, but in a really good way. It was amazing how strong the impact of one innocent touch shared with her could be.

Alyssa exhaled and her breath quavered a little as it came out. She put her hand on the door handle, and I knew I had to stop her. I didn't want our day to be over yet. Even though the morning had been heavy and hard, the afternoon shopping trip had been like nothing I'd experienced in a long time. The whole time we'd bantered, joked, and basically acted like we were actually friends. We'd fallen straight back into how it had always been for us. It just felt so fucking natural.

I had to think of some way to prolong our time together. I could only think of one. "Do you think I could meet her?"

As soon as the words left my mouth I realised it wasn't *just* a way to stay with Alyssa. I actually genuinely wanted to meet Phoebe. *My daughter.* I couldn't say if it was because Alyssa had told me about our similarities, or whether it was something I'd wanted all along but just couldn't admit to myself. With the words out in the open, a burning and urgent desire to meet my daughter had built.

Alyssa seemed to consider my words and stared at my face for a long time. She twirled the ends of her hair around her fingers—a nervous gesture from years ago—and frowned.

"I don't care how you introduce me. You can just say I'm a fucking friend of the family or whatever, but please, Alyssa? Please, let me do this?"

She considered me for another half a minute. "On one condition."

"You and your fucking conditions," I muttered, but tried to keep my tone light. I knew she had every right to be as fucking demanding as she wanted after what she'd been through. But fucking hell, it wasn't as if I wasn't trying my fucking hardest to do what she needed.

She rolled her eyes. "Just watch your mouth, please." Alyssa paused and I thought that she was just admonishing me for my muttering until she continued, "She picks things up very easily."

I nodded and smiled. "I'll try."

With her permission solidified, my heart pounded in my chest. Could I really do it? I was *going* to do this, but fucking could I?

Alyssa smiled at me quickly and then turned and opened her door. I was frozen in place. I took a deep breath and eventually found the strength to open my door and climb out too. When I shut the door, it was harder than I usually would and I cursed myself for slamming it. If anyone else had fucking done it, I'd have been all up in their face. At that moment though, I was dazed. Alyssa seemed to realise how lost and anxious I was.

"Are you sure you're ready to do this?"

I shook my head and took another deep breath. "No, I'm really not," I said, determined to be honest with her whatever the cost. "But I *want* to do this, and I don't know if I'll ever really be ready for the first time."

She played with the ends of her hair again. It was proof that the thought of me meeting Phoebe was as nerve-wracking for her as it was for me. "Would you rather wait until you've had some time to discuss it with someone else?"

Figuring she was referring to the agreement that I see a shrink, I shook my head. If I didn't do it right then, I'd always find some other reason. Some other excuse. Partly, I was worried about screwing up and saying the wrong thing. Underneath everything though, I knew what my fucking problem was: the knowledge that one little girl would likely have a pull over me one hundred times stronger than Alyssa did. That truth echoed into the very depths of my soul and it frightened the living shit out of me.

Alyssa grabbed hold of my hand. "You can do this. She's just a little girl. She won't bite . . . hard." She laughed.

I walked to the house, unsure of how my feet were moving because I sure as shit knew I wasn't telling them to. Alyssa pushed open the door. "Flynn? Pheebs?"

My heart thundered in my ears until it was drowned out by an excited squeal. "Mummy!"

The little girl from the photo, the miniature Alyssa with my eyes, rounded the corner. Her eyes widened and she froze in place when she saw me. Alyssa bent over and put her arms out and Phoebe ran into them. She wrapped her tiny arms around Alyssa's neck and Alyssa stood, pulling Phoebe up with her. She whispered into Phoebe's ear, "This is Declan. He's a friend of Mummy's."

When Alyssa said my name, Phoebe's face lit up into a huge smile. It looked just like my fucking smile. The sight was so surreal. Her eyes were bright as she declared, "Declan . . . Auntie Ruby's friend."

"What's that, sweetie?" Alyssa asked.

My heart started to thunder again. I wondered whether or not

Alyssa knew about that phone call and I didn't want her to be pissed at me if she didn't. It wasn't like I'd deliberately kept it from her, it'd just never come up.

Thankfully, the moment was interrupted by Flynn coming out from the hallway. "Hey, Lys. Oh, hi again, Declan."

I nodded, but didn't look at him. I couldn't look anywhere else. The vision of Alyssa and Phoebe together was too powerful for me to even try to tear my eyes from. Apart, they were each beautiful and held my heart captive, but the two of them together like that was enough to fucking cleave my heart in two at any thought of ever leaving again.

"Are you going to come to my birthday party, Declan?" Phoebe asked.

My mouth was dry, I couldn't even think of anything appropriate to say.

"Your birthday is a long way off, sweetie," Alyssa whispered.

I could hear in her voice the doubt that I would still be around then. I wanted to tell them both that without a doubt I would be there, but I couldn't. There was too much that was still unknown. Too much damage still to fix. The fact that I would be back in Sydney then was a big fucking issue too.

I stood and stared at Phoebe, and she stared back at me, that fucking grin plastered across her face.

"You've got blue eyes like me," she said, pointing at my face.

Fuck. The elephant in the room grew exponentially. I closed the distance a little.

"My hair's different though," I said, running my hand over my auburn spikes. I looked to Alyssa for guidance, because I had no idea how the fuck to talk to a child.

"It's pretty and red," Phoebe said. "My hair's brown."

I smiled. "It's pretty too. It looks just like your mummy's used to when she was little."

Alyssa had tensed and looked uncomfortable throughout our exchange. Even though I wanted desperately to alleviate the tension, there was only one way I could think of and I didn't want to fucking do it. Not yet. Still, I decided to man up and do it for

Alyssa. For the first time in fucking years, I did something I didn't want to do for the sake of someone else. "Well, thanks for the help today, Lys. I'll . . . um . . . I'll be heading off now. I'll see you later though, yeah?"

She nodded, the look of relief on her face both astonishing and fucking depressing. Feeling it was clear she didn't want me there, I turned to leave. Then I debated with myself for one second before turning and giving Alyssa, and then Phoebe, a quick peck on the cheek. I swept out the door before my resolve to leave dissolved completely. I pulled the door shut behind me, and then braced myself against it for a few seconds, knowing without doubt that my life was different to what it had been before. The simple fact was my life was no longer my own. It now belonged to the little girl with the turquoise eyes.

CHAPTER TWENTY-FIVE

SHRINK

MUM WAS OUT when I arrived home from dropping Alyssa off. I hoped like fuck she'd left me a spare key somewhere because I had no idea where my house keys were. I couldn't even remember if I'd taken them with me when I'd left for Sydney. Even if I had, I certainly hadn't brought them back up with me. I hadn't even thought to grab any before I left on my walk with Alyssa. I searched in all the usual hiding spots, but couldn't see anything. Even the letterbox was empty. I decided either Mum hadn't given it a second thought or, more likely, was probably punishing me for taking off in the car without telling her and then being gone for so long without a phone call.

I walked through the gate into the backyard to wait. Sitting at the outdoor setting, I pulled out my phone. For the first time in over a week, I turned it on. Mostly because I needed it to make a vital call, but I'd also decided it was time to face the messages from Bathurst and deal with the fallout. Despite the fact that almost two weeks had passed since I'd crashed, I still hadn't looked at them.

There was a steady stream of early messages from Morgan, all containing pretty much the same sentiments he'd offered when he'd arrived unannounced on my doorstep the night of the race. There were a few dozen from Eden, the latest one from just the day before. Somehow, she knew I was back in the country and wanted to catch up.

Fuck me.

The thought of having to explain to anyone from Sinclair Racing why I was in Brisbane was almost inconceivable. Especially when everything was still so fucking up in the air with Alyssa. I wondered how I could even begin to tell them about Phoebe or worse—Emmanuel. I was still trying to fucking understand it all myself, I didn't think I could explain it to anyone else.

I'd barely finished reading the texts and listening to the voice mails when my phone rang. Eden's number flashed up on the screen. For half a second, I thought about not answering it but I knew what Eden was like. The fact that the phone was even ringing at all and not going straight to message bank would tell her that my phone was on. If I hung up on her before talking to her, I'd never hear the end of it. She'd probably send me out on slicks when it was going to pour down with rain. It was early in the game that I'd learned it was best not to fuck with anyone who held your safety in their hands.

"Hi, Edie," I greeted, pretending everything was fucking sunshine and roses.

"Well, if it isn't the missing man himself."

"I wasn't missing, Eden," I explained with a slow measure. "I was in London. I know you know that."

"But you got back the night before last and I haven't had a single phone call from you."

Somehow, I just knew she was pouting as she said the words.

"I just decided I needed more of a break away from everyone."

"What do you mean? Wasn't that the point of London? Why'd you leave there if you still needed to be away?"

"Didn't really like it. It was too cold for me." God this lying shit was far too easy, especially over the phone.

"Sure." She didn't sound like she bought the lie as readily as I'd hoped. "So where are you now?"

"In Brisbane."

All I heard was her stunned silence.

"You there, Edie?" I asked, trying to stifle the amusement in my tone.

"You're in Brisbane?"

"Yeah."

"Seriously?"

"Eden, why on earth would I lie about where I am?"

"I just . . . Well, I guess, I just didn't think you'd go back there."

"I've come to Brisbane plenty of times." Which was technically true, although it was the first time I'd returned to Browns Plains. Usually I gave it as wide a berth as possible.

"Sure, I guess, usually with someone from here though. I can't remember you ever going there voluntarily. So whereabouts in Brisbane are you?"

Fuck, she was annoying. I could lie again, but I found I didn't really want to deceive her. She was the closest thing to a friend I had in Sydney. Fuck, she was the closest thing I had to a friend, full stop. At least until I could rebuild what I'd once shared with Alyssa.

"Browns Plains."

She laughed, a nervous kind of chuckle. "I *really* didn't think you'd ever go back there."

You and me both. I decided to play her for a bit and see if she'd admit to the whole talking about me to my mother behind my back thing. "Why not, Eden? My parents are here after all."

"I didn't think you got along with your parents?" I could hear the hesitation in her voice.

"Is that just a gut feeling?" I paused but not long enough for her to answer. "Or something you gleaned from your multiple conversations with my mother?"

To my surprise, Eden laughed. There wasn't a trace of embarrassment in her voice. "She told you about that, did she?"

"Some of it."

"Kelly and I have become close over the years."

Kelly? It was so weird hearing Mum's name come from Eden, as if they were long-time friends. I guessed they were, even if I'd only just learned of it.

"She's really lovely, and she was really worried about you."

"Yeah, when I went off the deep end four fucking years ago. That doesn't explain continued conversations."

I could almost hear the eye rolling going on at her end of the call. "You think I shouldn't care about her just because she's your mother?"

"Really, I don't give a fuck whether you're friends with her or not, I just don't like people sneaking around behind my fucking back. Especially not people who I fucking counted as a friend."

"Declan, of course I'm your friend. Morgan is too."

"Leave that fucking boyfriend of yours out of it. There was nothing friendly about his last visit."

She chuckled. "If you'd just given him a black eye in return like usual you wouldn't be so pissed at him right now."

I couldn't argue because she was right but regardless, I was pissed. Although at what exactly I wasn't sure anymore—the world in general would do. "I bet the three of you thought it was fucking hilarious talking about all my dirty laundry."

"Yes, Declan. You're right. We do nothing else with our time but talk about you." Each word was dripping with sarcasm. "I have no other possible reason for calling your mother."

I sighed. I really didn't need her giving me sarcastic shit. More than anything, I was regretting turning my phone back on.

Her tone snapped back to normal, if still slightly pissy. "It might surprise you to learn this, but the world doesn't revolve around you. Yes, you may have been the reason Kelly and I started to talk, but I honestly can't remember the last time you were discussed other than in passing. Anyway, I didn't call you up to fucking get abused."

"Sorry. I've just had a fucking stressful week."

She laughed. "You have had a stressful *year*."

She was fucking right about that, and I knew what I needed to do to start fixing that. "Eden?"

"Yeah?"

"Do you still have Dr. Henrikson's number?"

"Sure. Somewhere at least. I can find it for you if you like? I thought you stopped seeing him though?"

"Yeah, I did."

"So why do you want his number?"

"'Cause he's the only fucking shrink I want to talk to. Is that okay with you or did I forget to ask your fucking permission?" I snapped.

"Yes, of course. Sorry for fucking asking. I think it's a good thing you're going back to see him."

She honestly couldn't resist fucking sticking her nose into my business, could she?

"Can you just text me that number when you find it."

"Sure thing. So can we expect to see you back in the office soon? I know Morgan is hanging for a night out."

"I don't know, Edie, I'm not sure whether Danny wants me back before the testing in January. Besides, I'm not sure how long I'll be in Brisbane for."

"Mmmm? And what's so special that it's keeping you there for an extended stay?"

My heart hammered in my chest knowing the answer to that question. Well, the two answers. I wasn't sure if I was ready to talk about it all to anyone yet. Then again, Eden would be the most understanding, and it would be nice to have someone on my side of the fence knowing about it. For another minute, I continued my internal debate.

"My daughter," I finally managed to whisper when the "tell her" side won.

I got no response. I wasn't sure whether Eden had heard or not, but I sure as fuck couldn't speak again. Not without throwing up. My hands were shaking so badly that I could barely hold the phone up to my ear.

"Your *what*?" Eden whispered back; her voice had no more volume than mine.

If I'd had any doubts about Mum's story about Eden not knowing, they were swept away by the shock in Eden's voice. She wasn't that good of an actress.

"Phoebe." Her name gave me a little bit of strength. "My

daughter."

"Wow. Daughter. *You* have a *daughter*. Wow. That's just . . . Wow."

"I know."

"Do your parents know?"

I humphed.

"What?"

"They've fucking known all along. Ever since Alyssa found out she was pregnant."

"Wait, wasn't Alyssa your high school girl or something?"

"How the fuck would you even know that, Eden?" I'd never told her. Only one person in Sydney knew about Alyssa at all, and he was forbidden from telling anyone else under Doctor/Client privilege.

"It was just something your mum said, when I helped arrange the surprise meeting— Wait, did she tell you about that?"

"Yes, she fucking told me about that. Now, don't change the fucking subject."

"Well, being a father hasn't cleaned your language up any."

"Eden—" My voice was a low warning.

"Your mum said she wanted to tell you something about an ex-girlfriend. She'd hoped that the two of you might work things out. I didn't have the heart to tell her you were out screwing around all over town. She mentioned Alyssa's name then."

"Well la-de-fucking-da. I'm glad everyone knows all my shit."

"Declan, I'm hardly everyone. And I swear I knew nothing about your daughter."

"Whatever, Eden. I gotta go, all right? Can you text me that number?"

"Is that why you haven't been able to concentrate on the track? Because of your daughter?"

"No," I growled. "I only just fucking found out about her a week ago."

"Sorry. I had to ask."

"Please don't tell anyone. I just want to sort shit out for myself first."

"Sure thing, Declan. And I'll get that number to you soon."

"Thanks, Edie."

I hung up the phone and stared at it until the tone beeped to indicate that I had a new message. I pulled up the number and looked at the clock through the kitchen window as I dialled. It was just after four in the afternoon. Dr. Henrikson kept precise hours and closed the office at five. I figured I would have time to call quickly, and maybe schedule a phone hook-up for the following day.

The sooner I spoke to him, the sooner I could take Alyssa out on our first date. I rang the number and got an answering machine. I hung up the phone and as I did, I realised the time on my phone screen read just after five. I hurled the phone across the patio in frustration. I'd fucking forgotten that Queensland was too fucking backward to introduce daylight savings, so it was a fucking hour behind Sydney during summer. *Damn.*

It meant I'd fucking have to wait until the next day to schedule a meeting, which would put everything a day behind.

I walked over and grabbed my phone to assess the damage. It had busted apart when it hit the wood decking, but thankfully still worked when I pieced it back together again. I dialled Dr. Henrikson's number again. At least I knew he wasn't going to be there this time.

"Dr. Henrikson. It's DR. I want to schedule an appointment for a phone consultation. Soon. Today if possible," I knew he wasn't going to get the message that day, so I left the message in anticipation of him checking it in the morning. "Sorry . . . about the last session, I mean. Anyway, I'm not in Sydney, but if you call me to arrange a time, I can call you back for the session." I rattled off both my mobile and Mum's home number so that he would definitely be able to reach me. Vaguely, I wondered if he would actually call me back. Especially after what happened the last time we saw each other. It was hard to fucking believe that it was almost a year ago. Just after I won the championship. I thought back on that time in my life.

"I NEED tablets, Doc. I'm just not fucking sleeping anymore."

"Declan, we've discussed this before. Giving you sleeping tablets is not going to help in the long term. They are a short-term remedy. We need to find the root cause for your insomnia." Dr. Henrikson's slight British accent usually made his voice calming but in that moment, it just annoyed the fuck out of me. I didn't understand why he couldn't just give me the fucking prescription and be done with it. Each time I returned to his office, he'd been increasingly difficult about prescribing what I needed.

"I know the fucking cause, Doc. I can't stop my mind from ticking over without the help of the fucking tablets." I paced back and forth across his office.

He sighed. "You've supplanted illegal drugs with legal ones. I cannot in good conscience sign a prescription for a drug addict."

I rolled my eyes. "I'm hardly a fucking addict. I haven't touched the hard stuff for years now."

"You know a lot of people think that once an addict, always an addict. Besides, there are different levels of addiction and it's been my experience that it is a constant battle often lost at the most minor of infractions."

"I was never fucking addicted, all right? It was just a bit of fun and fuckery, and when it went too far, I came to see you. I gave it up."

"If you say so. Why don't we discuss what is keeping you awake at night."

I growled in frustration as I flipped around for a fresh lap in my pacing. "I told you, I just can't turn my fucking brain off."

His gaze followed my steps with a practiced patience. "You must be thinking *about* something? Is it to do with work? Are there any problems there?"

I stopped pacing long enough to give him an incredulous look. "Do you even fucking watch the news at all? I just fucking took the championship. Youngest driver ever to do it. So, no, there's no fucking problem at work."

The end of his blond moustache lifted as he met my look with a smug smile. "Well, there must be something? What about Alyssa?"

I rolled my eyes. "I fucking told you about her once because you asked about my past fucking relationships. I don't understand why you feel the need to fucking bring her up each fucking session. If I wanted to talk about Alyssa, I would fucking talk about Alyssa. I don't—so case fucking closed."

"Do you dream about her?"

I flinched, because I did. Every fucking night she was there. I'd managed to purge her out of my waking thoughts, but there were two times when she invaded my life. In my fantasies if I ever indulged in the use of my hand—which was why it was easier to go to a club and pick up an easy score—and at night when I closed my eyes. During those two times, Alyssa was all I could see. "I thought I just said case fucking closed."

He chuckled. "And that makes me want to talk about it all the more. You're not an off-limits type of guy. You've told me about your drug use, about your drinking, about the violent acts you can remember, and about your regular night-time activities. That makes me wonder why Alyssa is off-limits."

"Because she is," I snapped.

He raised his eyebrows at me. "That's all? 'Because she is.'"

"Yes."

"Why?"

"Why what?"

"Why is she off-limits?" he asked patiently.

I threw my hands in the air and started on my well-worn path again. "I don't want to talk about it."

"Why not?"

"Because," I snapped.

"In more than one word."

I sighed, and pinched the bridge of my nose. He was really starting to grate on my last fucking nerve. "Because she's in the past, that's why."

"Everything we talk about is in your past."

"She's in my past as in another fucking life. I don't talk about my parents either. I don't talk about any of my old fucking school friends. Because they all belong to another part of my life that no longer exists."

"But they do still exist, Declan. Don't you see that? You can try to cut that part of yourself off, but it's still there. It's still part of what makes you who you are today. So why won't you tell me about Alyssa?"

"Because I can't stand to think about her. Because thinking about her fucking stresses me out too fucking much. Because every time someone mentions her fucking name I feel like someone has ripped out my heart and lungs and I don't fucking like feeling like that. So shut the fuck up about Alyssa fucking Dawson!" By the end of my rant I was standing just inches from him, shouting while tears of rage pricked my eyes.

"Is it possible you still love her?" he almost whispered.

In the next instant, I had him pinned against the wall. To his credit he didn't even look afraid. "You are a fucking lunatic! Why the fuck do I pay you a small fucking fortune each fucking week? You don't do shit for me. You won't even give me the one thing I fucking need and yet you insist on harping on about the one topic I've said is off fucking limits." I shoved him into the wall and pushed away. "Fuck you, man, you're nothing but a two-bit fucking quack."

Turning away from him, I kicked his coffee table over before slamming his door open to leave. I stalked past the receptionist without a second glance. I hadn't shown up for another session since.

AS I sat, reliving the memory, I grew more unsure of what to do next. I took a deep breath and, recalling the agitation which had been such a constant in my life for so long, paced up and down the length of the patio. I had no idea how long it would be before Mum got home and until then, I was locked out and unable to change or eat or anything. I could go for a drive, but to where? The realisation of where I needed to be hit me like a lightning bolt.

I walked back to the front yard and grabbed a piece of paper from the car. Jotting down a note for Mum, I let her know I was going for another walk, that I'd be home later, and that my mobile was on. Before long, I was back at *our* park. Instead of heading to the table though, I moved toward the base of the giant tree which provided shade to a section of the park. Sitting on the roots, I tilted my head back and relaxed.

If I closed my eyes, I could almost pretend Alyssa was beside me. After a while, I twisted to lie on my back between the roots of the tree, feeling the cool, shadowed ground beneath me and enjoying the slight breeze in the air. I kept my eyes closed and felt at peace. For the first time in a long time, I was able to turn my mind off. I still saw Alyssa as soon as my eyes were closed, but I didn't fight it.

Instead, I spent my time revisiting all my favourite features; the way her fingers curl through the ends of her hair when she's nervous, the almost opaque colour of her skin, and the soft honey-gold gaze that burned me from inside in the best possible way. From there, my thoughts turned to Phoebe. I wondered how many traits she'd inherited from Alyssa. How much was she like me?

A spark of curiosity burned deep within me, and I realised I wanted to know more about her. I wanted to know everything about her. With that thought in my mind, I was determined that somehow Alyssa and I would make it work.

My mobile rang, startling me back to reality.

"Hello?"

"Declan. It's Dr. Henrikson. I believe you wanted to talk to me urgently."

"Fuck. I mean, shit, thanks for calling back. I just didn't expect you to call so soon."

"You asked me to call you back today. I assume you have something you need to discuss."

"I actually didn't think you'd check your messages until tomorrow. But, Doc, I have to apologise, for . . . well . . . for the last time we spoke. I guess I just didn't know what was fucking going on in my head."

"That is usually the reason for seeing a psychiatrist isn't it?"

I settled back to the ground with my eyes closed and the phone pressed to my ear. "I guess."

"I have to admit, I was a little bit surprised you decided to reach out to the two-bit quack again though."

"Shit, you know I didn't fucking mean that."

"I've known you long enough to know you don't say anything you don't mean, at least on some level. Enough about last time though. To what do I owe the pleasure now?"

"I need to sort some shit out. And trust me, I've got some deep fucking shit to sort out."

"Are you back on the drugs, Declan? Is that why you've been crashing?"

Why does every fucker have an opinion on why I've been fucking crashing? "No. I'm not back on the fucking drugs. I just need to fucking know whether you'll help me with some phone sessions over the next few weeks."

"I can probably pencil you in. I can have Lucy call you in the morning. Are there any particular times of day that would be better for you?"

"Any time is fine. I just need at least one a day for the next few weeks."

"Every day?"

"Yep."

He seemed to consider it for a while. "I guess if you want a session a day, I can get Lucy to squeeze you in."

I smiled to myself. An hour a day on the phone with Dr. Henrikson would be absolutely worth a date every night with Alyssa. After all, she was the one who made me agree to the condition of one date per session. She'd never specified how many sessions she wanted me to have though, or a maximum number. It was a loophole of her creation, I was just happily dancing through it.

I said goodbye to Dr. Henrikson and placed my phone on my stomach. Without his voice in my ear, I greeted my visions of Alyssa again. I must have started to drift off to sleep because a sound near my head jolted me back to consciousness. I turned my head to see what it was, and was greeted by a sight that made me leap to my feet in surprise: a pair of turquoise eyes, and a shining bright smile, set in a tiny little face surrounded by a curtain of brown hair.

CHAPTER TWENTY-SIX

TWO ON ONE

"FU—" I THREW my hand over my mouth before the word could come out. Truthfully, she'd scared the hell out of me. I hadn't expected to see Phoebe again so soon and I definitely hadn't expected her to fucking sneak up on me while I was lying beneath the tree which held so many perfect memories for me. I looked up and saw Alyssa standing timidly by our table.

I stared at Alyssa as if she were an apparition. Just moments ago, I'd had my eyes closed and was going over her face and body in my mind again and again. Seeing her for real, I realised my memory was not accurate. In my memory, Alyssa was beautiful. Standing in front of me she was fucking astronomical—nothing less than an Aphrodite.

Alyssa stared at me too, seemingly just as transfixed.

"Look, Mummy, it's your friend, Declan." Phoebe's voice suddenly filled the air between us, drawing my attention.

"That's right, sweetie," Alyssa cooed at Phoebe. She walked a few steps farther into the park. "I don't think we'll stay here tonight though, Declan probably wants to be alone."

"No," I said quickly. "Don't leave on my account." I wasn't

sure why Alyssa was there, so far from her house, but I didn't want to force her out. "Why don't you stay?"

Alyssa stared at me, no doubt trying to figure out how sincere I was.

"I need to talk to you anyway," I continued. "I mean—if that's okay with you?"

Alyssa looked undecided for a few moments. She glanced at Phoebe and I could almost see her weighing up her options. When she started walking over to me, I breathed a fucking sigh of relief. I sat back down on the grass and she sat beside me. After unloading a few toys from a backpack she was carrying, she threw a small soft soccer ball at Phoebe who squealed and started to throw it away and chase it around.

Alyssa watched me cautiously. "What did you want to talk about?"

"I did it." I smirked at her, knowing she had no idea what I was talking about. "I called Dr. Henrikson, my psychiatrist, and he's going to organise for me to start sessions tomorrow." I didn't want to tell her I'd arranged daily sessions just yet, otherwise she might try to stitch up the loophole.

She raised her eyebrow at me. "That was fast. I'd expected you to think it over a little bit first."

I shrugged. "What's to think over? I've already told you I want to make a go of this," I waved my hand between the two of us. "You've already told me that to do that I need to see a fu—" Her eyes narrowed and shot over to glance at Phoebe before settling back on me. Right, I've got to watch my fucking language. "—that I need to see a shrink."

She shook her head sadly. "It's not going to be a quick fix."

I rolled my eyes. "You think I don't fucking know that?"

I put my hand over my mouth once I realised I had let loose a fucking swear word. I was used to talking without swearing when I fucking needed to, like at press conferences and shit like that, but when it came to any emotive issues, the words tended to just fucking fall out without any conscious thought. I realised it was going to take a lot of effort to watch my mouth around Phoebe.

She stared down at her hands. "You've done a lot of hurtful things."

I sighed. "I know. And I can never really apologise enough for them all. But we had a good day today, didn't we?"

She nodded. "Yes." Her eyes remained fixed on her hands.

"What is it, Alyssa? Please talk to me."

"I keep waiting for it to happen."

"For what to happen?" I asked, confused at her change of tack.

"For the moment you run away."

I put my finger on her chin and directed it toward me until I could capture her gaze. "I'm done running, Alyssa. Running hasn't made me happy. It hasn't made anyone happy."

Her gaze penetrated through me, right through to the very depths of my soul—or at least the parts of it that were undamaged after my recent discoveries. She seemed to be searching for something. She shrugged and looked away. "We'll see."

The sadness in her voice made my jaw clench.

I knew there was no point fucking arguing. The only way to convince her that I had changed was to fucking show her that I had changed. And there was no time like now to start. "So are we on for tomorrow night then?"

"What do you mean?"

"Well, I've got a session with the doc tomorrow, so that means you owe me one date. If we're going one for one, like we agreed, it'll be easier to have the date on the same day as the session won't it? So we don't fu—so we don't lose count."

She laughed a little, but it wasn't a proper laugh; there was no joy in it. "Aren't you getting sick of me yet? You've seen me every day since being in Brisbane."

I brought my hand up to her face, wrapping my fingers around her cheek. There was a brief second when she closed her eyes and leaned into my hand. "And if I had my way, I'd see you every day the whole time I'm here." I still wasn't going to tell her my plan about daily dates, but I was damn certain I would make it work somehow.

She recoiled, but I wasn't sure whether it was from my words or my touch. I saw there were tears in her eyes and they were threatening to spill. "I can't . . . I'm not going to pretend everything is perfect—"

Phoebe selected that moment to interrupt. Apparently she was bored of playing by herself with the ball. I grabbed it from her gently and then cast what I hoped was a winning smile but really I had no idea, because I'd never been a kid person, so I had no fucking clue what I was doing or what to expect. "Do you want to play soccer?"

Phoebe scrunched her nose up; her blue eyes sparkled in the slowly fading sunlight. "What's that?"

"It's a game. You kick the ball up the field and try to get it in the goal."

She tilted her head to one side. "What's a goal?"

"In soccer, it's a piece of metal that's shaped like this"—I made the shape of a soccer goal with my fingers—"and it has a net on the back."

She looked up and down the field, obviously trying to find the goals. "There's none. We can't play."

"Sure we can." I pulled myself to a kneeling position and whispered into her ear, "We can pretend there are goal posts." Then I pulled back and furrowed my brow. "Do you know what pretend means?" She was fucking three, I didn't know what shit she did or didn't know.

She nodded enthusiastically. "It's when it's not real. Like my daddy, I pretend him all the time."

It was such an innocent statement, said with no malice or hatred, and yet somehow it hurt more than the worst fucking insult that had ever been hurled at me. How the fuck could a three-year-old girl know exactly what to say to break my fucking heart? I closed my eyes and took a shaky breath.

"Declan, you don't have to do this, we can go," Alyssa said, already halfway over to Phoebe.

I shook my head, steeled my resolve and plastered a fake smile on my face. "How about a game of two-on-one?"

Alyssa seemed to consider it for a moment and then nodded. I picked up my phone and slid it into my pocket. Then I grabbed her backpack and moved it over to the side of the park and we started our impromptu game of two-on-one soccer. Technically, it was Alyssa and Phoebe against me, but what happened in reality was that Alyssa or I would kick the ball softly to Phoebe who would boot it in any direction and jump up and down declaring she got it in the goal. She was too fucking cute to argue with.

The game continued for around half an hour or so until Phoebe decided she was bored with it and wanted to pick flowers instead. Who knew that three-year-olds could be so fucking fickle?

Alyssa and I walked slowly behind Phoebe as she started to duck in and out of the trees around the park finding flowers and yanking the tops off. Then she'd get bored with the one she'd picked and move on to another colour.

"Why did you come here, Declan?" Alyssa asked quietly.

"I don't know. Mum was out and I didn't see the point hanging around home when I couldn't even get in the fucking house."

"Please watch your mouth," Alyssa said, but she smirked, so there was no real anger.

"Sorry." I shrugged. "Habit."

She nodded. "You'll work on that, won't you?"

I grinned at her, before giving her a little wink. "I'll try."

She laughed at the reference to our previous conversation. "Fair enough. That doesn't explain why you came here though, just why you're not at home."

I stopped walking for a second, contemplating what she was asking. Why did I go to our park? Did I even really know? "I guess I just wanted to be reminded how good we were. We were good weren't we?"

She nodded. "Yeah, we *were* good."

"Until I fucked it up."

She smacked my arm with her eyes opened wide, motioning in Phoebe's direction, but then chuckled. "Yeah, until then."

We fell into silence as we walked side by side. I could hear Phoebe talking to herself and to the trees and to any-fucking-thing that would listen.

"Well, I told you why I'm here. Why are you here?"

"Phoebe and I come here almost every day. It's the one place that's just ours. Don't get me wrong, I am so grateful for all the support I get from Flynn and my family, but sometimes I think I just need some time to be alone with her. This place always held so many good memories for me." She kept quiet on the bad ones.

"I'm sorry for intruding on it. Are you sure you wouldn't rather I left?"

She shook her head. I reached out and grabbed her hand in mine. She didn't pull away which made me smile. She glanced over at me and smiled in reply. It was like it always had been—when I was with Alyssa none of the other shit mattered, nothing else mattered, but then we'd part company and all my shitty thoughts would come flooding back in.

Phoebe came back to us with three flowers in her hands. "Mummy, which one do you want?"

Alyssa put on a look of mock concentration. "Um, let me see. The yellow one?"

Phoebe beamed at her and passed her the yellow one.

It was still so surreal seeing the blend of Alyssa and me in a walking, talking little package. A fucking cute little package with the perfect mix of each of us. I began to wonder what she would look like as she grew, and instantly regretted the thought because she would get older—and no doubt prettier—and then she would date.

Fuck me.

I didn't even want to think about that but I couldn't help it. Questions came unbidden into my mind. Would she have her heart broken by some dick? Would she find someone who was good to her? Would she be the sort to go to clubs and fuck random arsehole strangers? God, I hoped not. It may have been hypocritical of me— in fact there was no fucking *may* about it, it *was* hypocritical of me— but she was too good for that. She was too good for every fucking man who walked this earth or ever would. My free hand went to the bridge of my nose as I tried to put the thoughts out of my head before I went fucking crazy. For some unknown reason, I had a sudden compulsion to lock her into a room and never let her back out again.

Alyssa seemed to sense my stress, or maybe she just fucking knew my tells too well, and gripped my hand a little more tightly with hers, as if trying to hold me in place. "What is it, Declan?"

I knew it would sound stupid to Alyssa, fuck it sounded stupid to me, but I wanted to be honest with her. I didn't want her to imagine the worst possible scenario for what was stressing me out. I looked at Alyssa, stress eating me alive from the inside. "She's going to *date*."

A look of shock passed across Alyssa's features for a second before she burst out laughing. She laughed so hard, for so long, that tears started to run down her face. Phoebe started to chuckle at Alyssa. I stood there open mouthed because that was not the fucking reaction I expected. My stress grew into aggravation as the laughter continued. The longer the laughter went on, the more my irritation grew.

"I'm glad you find it fucking amusing," I snapped.

Alyssa wiped a tear from her eye. "Sorry. It's just . . . well, for someone who wasn't sure he even was ready for this you've jumped on the protective ship pretty quickly."

She seemed to choose her words carefully. I noticed she hadn't used the words "dad" or "father."

"It's all right, Declan. That's years away. And when the time comes, I'll deal with it."

I shook my head and pulled Alyssa closer to me. "No. We'll deal with it. Together."

Alyssa dropped my hand and looked away with a frown. The shift in her demeanour was instant and confusing.

"What is it?" I asked, reaching for her arm.

"Just stop making promises you won't keep," she hissed back at me. "Especially around her. I can deal with another broken heart, she shouldn't have to."

"Lys, I—"

She shot me a glare that froze my blood and stilled my tongue. Every ounce of agony and anger she'd experienced poured from the momentary eye contact. Then, scooping Phoebe up into her arms, she made a beeline for her backpack.

Placing Phoebe on the ground near the bag, Alyssa knelt in front of her and whispered, "We're going home now, honey. Okay?"

Phoebe shook her head. "I want to play some more."

Alyssa closed her eyes and sighed. "Please sweetie, Mummy needs to go now. If you're a good girl we'll get a treat later, okay?"

Phoebe pouted but didn't complain. Alyssa started roughly shoving the toys back into the bag. I walked over and started to help but she pulled the bag off me.

"I can do it on my own, Dec," she said. Something told me she wasn't just talking about the bag.

"Alyssa, how can I get you to trust me?" I asked, needing an answer to that question more than ever before.

"I can't . . . I just don't . . ." Alyssa just shook her head. She waved her hand at me in dismissal, put the bag over one shoulder, hitched Phoebe onto her hip and practically ran from the park. "I don't know if I can."

"Now who's running?" I shouted after her. I was pissed. I knew I had no right to my anger, but I couldn't help it. My irritation was already at its maximum because of her laughter over my protective streak. Her running away only made it spike.

She didn't respond and just kept going, disappearing into the trees before long. The last thing I saw was my little girl turn and blow me a kiss before waving goodbye.

A big part of me wanted to chase after them, to make Alyssa understand that I wasn't going anywhere. Another part though, the small part I was trying to silence—the part that wanted to run from Alyssa and her magnetic fucking draw—told me to stay the fuck where I was because she wasn't worth it. Those two parts ripped at each other until I told the smaller part to shut the fuck up and then ran after Alyssa. I escaped from the trees just in time to see her taillights disappear around the corner. I ran down the road after her, but she was gone.

I didn't know what this meant for us. Did she just need space?

Should I chase after her or wait for her to call me? The one thing I needed was to try to find some calm, because my anger was still simmering through my veins, burning me from the inside. If I had chased after her sooner, it probably would have been a disaster. Any conversation we tried to have would likely have been explosive.

For a moment, I sat on the kerb and tried to gather my thoughts, but the longer I thought about the way Alyssa shut down after my promise, the more my doubt seeped into my every pore. The negative words rolled through me—she would never trust me, so why should I bother to try to convince her to? Eventually, I pulled myself up off the kerb and headed back to Mum's house. When I arrived, the front door stood open.

"Decided to grace us with your presence again, have you?" Mum asked.

"Mum, just fucking don't, all right. Not now." My mind was still twisted in knots and undecided over what I should do about Alyssa.

"Don't talk to your mother like that." Dad's voice came from the kitchen.

"Well, if it isn't the fucking invisible man," I snapped back at him. Then I ignored him as I walked into the kitchen and grabbed a can of Coke out of the fridge.

"Declan, you sit down at that table—" he started.

"Fuck off." I was ready to head back out the door again less than a minute after I arrived. Alyssa's mood swing had put me on edge; I couldn't deal with my parents' shit too. Without waiting for him to start again, I headed for the front door.

"Declan!" Mum called out as she chased after me. "What has gotten into you?"

Her brow dipped into a frown and she reached for me before hesitating. A ghost of doubt crossed her face, and I wondered whether she thought I was going to fly off the handle like I apparently had during my parents' trip to Sydney.

Pinching the bridge of my nose, I took a deep breath. "What the fuck do you think?"

"Why don't you just tell me what's wrong?"

"Alyssa. Alyssa's what's fucking wrong. Alyssa is what has always been fucking wrong." I turned away from her and took a couple of pacing steps, my hands clenching and unclenching at my sides.

"What did you do?"

I spun on my heels. "That's nice, Mum, real fucking nice. Of course it has to be something I've fucking done, doesn't it? She couldn't possibly have her own shit to sort out either? It couldn't possibly be anything but my fuck-up, right?"

Mum looked like she was going to say something more, but I didn't want to listen. All I could think was what a fucking waste of time the whole trip had been. All I'd done was rip open old wounds in my heart, tear some new ones in my soul, and it was all for nothing. Nothing had changed. I was still as empty as ever.

"You know what? I'm sick of everyone assuming the fucking worst of me. I know I've done some fucked-up shit, but seriously, don't I get any fucking credit for trying to fix it?"

"You have to understand that one day of interest doesn't make up for four years of neglect, Declan. It just can't. Especially considering how roughly you treated her when you first left."

Right . . . the three months I could barely remember. I closed my eyes and sighed. It did nothing for my sanity. I could only think of one thing that would, but doing it would be breaking the rules Alyssa had set for me. *Fuck her, and fuck her rules.* "Whatever. I'm going out. I don't know when I'll be back."

She nodded and then pressed a key into my hand. "Come home when you're ready."

"Yeah, maybe."

She frowned, but didn't say anything more as I climbed into my car and gunned the engine. I peeled off from the kerb with a squeal and drove into the ever-darkening horizon. Alyssa didn't trust me. My mother had lied to me. My heart had been shattered and broken. My soul twisted and destroyed. More than anything, I needed to get away. To blow off some steam. There was only one way I knew how—a decent night out. A night of drinking and debauchery.

It wasn't like Alyssa was trying to keep up her end of the bargain, so why should I? Would she even care if I just disappeared again? I doubted it. She had her perfect life already planned out, and it was clear from her, "I can do it on my own," that she wasn't including me.

Well, fuck her then.

Ten minutes later, I was tearing down the motorway in the direction of the Gold Coast.

Pushing the car past one eighty, I inched closer to home with every passing second.

CHAPTER TWENTY-SEVEN
UNFORGIVEN

TRAVELLING AT ALMOST twice the speed limit down the M1 toward the Gold Coast, my mind was filled with the past, and with past mistakes.

As I drove along the highway, I passed the rides at Dreamworld, the studios at Movie World and the waterslides at Wet'n'Wild. On autopilot, my body knew just where it wanted to go. I took the Smith Street exit off the highway and followed it through Surfers Paradise and onto the Spit. I was going to our old hangout. After I finally had my licence, halfway through year twelve, Alyssa and I would come cruising regularly to the Spit with Ben and Jade. It had always bored Alyssa to tears because cars had never been her thing, but she'd had Jade to talk to and had endured the rest of it for me. Of course the shitty Datsun I'd driven then was nothing compared to my Monaro.

I knew the Spit wouldn't be busy because it was a weeknight, but it didn't matter because I wasn't coming for company. In fact, I wouldn't have complained if I was the only car there. After pulling into the Sea World car park, I put the handbrake on, leaving the car running but not in gear. I locked my car so no fucker could disturb me.

Once I was settled, I thought about the last day and how much everything shifted and changed constantly with Alyssa. It was almost impossible to track where I stood with her.

Just that morning I'd had no idea what to expect, but then we'd agreed to try for an *us* and my hopes had skyrocketed. We'd had fun at the shops, like old friends, and then she'd frozen up when she introduced me to Phoebe and I'd taken the high road even though I hadn't wanted to. Then, when I thought things were finally turning around, it went to shit. Somehow, I'd fucked it up in the park when I hadn't even expected to see her there.

Why did I have to go there?

If I hadn't, maybe I'd know still know where the fuck I stood now. Instead, I was down at the Gold Coast, trying to capture old memories of a better time. All I got instead was a constant loop of all the ways I'd fucked up over the years. Alyssa, my career, everything. It had all gone to shit. The only thing that connected all those dots was me.

I turned my stereo on, threw in a CD and cranked it up. The sounds of Metallica thumped from the stereo. Closing my eyes, I let the general noise of the band, and James Hetfield's voice in particular, take over my mind. Just like I had as a teen, I let the angry words fill me, drowning out my thoughts completely. Tapping the drumbeat on my steering wheel, I allowed the music to do its job and distract me. It worked. At least until track four came on, and I felt like the song had been written for me and everything came flooding back.

Singing along at the top of my lungs, I vented my frustration through song. I was just fucking glad I was alone in the car park.

Just as I was finishing the last chorus, with an extra flourish on the "drums" on my steering wheel, I spotted a security guard wandering over. I turned down my music and pushed the button to wind down my window.

He noticed he had my attention when he was halfway to my car.

"Sorry, son, this is private property. You can't park here."

I nodded and waved to let him know I would be going. I pushed repeat on the CD player before putting the car in gear and driving off. I spent twenty minutes circling the Gold Coast, not knowing what the fuck to do or where the fuck to go. In the end, I drove around the streets that were closed off to become a racetrack once each year. Those streets, I knew fucking well after four years racing there in both production cars and ProV8s.

Those streets, I understood even if nothing else made sense.

I clung on to the corners in my car, craving familiarity. Only there was nothing familiar there anymore. The track was cleared, the stands dismantled, and the crowds tucked in their beds all around Australia and the rest of the world. The roads were just that—roads. I longed for the comfort of my race gear, the feeling of power that came from throwing the race car around the track. I ached to feel in control of something—*anything*—rather than just feeling like a passive bystander in my own life.

Parking in Surfers Paradise, I walked along the beachfront until I reached Cavil Avenue and the nightclubs that lined the road. They were ones Alyssa and I had always talked about visiting after we turned eighteen, but we'd never made it. I doubted she had even after I left; the twins were born shortly before my own eighteenth and her birthday was almost two months after that. Grief and a three-month-old would hardly have put her in the mood for clubbing.

On a whim, I walked inside one. I didn't notice what the name was; didn't really care. Something to do with moons or stars or some shit. I just wanted a drink. I longed for control, but if I couldn't have it, oblivion would do.

It cost me a ten fucking dollar cover charge to get into the club. I ordered a double whiskey and a Corona and was out another twenty. I downed the whiskey in one gulp and chased it with the beer. At that rate, it would cost me too much to get sufficiently blotto. Once, I wouldn't have blinked at the cost, but with my recent fines and pay suspension, I had to give a shit about things like that.

Even though I had no idea where things stood with Alyssa, I wasn't interested in chasing tail; for once my libido was tucked away—or perhaps I'd just left it in Browns Plains with Alyssa. On top of that, the music was shit. All in all, there was no fucking way I would be able to relax in the club, so I left. Instead, I pulled into the first bottle-o I saw and bought two small bottles of whiskey.

Within minutes, I was back on the highway. I put "Unforgiven II" on repeat to drown out my thoughts, and drank deeply from the bottle as I drove up the highway back to Browns Plains. It was only when I turned off the highway that I decided I couldn't leave it like it was. I drove straight to Alyssa's house. I wasn't happy with the way things had ended in the park and I needed to know where we stood. I just needed to get her to understand how much I needed her now. How inescapable she was for me. That I wasn't making any promises I didn't fully intend to keep.

I hadn't realised I had downed three quarters of the first bottle until I climbed out of the car and my legs didn't work quite the way they were supposed to. I staggered across her front lawn and banged on her door. "Alyssa!"

There was no answer from the dark little house, so I banged again and shouted louder.

There was still no response. I tried for a third time and a light came on. Unfortunately, it wasn't a light in Alyssa's house but her neighbour's. Less than a minute later, someone came out of that house. An old lady wearing a floral nightgown and a hideous pink velvet robe stared down her nose at me with a mouth pinched into the shape of an arsehole.

"What are you doing banging like that at this hour of night?" the nosy old bitch asked.

"I gotta talk to Alyssa," I shouted at her. I couldn't seem to figure out how to find the volume control for my voice.

"Well, she's not there." The old bitch started to shut her door, closing my one connection to answers at the moment.

"Wait! Do you know where she is?"

Mrs. Nosy looked me up and down as if I were some animal pissing on her roses. "It's not really my place to say."

Sure, as if you don't fucking gossip all up and down this town.

I didn't recognise this old woman, but I knew her type well enough. Luckily for me, I also knew how to charm them. I took a few steps toward her yard, careful not to actually enter it because that would put her off-side. I put my best smile on my face, hoping like fuck it worked but too drunk to tell for sure. "Please, it's really important. I have to talk to her, or at least get a message to her."

Mrs. Nosy looked me over again. "I know where she is. I can get a message to her for you."

"Tonight?" I interrupted.

She rolled her eyes. "It's too late to be politely calling on people, son."

"It's really urgent." I didn't know why it was so fucking urgent, just that I needed to see her again and I felt that if I didn't do it now, I'd never have another opportunity to try. I knew I was being irrational, but I couldn't turn it off. A night of panic attacks and haunted dreams would be my reward if I refused to chase Alyssa right then. I wondered if it was just the words of the songs I'd been listening to that had me so worried, but I needed to see her to know that she would still try for there to be an *us*. I didn't understand why she'd walked away from me at the park. Why she didn't see that I was trying and just allow me the fucking opportunity to show her how devoted I could be if she'd just let me. Why she ran every time the future was mentioned in passing or I told her how beautiful she was.

"Look, young man. I know Josh and Ruby wouldn't appreciate getting a phone call this time of night—"

I didn't listen to the rest of her sentence. I knew enough for now. I stumbled back to my car and climbed in. I pulled out my phone and brought up the Internet. I flipped to the White Pages and entered Dawson of Browns Plains. There were fifteen names but only one J and R so I drove to the address listed for them. Why fucking call if I could just turn up? At least that way I could turn on the charm and have some chance for success—however limited that might have been.

I finished the last of the bottle on the way to Josh's. I needed liquid gold courage in order to be able to face him again. I could clearly remember the pain of our last meeting—a beating that severe takes a lifetime to forget. I parked the car one street over from their house. There was no point putting my baby in harm's way if Josh decided to try to knock my block off. I wouldn't put it past Ruby to fuck up my car somehow either.

I walked the short distance to Josh's house. It seemed to take forever, but I wondered whether that was because each of my steps seemed to take me farther sideways than forward. I checked each letterbox carefully, taking all my energy to focus on the numbers to make sure I got the right house. Once I was certain I had the one I needed, I thanked the Lord because the house was still mostly lit up. Someone had to be awake at least. I banged on the door once, but didn't call out for Alyssa. That would be a sure-fire way to make sure she wasn't the one who answered.

The porch light came on above me and it drew my attention. I stared at it for a few moments, blinking. I didn't even hear the door open, but I did hear the sigh. It was the smallest sound in the world but from the most important person.

"What are you doing here, Declan?" Alyssa asked, sounding tired. "I thought we were going to meet up tomorrow night."

I smiled a little. "You still want to meet tomorrow?" I squeezed my eyes shut and then opened them quickly to try to focus on her.

"Jesus Christ, Declan! Are you drunk?"

Oh . . . fuck. Not drinking was one of her fucking requirements or some shit . . . wasn't it? I scratched my head trying to remember. I recalled something along those lines. *Shit*! I shook my head enthusiastically. "Nope. Not me." A chuckle escaped my lips.

Alyssa pushed me away from the door and stepped out herself, pulling it closed behind her. "Declan, how stupid do you think I am?"

I was confused by her question. "I don't think you're stupid at all." Reaching out to stroke her hair, I continued. "I think you're pretty."

"I'm going to ask you another question and you need to think *very* carefully about how you answer it, okay?"

"Wait, was that the question?"

She sighed and pressed on. "Have you been drinking tonight?"

I nodded. I'd remembered I was allowed to drink, just not get drunk.

"Well, at least you're not trying to lie to me anymore."

I scrunched my eyebrows. "I may be a fuck-up, Alyssa, but I've never lied to you. Well except maybe when I told you I didn't want you anymore."

She pinched the bridge of her nose but remained silent.

"I never stopped wanting you. Never. I never stopped seeing you. Never ever."

I stepped closer to her and put my hand on her shoulder to steady myself. I rested my mouth against her ear.

"I never stopped loving you. You're in my dreams every night."

My vantage point gave me a good opportunity to drink in all her features, and I found that was more satisfying and helpful than the entire bottle of whiskey had been. I pulled back a little and examined her whole face. A lone tear ran down her cheek. Lifting my hand, I traced my finger across her skin to wipe away the tear before cupping her face. Her eyes closed and her lips parted. I guided her face closer to me. I gave her plenty of opportunity to pull away, but she didn't. The instant our lips met the haze lifted from my mind.

Her lips were moist and warm as they brushed against mine. Her tongue pressed forward into my mouth and made my breathing speed. I shifted my hand from her cheek to the back of her head. I wrapped my other hand around her waist and pulled her tightly to me.

Her hands came up into my hair and tugged at it gently. My mind was sending my body all sorts of crazy impulses. Some part of me realised that this was a mistake. I was pushing her too far and I needed to back off. I savoured her taste for another few seconds before gently pulling away from her lips and resting my forehead on hers. After the magic was broken and we'd parted, I kept my eyes closed. I didn't want to see the expression on Alyssa's face. I knew it didn't matter what it was, it would kill me. If it was revulsion, it would mean I was fucked when it came to second chances. If it was need, it would drive me to decisions I needed to avoid.

"I'm sorry," I whispered. "I shouldn't have done that."

Alyssa responded by pulling her hands, which were still in my hair, toward herself and forcing my lips back to hers. She kissed me fiercely and I responded, wrapping both my arms around her waist and lifting her against my body. Before I was ready to let go again, Alyssa's hands dropped out of my hair and she broke off the kiss.

"I'm sorry," she whispered. "I shouldn't have done that."

I chuckled. "That was my line."

She laughed softly, without any mirth.

"I am sorry for everything I've ever done to you, Alyssa. More sorry than you will ever know."

"Even for the email?" Her voice held a little resentment.

CHAPTER TWENTY-EIGHT
SPIRAL

"WHAT DO YOU mean?" I asked, wondering what the hell she could mean by her question.

"For the reply I got to the email asking you to call me."

"You never emailed me asking to call you. You called me asking to call you but never emailed."

"I did. You even responded." Her voice was thick with emotion.

I shook my head trying to clear the cobwebs that were quickly settling back over my mind. Email. Mum had mentioned something about an email too. What was that? That Alyssa had been in tears for hours after receiving it. I was afraid to ask the obvious question, but I had to. I had to know how badly I had hurt her if I ever wanted to make it right. "How did I respond?"

"With photos and video attached of you screwing three other women. At once. And the email message said that I could go fuck myself, because you were no longer interested in talking to me." Alyssa's gaze fell to the ground as she fought back tears.

I guided her face to look back at me and met her gaze as best as I could. "I'm sorry. You'll never know how big an impact you've had on me. How big the hole in my heart was when I left. I fought against it, because I was consumed by you. Fighting it just made me hurt you over and over. There's nothing I can say other than sorry, but I'll say it a hundred times if I have to. A thousand. I'll apologise every damn day for the rest of forever if that's what it takes for you to forgive me."

The tears were flowing freely down Alyssa's face now and she began to sob. I wrapped my arms around her and clutched her tightly to my chest. I could feel all of her curves moulding to the front of my body and found myself instantly hard. I dropped my arms and stepped back quickly, landing on my arse but unsure how I got there.

Alyssa sighed. "Why do you have to be drunk to have this conversation? You probably won't even remember this in the morning."

I smirked at her. "I mingh't . . . mightn'n . . . might not, but you will. And that's what's important."

I waved my arm in the air to punctuate my point and she laughed. After I'd offered her what I hoped was a sexy wink, she shook her head a little as her laughter continued.

She held out her arm to me to help me off the ground. "Come on, Casanova, let's get you up."

I didn't think it through before I put my hand up to hers. As soon as her hand was in mine, I pulled, trying to help myself up. Instead, I succeeded only in pulling her on top of me. The weight of her body on just my upper torso pushed me to the ground and I instinctively wrapped my arms around her to stop her from getting hurt. We were soon a pile of jumbled limbs and laughter.

When we settled, I was lying on the ground and Alyssa was above me staring intently into my face. She dipped her face again and pressed her lips to mine for the second time that night. I reciprocated hard, my body taking over and drinking in every bit of her it could. My hands roamed up the back of her shirt. She moaned against my mouth and that was all I needed. I rolled us together so I was on top of her and kissed her fiercely. Our tongues danced with each other and we both began to explore each other's bodies.

I broke off the kiss and raised my head when I heard the front door open.

"Lys, you all right out here?" Josh asked quietly from the porch. Then his eyes focused on Alyssa and me. His voice was full of rage as he shouted, "What the fuck, Reede?"

I extricated myself from Alyssa's arms as quickly as I could and crawled backward. I lost control of my limbs and ended up on my arse for the second time. I raised my hands up in an attempt at defence, but knew it was futile in my current state. I wasn't even able to find my own fucking voice.

"Josh, stop!" Alyssa seemed to come to her senses quickly and stood, holding her hand out to him.

"What the hell do you think you're doing?" Josh snapped.

Alyssa's voice was thick with both rage and embarrassment. "Josh, I'm a grown woman. I can make my own choices."

"You're lying underneath Reede in the middle of our fucking lawn, Alyssa. That's not a wise choice."

"I—I fell. Alyssa was helping me up." I found my voice finally. Even I recognised how piss-weak I sounded.

Josh scoffed. "Sure, that's what it looked like. I swear to God, Reede. Give me one good reason why I shouldn't fucking knock your block off right now?"

"Because I came over to fucking apologise to Alyssa," I shouted, managing to push myself up off the ground.

"You'll never be able to apologise enough for how much you hurt her."

For some reason, I took a few steps toward him. It seemed my brain had overridden my sense of self-preservation. "You think I don't know that? You think I don't realise that nothing I ever do will erase how I've made her feel? But how about the shit that you did?"

He seemed amused that I was coming at him and confused by my words. "Like?"

"Don't give me that 'like?' crap! Like fucking kicking my arse for no fucking reason. You don't think that hurt Alyssa too? Especially considering your fucking beating was a big part of why I signed the contract and went to Sydney." I was right in his face now. I was ready for him to take a swing at me. Practically begging for it.

Instead, he just laughed and shook his head. "Keep telling yourself that. You can't even own up and say that you made a decision because it was the one you wanted to make."

"Of course it was the fucking decision I wanted to make. Why the hell would I want to stay in this shithole town and be a fucking housebound husband when I can go live every fucking male's dream driving race cars?" I realised how bad the words sounded the instant they left my mouth. I turned quickly to look at Alyssa, but all I saw was her back as she pushed past Josh and ran back in the house.

Josh just stood there looking smug. "I think it would be best if you left now, Reede."

"No. Fuck you. I'm not leaving until I talk to Alyssa again."

"What if she doesn't want to talk to you?"

"I don't fucking care. I need to tell her that she's the reason."

"She's the reason for what?"

"For me—no, fuck it! I'm not explaining anything to you. I don't owe you shit. I owe Alyssa explanations. Explanations I don't even fucking understand myself."

"I'm not getting Alyssa for you."

"I'll talk to her again. I'll wait here all fucking night if I have to."

"Do what you want." He shrugged and turned back into the house.

I walked up to the door and put my hand on it, unsure what to do next. If I knocked, there was every chance that Josh would answer. Which meant there was every fucking chance he would knock my head off. The alcohol haze over my head didn't help the decision-making process. The only thing I knew for sure was that I was unable to leave. I couldn't even if I tried. In the end, I slumped against the door and rested my head against the doorjamb.

At some point, I must have fallen asleep because I was woken by the sound of a woman's screams. I stood and stretched out. Every part of me ached from the uncomfortable position I'd been in. My head ached most of all. The screams came from the room with the window just down from where I was standing and I just knew who it was who'd screamed. It was strange how I could recognise any sound Alyssa made. It was as if it registered in some part of my brain that was reserved only for her.

I tapped gently on the window, hoping I could wake her from what I assumed was a nightmare. The curtain slid back to reveal Alyssa's confused face staring at me. She opened the window a little.

"Declan, what are you still doing here?"

Fucking Josh. I knew he wouldn't tell her. "I've been waiting for you to come back out, so that I can explain."

She rubbed her forehead as she assessed me.

"Dec, what . . ." She trailed off with a sigh, as if whatever she was going to ask hadn't been that important. When she continued, she sounded exasperated, as if I'd been wearing on her last nerve and had just destroyed it. "I'm not going to talk to you about this while you're drunk. Can you just ring me later or something?"

Her voice held the same finality I'd heard so many times when we were kids. The confirmation we'd reached tipping point and I'd pushed her too far. It almost felt like she was about to tell me to get out of her life just after I'd realised I needed her in mine. "W-will you talk to me if I call?"

"Yes." She frowned and started to slide the window closed. "For some reason, I can't avoid you. Even when I want to." Her words floated to me less than a second before the window clicked shut.

Bile rose in my throat. I didn't think she'd intended for me to hear the statement, but it was impossible to ignore now that I had. She wanted to avoid me. The words were knives to my heart, slashing at the still-fresh wounds on my soul. I couldn't take it anymore. Certain aspects of my life might have been fucked up, but I'd never felt so much—good and bad—as I had in the last few days and I was ready to turn it all off again if that's what she wanted. "Fuck it!"

Without looking back, I turned and headed for my car. The thought solidified that maybe I *should* just give up and go home—

take whatever consequence was coming to me.

If she wanted to avoid me, that was fine by me. I would just have to cope with it the best way I knew. My life had been empty, but so had I. As far as I was concerned, empty beat the constant fucking ache in my heart since the moment I'd seen Alyssa on the plane.

The night was filled with heavy, black clouds, just like the ones that surrounded my fucked-up soul. Even though I prayed that they'd hold long enough for me to make my retreat, I'd barely reached the end of Josh's street before it started to spit. As if the sky itself wanted to take its shot at me, the raindrops grew heavier with each step I took and by the time I was halfway back to the car, it was bucketing down. Fat drops hit the road in loud splats, and soaked through my clothes in no time.

By the time I reached my car, I was soaking wet and pissed off. I threw open the door and grabbed the second bottle of whiskey from the passenger seat. With barely a consideration of all the reasons I shouldn't, I threw back a mouthful.

Instead of helping, and easing the pain, it just reminded me of Alyssa's ridiculous rules for trying for an *us*. A fresh wave of nausea rolled through my stomach. Even the booze couldn't give me comfort now.

Alyssa had charged back into my life, fucked everything up and now she wanted to avoid me. Worse, I couldn't even soothe the ache in the usual way.

Fuck her.

Holding the bottle of whiskey by the neck, I drew back my arm and tossed it at the kerb across the road. The loud crash as it hit the cement offered a momentary salve that lasted only as long as the sound hung in the air. I wanted to do more damage. Needed to burn down the world, to lash out and tear open scars at least the size of the one on my heart.

Just as it had with every other crossroads in my life, part of me screamed to run to get the fuck away from it all. Before I'd even considered what I was doing, I was in the car and the engine was running.

It was only when I put the car in drive that I stopped. I froze because I didn't want to run. Not this time. I wanted her. More than that, I wanted to *deserve* her. With a new determination burning through me, I glanced back in the direction of Josh's house.

"I will earn you back, Lys," I said, as if she'd be able to hear me despite the distance between us. "Whatever it takes."

Putting the car in first, I drove away even as a plan for winning Alyssa back formulated in my alcohol-addled brain.

Without really planning where I wanted to go, I headed for my parents' house. No doubt Mum would be waiting to lecture me like I was a teenager again, but I'd deal with it. I'd take all the shit in the world for Alyssa. And I'd take it all twice for the little girl with turquoise eyes.

For my daughter.

For Phoebe.

It was her name that burned through my heart and a vision of her that danced behind my eyes as something darted onto the road in front of me. I smashed my foot against the brake. The rain slicking the bitumen made it difficult to wrestle the Monaro back onto the road.

My heart was in my throat as I lost control of the car and it went into a slide. I tried to correct but pushed too far in the opposite direction and the tail spun loose. With my usual instincts dulled by the whiskey, I couldn't stop the car from pirouetting into the opposite lane just as a pair of headlights came around the corner in front of me.

I lifted my arm up to shield my eyes from the light seconds before I heard the impact.

I lurched forward against my seatbelt with a sickening crunch.

Seconds later, everything went black.

THE STORY CONTINUES IN

DECLAN REEDE:
THE UNTOLD STORY #2

ABOUT THE AUTHOR

Michelle Irwin has been many things in her life: a hobbit taking a precious item to a fiery mountain; a young child stepping through the back of a wardrobe into another land; the last human stranded not-quite-alone in space three million years in the future; a young girl willing to fight for the love of a vampire; and a time-travelling madman in a box. She achieved all of these feats and many more through her voracious reading habit. Eventually, so much reading had to have an effect and the cast of characters inside her mind took over and spilled out onto the page.

Michelle lives in sunny Queensland in the land down under with her surprisingly patient husband and ever-intriguing daughter, carving out precious moments of writing and reading time around her accounts-based day job. A lover of love and overcoming the odds, she primarily writes paranormal and fantasy romance.

Comments, questions, and suggestions for improvements are always welcome. You can reach me at writeonshell@outlook.com or through my website www.michelle-irwin.com. Thanks in advance for your correspondence.

You can also connect with me online via
Facebook: **www.facebook.com/MichelleIrwinAuthor**
Twitter: **www.twitter.com/writeonshell**

Printed in Great Britain
by Amazon